# DIAMONDS IN DISGUISE

*Recent Titles by Tessa Barclay from Severn House*

*The Crowne Prince Gregory Mysteries*

FAREWELL PERFORMANCE
A BETTER CLASS OF PERSON
A HANDFUL OF DUST
A FINAL DISCORD
TO DIE FOR
DIAMONDS IN DISGUISE

*Romance and Saga Titles*

THE DALLANCY BEQUEST
A LOVELY ILLUSION
RICHER THAN RUBIES
THE SILVER LINING
STARTING OVER
A TRUE LIKENESS
A WEB OF DREAMS

# DIAMONDS IN DISGUISE

A Gregory Crowne Mystery

## Tessa Barclay

This first world edition published 2009
in Great Britain and in the USA by
SEVERN HOUSE PUBLISHERS LTD of
9–15 High Street, Sutton, Surrey, England, SM1 1DF.
Trade paperback edition published
in Great Britain and the USA 2009 by
SEVERN HOUSE PUBLISHERS LTD

British Library Cataloguing in Publication Data

Barclay, Tessa, 1925-
   Diamonds in disguise
   1. Crowne, Gregory (Fictitious character) - Fiction 2. Art
thefts - Investigation - Italy - Rome - Fiction
   3. Detective and mystery stories
   I. Title
   823.9'14[F]

ISBN-13: 978-0-7278-6736-0   (cased)
ISBN-13: 978-1-84751-119-5   (trade paper)

*All Severn House titles are printed on acid-free paper.*

Typeset by Palimpsest Book Production Ltd.,
Grangemouth, Stirlingshire, Scotland.
Printed and bound in Great Britain by
MPG Books Ltd., Bodmin, Cornwall.

# ONE

**M**r Crowne was listening to a clarinet playing on his headphones. The clarinettist was a client for whom he was arranging a recital in a prestigious little hall in Bonn, and the problem of the moment was to decide which pieces of music to put in the programme.

Across at her desk in the little office, his assistant Amabelle was waving, mouthing words at him. He left the cadences of Schubert, took off his headphones, and heard the dreaded words: 'Your grandmother is on the phone.'

It was seldom good news if the ex-queen mother of Hirtenstein wished to speak to him. She disapproved of her grandson for several reasons; she generally wanted to scold him. Sighing, he got up to accept the phone from Amabelle.

'Good morning, Grossmutti.'

'Gregory, I want you to come to Rome at once.'

Well, that was a surprise. She rarely wanted to be with him. But he couldn't go to Rome. He had business to attend to elsewhere.

'And it's extremely important to check this before it gets out to the newspapers,' Queen Nicoletta was saying over his attempts at protest.

'Before what gets out?'

'I can't discuss it on the telephone. I want you here to have the situation explained to you confidentially by Signor Ardicci.'

He had the good sense not to ask who Signor Ardicci was. His grandmother took it for granted that he would know why she was in Rome and what she was doing.

Although there was a coldness between Mr Crowne and herself, she knew that her son, the ex-King Anton, kept the ex-crown prince informed of her activities. Exiled long ago from their homeland, the family had made their home in Switzerland. His father taught horsemanship up to championship standards, and his grandmother decorated the homes of the rich in the opulent style she had made her hallmark.

As for him, the youngest member of the family, he made his

living by arranging concerts and recitals of classical music from a small office in the old quarter of Geneva. He travelled frequently, but this invitation to Rome held no attraction for him.

Haughty and high-handed, Nicoletta still believed she could make demands and have them attended to at once – and on the whole her son and her grandson went along with that, for the sake of peace.

'You're . . . er . . . decorating some rooms in his villa?' he ventured.

He searched his memory for what his father had told him. Ruggiero Ardicci was a politician. A rich politician. For the moment he was out of favour – the reason eluded Gregory, because Italian politics never figured very largely in his life. But one thing he did know about him, because it had to do with music. Signor Ardicci had married Irina Grushenka, a Russian opera singer of some repute.

'It's Grushenka's house you're decorating, right?'

'Never mind about that,' scolded Nicoletta. 'I'm not ringing to ask for help with the décor, Gregory! It's something quite different – I want you to make use of that peculiar talent you have for finding out things.'

'You mean something diplomatic? You know I don't want to get involved in—'

His grandmother made a sound of irritation. 'Will you just do what you're told, for once?' she exclaimed. 'You're needed here, in Rome, and the sooner the better!'

Amabelle was looking at him with some concern. She could hear faint strains of the voice on the phone, and she knew – although she never mentioned it – that the ex-queen could be a great problem to her employer. Something over a year ago, Nicoletta had somehow succeeded in breaking up the relationship between Gregory and the woman he loved, Liz Blair. Exactly how, Amabelle had never quite fathomed, but for months he had been very unhappy.

And now here was the old lady, meddling again.

'Grossmutti,' said Gregory, 'I've got musical events happening in four different countries at the moment and two about to happen next week—'

'Well, they're happening, you say, so that's no problem. And if anything needs your attention, you can deal with it just as well from Rome as from Geneva.'

There was truth in that. Moreover, she sounded upset. And it took a lot to upset Queen Nicoletta. He was accustomed, since his boyhood, to looking after his grandmother when she was upset.

'I suppose I *could* come . . .' he murmured. Rome was a city he loved, yet it was the beginning of August. The place would be like a pizza oven. But was that a reason for refusing to help Grossmutti?

While he was still having this inward debate, his grandmother was issuing orders. 'Signor Ardicci has arranged your flight. You can pick up the ticket at the check-in desk. The next flight is at four o'clock so make sure you don't miss it, my boy. There will be a car to meet you at Leonardo da Vinci. I don't know how long this affair might take so bring clothes for . . . let's say, a week.'

He was still trying to think of a convincing reason to say no when she hung up.

His assistant looked at him in inquiry.

'I'm going to Rome,' he sighed.

He spent the next hour ensuring that she knew what needed present attention. She would of course keep in touch by telephone if there was an emergency. In his apartment he threw some suitable warm-weather clothes into a travel bag, scribbled a few reminders to himself, made an important phone call, then took a taxi to the airport.

Sure enough, everything had been arranged, including the car at the airport – an elderly man in a dark suit was holding up a placard, with the name Mr Crowne.

This was the name the crown prince used to shield himself from nosy reporters. It always surprised him to see there was an avid interest about royalty and ex-royalty, even in republican countries – or perhaps especially there. From time to time his name would appear, coupled with some other minor royalty, female, and of course there would be prophecies of a forthcoming wedding. Had they but known it, they were wasting their time. For Mr Crowne was pledged heart and soul to a commoner, and it was to her that he'd telephoned before leaving Geneva.

'Rome?' Liz had said. 'What, in mid-summer temperatures? Are you nuts?'

'Well, I couldn't really say no.'

'Who was it that talked you into this?'

'Er . . . well . . . it was my grandmother.'

A silence. His grandmother had been extremely rude to Liz Blair on a past and very public occasion, causing Mr Crowne and his beloved to quarrel and part for many months. So it was natural that she should be less than delighted at hearing his news.

'There's some sort of problem where she's at work, you see, Liz. It's an Italian politician – or perhaps he's more of an ex-politician – anyhow, she sounded really unhappy so I thought I ought to go.'

'Ha,' said Liz.

'What I thought was . . .'

'What?'

'Perhaps you could come to Rome, too.'

Another silence.

'You don't have to meet Grossmutti. She's living at the Ardiccis' villa and you could be in some lovely hotel in Rome with a spa and all that kind of thing.'

Still no reaction.

'Of course if you don't want to, I won't try to talk you into it.'

'Mmm . . .'

'It can be great in Rome even in high summer, in the evening, sitting outside a café with a glass of wine, and perhaps a guitarist playing something romantic.'

He heard her begin to laugh, and knew he had won. 'Can't be for a day or two,' she said. 'How long are you going to be there?'

'Grossmutti said perhaps a week.'

'Today's Tuesday. I could maybe get away by tomorrow evening.'

'Marvellous. Ring me and let me know. I'll fix up a hotel and meet you off the plane.'

He was reviewing his knowledge of Rome's hotels now as the limousine made its sober way towards Tabardi, on a minor road somewhat in the direction of the Pope's Summer Palace.

The sky was almost fully dark, but a half-moon showed the glimmer of white stone buildings, sometimes with illumination to mark their touristic importance. Here it was cool; his driver had the windows half open to let in a soft, cool breeze.

Gregory had an idea that there was a lake not far off although the area was unknown to him so far. Much travelled, he knew mostly opera houses and concert halls in town centres.

By and by the car turned into a narrow road, paved although in some distant era. There were bushes and some saplings along its sides, but then came a pair of handsome wrought-iron gates which swung open at an electronic signal from the car. They swept up an incline towards a villa whose windows shone with welcoming light.

Its door, reached by a flight of four shallow steps, was wide open; in its frame stood his grandmother and a short, grey-haired man in a finely tailored suit of Italian heavyweight silk.

The driver opened the passenger door. Gregory Crowne stepped out. His host hurried down the steps to greet him. 'My dear sir,' he exclaimed, taking Gregory's hand in both of his, 'how kind you are to come to my aid! Welcome, welcome, to Villa Stefani – and here is your grandmother whose good offices brought you to us.'

Gregory allowed his hand to be vigorously shaken. *What a windbag!* he thought. But then, the man was a politician, after all – or had been, until some unfortunate turn of Italian affairs had seen him fall from favour.

If the prince had tried to say thank you for his welcome, the words would have been swept away by the torrent from Signor Ardicci. His grandmother had descended the steps, bringing with her Signora Ardicci, but she made no attempt to introduce her. The two women stood by until Ardicci ran out of breath, then followed meekly as he led the group indoors.

'So here is my humble home, Your Highness— Ah! I forgot. I mustn't call you that. But I am so honoured, sir—'

'Ruggiero dearest,' his wife intervened, 'our guest is surely tired after his journey. You would like to be shown your room, sir, would you not?'

'Ah, of course, my angel. Mr Crowne, this is my wife, Irina – perhaps known to you, as you are a music-lover?'

Gregory took the hand she offered, bowing over it. 'Who doesn't know Irina Grushenka? It's so wonderful to meet you, madame.'

She smiled, colouring a little with pleasure. Her dark eyes sparkled. 'Thank you, Mr Crowne. It's nice to be remembered.'

'But you haven't really retired from the stage, have you? That would be such a loss!'

'Too kind,' she murmured, with a sigh behind the words.

Irina Grushenka had had a good career in opera although it would have been untrue to say she enjoyed the highest praise. The voice was good, but sometimes had been used carelessly. She'd had a reputation for being . . . well, a little difficult. Not temperamental, but apt to shy away from modern works, from anything challenging her religious beliefs.

But of course, one didn't allow that to interfere with good manners. Mr Crowne had flattered her a little, and knew she was well aware of it. She'd married and left the stage because her career was flagging.

'Our dear Floria will show you your room, Mr Crowne,' she went on, turning her head and making a little gesture to usher 'our dear Floria' forward. She proved to be a middle-aged lady with rather thin greying hair arranged in a very smart style. Her dress was black and perhaps not in the very latest fashion but it had cost a substantial sum when new. Housekeeper? Dependent relative earning her keep by being useful?

'How do you do?' said Mr Crowne, ready to offer his hand if she offered hers.

But she turned towards the marble staircase, saying, 'Ernesto will bring your luggage. This way, *signore*.'

They went upstairs, with ex-Queen Nicoletta following in their wake. By no means young, Mr Crowne's grandmother toiled a little at the ascent. They all went into the bedroom, a very fine room: high ceilings decorated with floral plaster-work, a bed hung with a tester of thin embroidered silk, a pale Chinese carpet on the floor and a suite of nineteenth century furniture that looked like French Empire.

Floria Massigna trotted about in an efficient manner opening doors to the bathroom and the walk-in wardrobe. 'And of course, *signore*, if you require it, here you have access to the internet.' She touched a computer on the handsome little walnut bureau and then the telephone handset. 'If you require anything from the staff, you can call from this instrument. Ernesto will answer, and if he is absent, then his wife, Cristina.'

'Thank you.'

'Rini asked me to say that dinner will be at eight-thirty.'

She glanced at Nicoletta. 'Perhaps, *signora,* you will be so good as to show him the dining-room?'

'Certainly, Floria. Thank you.' This was dismissal, and Floria recognized the queenly tone. She gave a little dip of the head and left.

When the door had closed on her, Nicoletta said with some commiseration, 'She's a cousin or something. Poor thing, her nose was put out of joint when Ruggiero re-married. She used to keep house for him, I gather, and it was quite a nice little spot for her because it seems he used to entertain a lot when he was in the political swim.'

'Now he's not?'

'No, it seems not. Don't ask me to explain, Italian politics are beyond me. But besides the usual in-fighting, there's some little hassle about religion.'

'Really? In this day and age?'

They were speaking English, in deference to the fact that this was a polyglot household with English the language they all had in common.

Nicoletta wagged a knowing finger. 'Oh yes. The Prime Minister is a deeply religious man, and a Catholic. Ruggiero married a woman who's devoted to the Russian Orthodox church. And you may not have noticed but the Vatican is rather cross with the Orthodox Church at the moment.'

'So that puts Ruggiero out of favour?'

'It doesn't help, *mon ami.* But it's not religion I want to talk about. I want to explain something before you hear the story from Ruggiero and Rini.'

'Rini – that's short for Irina, then.'

Nicoletta shrugged her handsome white head. 'It was supposed to help her dissociate herself from the Russian government, though how it helps to shorten your first name when your surname is Grushenka, heaven only knows. But part of her career was in the United States, as of course you'd know – and there, it didn't help to be a Russian after the present regime took over.'

'So what is this that you want to explain?'

'Gregory, you should take everything they tell you with a pinch of salt. When Rini is asked to talk about something she doesn't want to, she tends to take refuge in whimpers and a suggestion of tears. Ruggiero, of course, melts at the sight.'

'What kind of things doesn't she want to talk about?'

'Well, the diamonds, for a start.'

Gregory raised his eyebrows. 'Diamonds?'

'A necklace she was given by some mad admirer when she was about twenty.' His grandmother pouted and looked dubious. 'She's beautiful, of course – all that mass of dark hair and those great sparkling eyes. But you know, although I can't compare with you as an expert on these things, I don't believe I ever heard of her as a great prima donna, like, for instance, Maria Callas.'

'Quite right. She had a voice, and was a pretty good actress. But I think any diamonds she received were probably for something other than singing.'

Grossmutti giggled. '*Méchant*! But then a little naughtiness is always helpful in the publicity world, no? Well, the diamonds are worth a great deal of money, even more than they used to be because with the so-called emergent nations developing a taste for luxury, it seems diamonds are greatly in demand.'

'And so what about the diamonds?'

'They've disappeared.'

'What?'

'Vanished. And she is *distraught*!'

There was a knock at the door. Ernesto appeared bringing Gregory's luggage – a travel bag of clothes and a briefcase with his planner and some business documents. The man carried the clothes bag to the walk-in wardrobe, set it down, and looked in inquiry.

'Would you like me to unpack and hang your clothes now, sir?' he asked in heavily accented English.

'Not at the moment, thank you.'

'If you need anything, please ring, sir.'

'Thank you.'

When Ernesto had gone, Gregory went back to what they'd been discussing. 'You say "distraught" – is there anything behind your word? More than misery at being robbed?'

'I don't know. All I can tell you is that when she discovered they were gone, she was almost in hysterics.'

'Can you think of a reason, other than the normal one?'

'I was wondering if the man who gave them to her was someone she loved very deeply.'

Gregory looked at her with unconcealed surprise. 'Coming from you, madame, that's very romantic.'

'Ha! I wasn't always in my dotage, my child. I've been head over heels in love in my time.'

That might have been so. In the old days, when she was Queen of the little state of Hirtenstein, Queen Nicoletta's name had been murmured in more than one scandal. But even so, the prince couldn't imagine his grandmother getting hysterical over a lost gift from a beloved.

'So,' he said, in a tone that meant he wanted to get down to brass tacks, 'what are the police saying?'

'The police have not been informed.'

'No?'

'No. My dear, it's to do with the politics. I think Ruggiero doesn't want any police involvement because of course that means the press, and he doesn't want the attention. He's angling for some diplomatic post, I think, so it seems he doesn't want the spotlight turned on him and *his Russian Orthodox wife*. You see?'

'Grossmutti, you shouldn't have brought me here. I'm not interested in saving a politician from his problems.'

She made her way towards the door. 'Wash your face and hands, child, and change your clothes. Dinner will be announced quite soon.'

'What's the matter?' he asked, perplexed by her tone.

'Gregory, I came here to re-decorate the ballroom, the drawing-room, and the dining-room. Three weeks after my arrival, diamonds worth nearly a million dollars go missing.' She jutted her chin. 'I am not a suspect, I believe. Yet I would like this matter cleared up, you know.'

'Oh.'

'The Hirtensteins have no money. That's common knowledge. There could be unpleasant comment if this story leaks out and I could be—' she broke off, shuddering, '*named* in the newspapers.'

'I see. Of course. All right, I'll wash and change. And then we'll see what the Ardiccis have to say.'

'Tap on my door when you're ready. I'm the next door but one.'

When they went downstairs together, they found the Ardiccis in the drawing-room, sipping aperitifs. Floria Massigna was there too, proving her family connection.

They had changed, but not into evening clothes, in deference to their guest whose luggage had suggested only a few necessities. Nicoletta had satisfied herself with the addition of a velvet jacket to her day dress. The effect of the gathering, nevertheless, was of status and respect for tradition.

The dining-room, recently redecorated by Grossmutti, was rather splendid. Her usual style was European Biedermeier, but for this house she'd gone for classical Roman – a bust of some patrician lady stood on the marble mantelpiece, there were triumphal garlands above the doors and window frames. Not at all bad, thought the crown prince.

Ruggiero Ardicci offered drinks. When they had settled in armchairs, he cleared his throat. 'Your grandmother has no doubt given you some idea of our problem, Gregory.'

'Only that some valuable property has gone missing.'

'Aha. Well, the "property" is a set of diamonds. They belong to Rini. We are very anxious to get them back.'

'But I would have thought your best plan would be to call—'

'The police. No, no, my dear friend, that would be extremely awkward for me. Politics, you understand?' His glance moved from Gregory to Nicoletta.

'I gave him some notion of the difficulty of that move,' she said. 'But of course very little detail.'

'Could we leave that for the moment?' Gregory suggested. 'It might be easier to tell me about it from the beginning.'

Ruggiero looked at his wife. She took a sip of Recioto Amaroni before beginning, rather hesitantly. 'The diamonds aren't strung as a necklace. I seldom wore them because they were . . . somewhat ostentatious.' With a finger she traced a line at her throat. 'What in casual terms is called a choker.'

She paused. Gregory waited for the rest but she seemed reluctant to go on. After carefully setting her glass on a side table, so as to gain time, she said: 'I had them made into a frame for a little picture I own.'

He tried not to look surprised. Ostentatious diamonds, made into a picture frame? What on earth could that look like? He carefully avoided catching his grandmother's eye, and asked in a neutral tone: 'Was this picture hanging somewhere – in a public room?'

'No, it was hanging on the wall in a corner of my boudoir.'

'Yes?'

'Above my prie-dieu.'

The prince was entertaining very unkind thoughts about his grandmother for having dragged him into this. It sounded stranger and stranger the more he heard.

'It's a religious picture,' Rini explained in a low voice. 'Of Saint Olga.' As she said the name, she crossed herself.

Gregory had never heard of Saint Olga. That wasn't surprising, because the family religion, if it had one, was Lutheran, and Lutherans are not very approving of the worship of saints.

'Rini has a special reverence for Saint Olga,' Ruggiero put in.

'It was her feast day last month. She was the first saint of Russia,' his wife declared, lifting up her head and looking about with eyes that glowed with pride. 'She was a queen of my country in its very early days, and so she is revered as the patron saint of rulers and statesmen. You understand? She is the protector of my Ruggiero. If I am faithful to her, she will save him from his enemies, and she'll restore his health.'

This outburst had something in it of both apology and defiance. Gregory could see that she knew very well how strange it had sounded – diamonds framing a little religious painting. But she believed in what she had done, believed that in honouring her saint, she was helping her husband.

'So then,' Gregory said, 'who besides yourself had access to the painting?'

'No one! No one but myself and Ruggiero.'

'You keep the room locked?'

'No, but the painting is in the far corner of the boudoir, and the corner is partitioned off by a folding screen.'

'So the household staff – the maid, for instance – would see it when she cleaned the room.'

'No, because I look after my prie-dieu myself. Cristina has strict instructions not to go near it.'

'But you had work being done inside the house – redecorations. Could some of the workmen have gone up there?'

'No, not at all,' his grandmother declared. 'All the work was on the ground-floor rooms – this room, the dining-room and ballroom. The workmen had no need at all to go upstairs and I was supervising them very closely, Gregory.'

He knew this to be true. Nicoletta was quite a tyrannical overseer.

'Besides,' Ruggiero said, 'we feel it was not a casual event. We think the thief must have had – what is it called? – inside information. No one would have thought of looking for real diamonds framing a little picture, without having inside information.'

'You may be right there. So the next question is: who made this diamond frame for the picture?'

'Exactly. We can give you the name of the picture-framer, Gregory. And we want you to visit him and question him very tactfully, so that no gossip can be aroused. And if he has the picture, or knows who has taken it, we want you to buy it back for us. At any price, and very quietly.'

# TWO

Gregory's first impulse was to set down his drink and ask to be driven back to the airport at once. He had no wish to be involved in some shady deal with a jewel thief, even if he knew how to contact one. If anyone had been watching him, they'd have seen the frown of distaste on his long, fair-skinned face. Even his attitude would have been enough to show his displeasure. His rangy body was tensed to spring up in revulsion.

But at that moment Ernesto came in to announce dinner. Everyone rose just as he did, his grandmother took his arm to be escorted to the dinner table, and the moment for immediate protest had gone by.

The table was candle-lit. The candle flames in their glass protectors did not waver although the French windows were open to allow the muslin curtains to sway in the cool air of the Castelli Romani.

Porcelain and silver glistened on the pure white of the cloth at one end of a long walnut table. Ruggiero drew out a chair for his wife, Ernesto did likewise for Floria, and at a sign from Nicoletta, Gregory saw her into her place. He took his seat in the remaining chair.

A middle-aged woman in cap and apron came in with the *antipasti* on a great silver tray. Ernesto poured wine – a bright stream from a bottle with a label unknown to Gregory.

Gregory waited until the servants had withdrawn. Then he said: 'I was startled by your request, Signor Ardicci. I must tell you that I don't have the kind of knowledge that could be helpful to you.'

'Gregory!' scolded his grandmother.

Ruggiero Ardicci looked concerned. 'I was wrong? I gathered from Madame von Hirtenstein that you had had considerable success on previous occasions.'

He acknowledged the compliment by a slight inclination of the head. 'But on none of those was I asked to buy back stolen goods, *signore*.'

'Please, I beg you, call me Ruggiero, and if I may I'll call you Gregory. Your grandmother has used that name, it's familiar to me now.'

'Whatever name you call me by, I shan't enter into negotiations with a thief.'

'Darling,' murmured Rini, 'I think we have been tactless.'

'Hmm.' Her husband chose an item from among the little slivers of ham and avocado and salted fish. He chewed for a moment then said: 'I apologize, Gregory. I'm out of practice, it seems. Clumsiness is not a useful thing for a politician.' He arranged his sallow features in a smile intended to be winning.

'Child, you're being difficult,' Nicoletta declared. 'You can surely help to find out where the diamonds are now, who has them, whether they would be interested in selling.'

'I haven't any connections in the Roman underworld, Grossmutti.'

'Oh, nonsense.' It was a snort of irritation. 'You have friends everywhere! Perhaps you can't lay your hands on a jeweller who would accept stolen goods, but you have friends here who could tell you which jeweller it might be.'

There was truth in that. Gregory knew people in practically every city that boasted a concert hall or an opera house. They were what Liz Blair called his 'musical Mafia'. He knew instrumentalists, singers, composers, costume designers, gossip writers who specialized in watching the famous, record collectors, collectors of programmes or photographs or autographs – dozens of people who shared his interest in the world of classical music. Probably, among that crowd, there would be someone who knew someone who might guide him towards a likely pawnshop or jewellery store.

'I would wish to recompense you for any work you did on my behalf,' Ruggiero said, with enough hesitation to make it seem he was being tactful.

'My dear Ruggiero,' cried Nicoletta, 'that needn't be thought of!'

Ruggiero gave Gregory a sly glance, as if to say, 'We'll sort that out ourselves, eh?'

He raised his glass. 'Let's drink to our agreement.'

Gregory stifled a sigh, then raised his glass. He'd put in a couple of days and then announce defeat. Better that than have his grandmother reproach him for being selfish and pig-headed.

The meal continued with a faint sense of strain in the air. Ruggiero, understanding that he had offended his guest, exerted himself to be affable. He talked about the villa and its history, with a hint of pride as if he'd put it up himself.

'It was built to a design by Durand – do you know him? No? Oh, greatly respected in the late eighteenth and early nineteenth century. Our little place' – this with a modest shrug – 'is one of the projects that he himself supervised.' Here followed a little lecture about architraves and pillars Doric or Tuscan, until his wife suggested they should take coffee in the drawing-room.

Not to be deflected, Ruggiero began again when they settled there. 'The stables here are interesting. Built after the villa was finished, but quite a clever imitation in miniature of Durand's style. Do you ride? I'll show you the horses in the morning.'

'It would be quite a good idea to show me where the missing picture was hanging,' Gregory suggested.

'Ah? You think so?'

'It might give me some idea how the thief found out about its existence.'

'There you are, my dear,' said Ruggiero with admiration. 'I knew it was a good idea to ask for help. Perhaps you'd like to show Gregory where . . .?'

But Rini was unwilling. She let her head sink as if to avoid his gaze, then said in a mournful murmur, 'But dearest . . .

You know how precious the place is to me. And . . . you know . . . it's in my boudoir . . .'

Nicoletta let a flicker of irritation appear for a moment before suggesting that Floria might conduct her grandson to the spot. 'You know the place, I imagine, *signorina?*' she said to her.

'I supervise the cleaning of the house,' Floria agreed. 'I have never myself ventured behind the screen, of course, since the picture was placed there. No one has.' There was a suggestion of ruffled feathers in this report. Clearly Signorina Massigna had no great affection for the lady of the house.

A little time elapsed while they nibbled *petits fours* and Ruggiero drank a special liqueur which was deemed to be good for his health. Then Floria led the way upstairs to the bedroom floor, taking him through some double doors to a splendid apartment in the east wing.

The room they came into first was a sort of little antechamber, with a writing desk, a bookcase, a trio of armchairs in willow-green tapestry, and doors opening off it on three sides. Floria led the way to one of these, opened it, and ushered in Mr Crowne.

This was the boudoir: walls painted with a faded scene of fauns and nymphs dancing, soft creams and pinks in the curtains and on the upholstery of the eighteenth-century Italian furniture, and in one corner, a folding screen extended to seal off its contents.

Floria turned back one of the folds of the screen, inviting Gregory to pass on into the three-cornered cubicle it formed. She herself didn't follow.

Gregory found a prie-dieu, a very old article of dark wood, with a cushioned base to kneel on and a stand with a shelf attached. On the shelf was a little vase containing some wild flowers and leaves, now somewhat wilted, and a prayer book. He bent to see its title. The name was in gold, in Cyrillic letters.

He looked up to examine the walls. There was no brighter area such as would be left if a picture had hung there a long time. There was a plain wooden crucifix there now, the Byzantine cross with its three bars, the lowest one slightly at an angle. This was where the painting must have hung.

When he emerged into the main room, Floria was flicking over the pages of a magazine on one of the little tables. Impatience was evident in every twitch of her fingers.

'*Signorina*, as far as you know, is everything just as usual?'

She raised her eyebrows. 'I suppose so. I believe you found a prayer-stall, with some flowers – only meadow flowers, because Saint Olga lived before the days of cultivated roses and lilies. Or so one is told.'

'And the painting? Did you ever see it?'

'Only when it first arrived. That was about a year ago, I think. It was brought in a little wooden box, which Ernesto had to use his tools to open. Inside was a purple velvet case embroidered with a golden cross – the Orthodox cross, of course – the case opened as if it had two little doors. Rini opened it with a lot of fuss and weeping, kissed the painting, then shut it up again very quickly.'

'Can you describe the painting?'

She hesitated. 'I only caught a glimpse. It wasn't very big.' She held out hands cupped together to form an oval about seven inches wide and suggesting perhaps eight in height. 'About that size, perhaps a little more.'

'A miniature, in other words?'

'I believe it would be called that.'

'Did you see the saint's portrait?'

'No, I couldn't see that. I just got the impression that there was a face in what I suppose you'd call flesh colours, with perhaps a golden crown, and the rest mostly rather dark.'

'But it didn't have the frame of diamonds?'

'Oh, no, that was done a few weeks later. Ernesto had to fasten up the wooden box again and it was taken off by Rini to whoever was going to make the frame.' She sniffed. She didn't actually say, 'Dreadfully bad taste,' but it was in the down-turn of her lips.

'What do you think made her use her necklace for the frame? It seems . . . a little bizarre.'

Thus tempted, Floria gave in to gossip. 'Oh, well, my cousin had been really rather ill at the time.' She paused, and Gregory wondered what that had to do with making a diamond frame. Seeing his puzzlement, she went on. 'He suffers, you see – his digestion has become somewhat weakened recently, and the doctor says it's due to his past – the political life – too many banquets and late-night plotting over whisky and brandy – you know the kind of thing.'

'That's understandable.'

'Rini has never really understood Ruggiero's health problems. He needs a bland diet, and something to settle the stomach after a meal. I make him these little *digestifs*' – she gave a little self-satisfied smile – 'little additions to the liqueurs he likes to drink, nothing much, but I have something of a talent for it.'

'Oh, yes. I believe I saw something special in his glass after dinner.'

'Yes, Calvados with just a few herbs steeped in it – very soothing to the stomach. That has helped him. But now with the anxiety over the New York post—'

'*The New York Post*?' Gregory was thinking of a newspaper.

'There's a diplomatic post becoming available soon – Ambassador to the United Nations in New York – and Ruggiero would dearly love to get it. Here in Rome, you see, he has many rivals, but to be in New York would help him greatly. He could make new contacts, extend his possibilities . . .'

'You take a great interest in his career, I see.'

'Oh, yes, after Camilla died – my cousin, Camilla, they were married ten happy years but then alas . . .' She sighed. 'I took over as head of this house and I have always paid great attention to his well-being. But Rini – well, she loves rich food. Our menu isn't always suitable for someone with a delicate digestive tract.' She paused, her lips curling in disapproval. 'Perhaps she's making up for years of eating in a dressing-room or at inexpensive cafes. Before she married Ruggiero, you know, she wasn't greatly in demand at the main opera houses.' She gave him a glance inviting agreement. 'You are involved in the music world, I gather. Rini wasn't exactly in the top rank, was she?'

'Perhaps not.'

'Well, never mind that, the fact is that Ruggiero was suffering quite a lot of pain because of the rich food. The doctor suspected a stomach ulcer at one time. Rini thought that Saint Olga would intercede for him if she made some great devotional offering, and that's how the diamond frame came into being.'

'I recall she said it was a "choker"?'

'Yes, two chains of gold half an inch apart, holding about a dozen diamonds – I'm no expert but I remember Camilla's engagement ring had a diamond about that size and I think it was about one and a half carats.'

She looked at him for confirmation, but he shook his head. He'd seen his royal relatives wearing diamonds at events such as weddings and christenings, but had never inquired about their value.

'So she had the diamonds taken out of the chain and made into a frame for Saint Olga's portrait,' Floria said with a shrug.

Gregory didn't inquire whether there had been an improvement in Ruggiero's health as a result. Instead he asked: 'Ernesto drove me from the airport, and helped served dinner. Cristina I gather is the cook. What other servants do you have?'

'None that live in. Ernesto and Cristina don't actually live in. They live in the lodge, just inside the main gates. There are two regular members of staff – a daily maid, and a boy who looks after the horses and helps care for the garden. I hire others as they are needed – caterers for a special occasion, waiting staff, and a team once a month to take on the major cleaning that Sara can't do.'

'Do you think any of those could have taken the painting?'

She shook her head emphatically. 'In the first place, *signore*, I don't think they know the painting exists. Access to Rini's boudoir is strictly limited. Sara cleans it, but I supervise her. I don't think she has ever even seen the prie-dieu.'

'Do you supervise Ernesto if he comes up to the bedrooms? He brought up my luggage?'

'Ernesto . . . yes, he comes up to the bedrooms, and takes Ruggiero's shirts for the washing-machine, things like that. I doubt that he has ever come in here, and if he has, I doubt if he has looked behind the screen. Cristina, now – her work is confined more or less to the kitchen. She has no opportunity to go upstairs. He and Cristina are rather dull people – peasant stock, you know, not apt to do anything that would seem presumptuous for fear of losing their jobs.'

'And the stableboy?'

'Oh, he's practically a horse himself! Thick as a marble pillar but a gem with the animals. No, I don't think he's even come into the house – he spends all his time in the stable and the garden.'

'That leaves the workmen who were doing the redecorations.'

'Ah, your grandmother hired them. From a very reputable firm in Ostia.' Floria smiled. 'They worked in the drawing-room and the dining-room. The ballroom had not had anything done to it when the theft was discovered but she at once cancelled the work—'

'Really? I didn't know that.'

'Well, that was at Ruggiero's request. He was afraid that somehow they'd get some hint that there was trouble here at Villa Stefani, and talk about it to the gossip columnists. Perhaps it was unjustified, but the work can be resumed once this business has been cleared up.' She looked at him expectantly, as if asking him to say it would soon be done.

Gregory was unable to give her the assurance. He felt somewhat out of his depth – or out of his comfort zone, perhaps. He knew nothing about gemstones, had not felt any great fellow-feeling for Ruggiero, and wished he'd never got involved. But having agreed to look into it, he'd keep his word.

'I think I'll settle down with the telephone and contact a few friends in Rome,' he muttered. 'To see what I can set up for tomorrow. Thank you for showing me the crime scene.'

'When you telephone please use the landline, *signore*. Mobile phones don't work well within the villa – you have to go out into the old vineyard to get a good signal. If you press M1 on the numerals, you will automatically get an outside line.'

'Thank you.'

The first 'contact' he wanted to make was not with anyone in Rome. He called Liz Blair in London. She answered with a cheery: 'Hello, chuckie!'

'Chuckie? What kind of a word is that?'

'Oh, it's from the universal language of my schooldays – very much in my mind at the moment because I'm sketching a copy of what looks like a school blazer that's a hot tip for next spring.'

He never could keep track of her fashion work. One minute she was off supervising a fashion show in Majorca, the next she was at her drawing board providing a knocked-off copy of someone else's inspiration.

He could picture her there – light-brown hair falling forward as she worked, a frown of concentration on her brow, hazel eyes focused on the lines drawn by her charcoal pencil.

'Are you busy, then?' he asked. 'Have I interrupted you while you were conversing with your muse?'

'Ha ha. How are things at the Villa Tormentata?'

'It's not exactly tormented. It's more in panic than anguish. I can't say I feel close to any of the residents. I wish I hadn't come.'

'Er . . . mm . . . How's Grandmama?'

'Upset. There's been a theft and it's made her anxious.'

'That she might be arrested?' she asked, stifling a giggle.

'Now, now, behave. She might get mentioned in the gossip columns because Ardicci is . . . well, I don't know exactly what cabinet post he used to have but he got fired, and now he has diplomatic ambitions. The press are likely to be interested in him. Never mind that. I'm going into Rome tomorrow, sweetheart, so I'll take a look at one or two of the hotels—'

'No, no, don't bother, Greg. I've fixed that up for myself. If I'm in Rome on business, I generally stay at a comfy little hotel not far from the Via Sacrata, the Pastorella. I'm flying tomorrow evening and you'll find me there about eight if you care to linger in that neighbourhood after you've carried out your day's work.'

They had a little discussion about their meeting and then she asked, 'What are you actually going to be doing in Rome? Is there a suspect or what?'

'Nothing so helpful! Something's gone missing and as far as I can tell, nothing sensible has been done about it. In a minute I'm going to telephone a few friends, to see if they could suggest a jeweller or someone that might buy some stolen stones.'

'Stolen jewels, eh? A diamond tiara?'

'You wouldn't believe me if I explained. But it seems to be the general idea that these will be loose stones by now. I thought I'd ask Mario Zetto – he works for a little magazine that reports on nightclubs and things like that.'

'You mean things that aren't quite respectable . . .' Her words trailed off. 'I do believe I might be able to help you there, love.'

'You mean you know someone who is not respectable?'

He knew she was smiling to herself when she replied. 'Us girls in the fashion industry aren't altogether little Snow Whites. There's a guy in the Roman world of bling—'

'*Bling?*'

'Flashy jewellery, sweetie. The stuff worn by WAGS.'

'Wags?' It was yet another baffled query.

'Wives And Girlfriends.'

'Wives and girlfriends of whom?'

'Footballers and rock stars, people like that. Eduardo's good at that sort of thing. He's been known to supply ruby earrings and gold bracelets that . . . if you get my meaning . . . might have been part of someone else's jewellery box.'

'You think he handles stolen goods?'

'We–ell, I think he perhaps buys things that have been broken up from stolen goods – gemstones taken out of their settings, bits of gold-work that can be re-used without too much bother.'

'Is Eduardo his business name?'

'He's Eduardo Fernaldi. I've never met him, so I don't know where he hangs out but he's sure to be in the Rome phone book. His firm's called *Cose Raggiante*, whatever that means.'

'Shiny Things. That sounds very promising. My darling, you really are a wonderful woman.'

'And don't you forget it! Listen, Greg, I must get back to that bothersome blazer. The manufacturer wants to see some ideas by midday tomorrow.'

'Of course. I'm sorry to have disturbed you at work. Until tomorrow at the Pastorella.'

When he had disconnected he considered asking Inquiries for the telephone number of *Cose Raggiante* but decided against it. It was too late in the evening to ring a stranger. Instead he looked in his personal planner for Zetto's number, and was greeted with a friendly but rather drunken '*Come sta, caro fratello mio?*'. The words were only just audible over the sound of some fierce percussive music.

'I'm fine, thank you, Mario. Is this a good time to talk to you?'

'Ah, talk to me? You wanna get in touch with La Valdina? She's inna first stages of a new love affair, so you won't be able to p'suade her to go to Berlin or Rio de Janeiro for some stupid concert—'

'Mario, Mario, you've had too much to drink.'

'Course I have. I'm at Club Tamburo. I don't come here for the *band*, that's for sure. So whaddaya want?'

'I only want to ask you a simple question. Do you know anything about a man called Eduardo Fernaldi?'

'Who? Oh, you mean Signor Scintillio? Why d'you wanna know anything about a show-off like him? He can't play a *ninstrument*, you know. He can only make glittery things.'

'That's why I want to talk to him.'

'Gonna buy something for your girlfriend? She won't wear it if you do.'

'I just want to talk to him.'

'Grego, he'll make you buy something. A name bracelet or something. You don't wanna name bracelet.'

In the end, Mr Crowne extracted the information that Eduardo Fernaldi liked to hang out at a smart restaurant in Via del Corso eating a late lunch and showing off his 'bling'.

'Not every day, y'unnerstan, Grego. Too hot and stuffy in Rome – he's got a pad on the coast, nice breeze, y'know. But he needs to be in touch with the fash'n industry 'cos the autumn shows will be on soon.'

Satisfied that he had done enough for the moment, the prince went to bed.

Next morning, with an air of proud ownership, Ruggiero showed him round the property.

'You see, my friend, this is an old building. There are many doorways, but all of them have alarms. Still it might be possible, perhaps, for a thief to hide in the garage some time during the day, and so be able to get into the house once we were all asleep.'

There was a connecting door, with no alarm. True enough, an interloper could have been lying down comfortably in the back of one of the cars until the right time came.

The stables, built like a rustic version of the villa as promised, offered no connecting entry to it. A visit there gave Greg the chance to speak to the stableboy, Armeno. Floria's verdict was correct: Armeno's answers to Greg's gentle questions showed him to be slow-minded, almost child-like – not at all the kind to steal anything, let alone something hanging in a holy corner on the upper floors of the house.

After admiring the shining coats of the two horses that were Armeno's joy, they went on a round of the gardens.

A loggia led out to the part that was known as 'the old vineyard', now empty of vines except for one at the top of the slope. 'My family used to make wine,' Ruggiero explained, 'not for sale, only for personal use. I expect it was rough, but full of flavour. The vines were taken out before I was born, but you see, here's one of them, a fine old survivor, and still giving us grapes every year.'

The vine formed a sort of arbour at the top of the slight southern facing incline. An old wrought-iron chair stood in the shelter of its leaves. Bunches of grapes were visible among them, gleaming plump and red. Ruggiero touched one with a finger. 'Ready to eat, I think. I love to sample the first grapes. Sentimental, isn't it?' Smiling, he led the way across a parterre where little patterned beds of lavender and thyme sent their perfume into the air.

At the far side of the paved area was the driveway to the gates. They walked along it, to the lodge. Ernesto was up a ladder, busy with shears, clipping the evergreen hedges that bordered the drive. These were tall, to give some shade on a day of fierce sunshine.

At sight of his employer, Ernesto set the shears on the top step and came down hastily. 'Good morning, *signore*.'

'Good morning, Ernesto. I'm just giving Signor Crowne a little tour of my domain.' Ruggiero always used Italian with the staff.

'Yes, *signore*. Everything satisfactory?'

'Oh, certainly. We just came from the pergola. The grapes are almost ready to be picked, eh?'

'Yes, *signore*.'

'A day or two, then.'

'Yes, *signore*.'

'You have a lot to do, Ernesto,' Mr Crowne remarked. 'And you seem to do it well – the garden looks lovely.'

'Thank you, *signore*.'

He was a man of middle-age, sturdy and with a broad, sunburnt face, not handsome but full of character. He spoke very briefly, almost as if avoiding vocal contact. The prince got the impression that Ernesto had no great love for his master.

'I imagine you've worked here a long time,' he ventured.

'Me, *signore*? No, no.' He glanced at Ruggiero from under dark brows. 'Signor Ardicci was so good as to give me and my wife employment at the villa and a place to live, about a year ago.' He nodded towards the lodge, a pleasant house in the same trimmed-down version of the villa.

Greg thought that probably there was some ancient tie between the families. He imagined that to be employed at the villa was a privilege in these parts, not likely to be awarded to a stranger. It was true that the area held several big tourist attractions, but that was seasonal work. Unemployment was a problem in Italy at present and having a job like his was fortunate. Yet Ernesto seemed almost careless in his manner towards Ruggiero.

Was this the kind of man who might steal a diamond-bordered miniature?

# THREE

As they went back into the Villa Stefani, a little woman, plump and elderly, was at work with a soft-haired brush cleaning a small marble statue on a side table. She shifted out of their way as they came into the hall.

'Good morning, Sara,' carolled Ruggiero. 'How are you this fine day?'

'V–very well, signore,' she stammered. 'Tha–thank you for asking.'

'Lovely, lovely!' He strolled on into the drawing-room.

Mr Crowne lingered a moment. 'It's delicate work, caring for antiques,' he suggested.

'Oh, y–yes, *signore*.'

'Is it your speciality?'

'Who – m–me? Oh, no, *signore*. B–but I,' she hung her head and mumbled the rest, 'I love do–doing it.'

Floria appeared, coming from somewhere at the back of the house. Sara immediately picked up a little hold-all of tools and scuttled away.

'Was she bothering you, Gregory?' asked Floria.

'No, no, not at all. I was just asking about her job, looking after these precious things. She seems quite devoted to it.'

Floria's expression seemed to imply that this was only what she expected. Gregory was satisfied that Sara, with her nervousness and her uncertainty, was an unlikely suspect for the theft of the painting.

The two of them went into the drawing-room to join Ruggiero. They found him with Nicoletta and Rini, settling down to mid-morning coffee.

'Now what do you think, Gregory!' cried Ruggiero. 'This dear lady is saying she wishes to go back to Geneva. Tell her she must stay.'

Gregory said nothing but instead turned to his grandmother for clarification.

'I feel it would be best if I were to take myself from the scene,' she said. 'I don't want to do anything to the ballroom until this little contretemps has been cleared up. I'm sure you agree, my child.'

'Whatever you wish, Grossmutti.' Inwardly he was pleased to hear of her decision. Liz would be arriving in Rome this evening. God forbid that they should at any time come across one another.

Rini and Floria joined in to re-enforce Ruggiero's objection but out of mere politeness. The ex-queen mother maintained her wish to go. When the coffee was finished she went upstairs to pack. Her grandson said he intended to take himself into Rome by train to Termini Station, but this was greeted by cries of amazement.

'No, no, not at all!' cried Ruggiero. 'Madame Hirtenstein has to fly from Ciampino. Of course Ernesto will drive you both, and will take you on into Rome after dropping her there.'

He could see it was no use arguing. But he intended to hire himself his own transport. He had no wish to hamper his freedom by depending on Ernesto.

They drove off as planned, down between the high hedges to the gates, which opened at the electronic command of Ernesto. The road outside was edged with the undergrowth and trees that enjoy stony soil, what is known as *alberini selvaggi*, and its surface wasn't of the best.

On the journey to the airport the passengers dropped into German, a language they often spoke at home in Geneva because

Nicoletta had been Austrian by birth. This was so as to prevent Ernesto from understanding them.

'You mustn't let Ruggiero annoy you, Grego,' she said. 'He's a bit of a fool but all the same, he has some standing in this country.'

'I'm not taking any of this too seriously,' he replied.

'But you *will* try to find out who has the jewels?'

'That's why I'm going to Rome. To look for a man who seems to buy things that aren't exactly honestly on sale.'

She gave him a wry smile. 'What a strange thing, eh? You and I are employed by this man, who'd be beneath our notice if we were where we really belong.'

'What, back in dear old Hirtenstein, with the peasants kissing our hands?'

It made her laugh. 'You know the place is full of bankers and stockbrokers these days. But yes, I wouldn't mind having my hand kissed by inhabitants like those!'

They parted on good terms. As Ernesto held open the car door for him on his return from the departure hall, he inquired, 'Whereabouts in Rome would you like to go, *signore*?'

'It's a restaurant in the Via del Corso called La Gazza.'

'Ah . . . I don't think I can wait for you there, sir. I'll drop you and then if you say when you want to be picked up—'

'No, no, that's not necessary. I'll make my own way back.'

'But Signor Ardicci said—'

'That's all right, Ernesto, tell him I didn't want you to wait.'

'Very well, *signore*.' He looked quietly pleased at having to tell his master that Mr Crowne had changed the instructions.

La Gazza – suitable name for a place where a man showed off shiny things, because magpies are well known to collect bits of silver paper and glittery objects. Its façade was pleasant enough though painted rather brightly in irregular patches of black and white. A black-and-white figure of a magpie showed a list of the day's special dishes on its surface.

As he entered, he was greeted by the head waiter. 'Signor Fernaldi?' he inquired. He was ushered into the cool depths of the restaurant, to a table where a tubby young man sat alone with a little array of fake jewellery in front of him. He was clad in a short-sleeved shirt of dark-red silk with a row of little enamelled studs along the edge of its collar.

He looked up. The waiter bowed and moved off.

'Eh!' said Fernaldi. *'Sei svedese, tu, no?'*

Mr Crowne rejected the idea he was Swedish. 'I'm from Geneva,' he said. 'Gregory Crowne.'

Fernaldi grinned. 'Swiss, eh? Too bad. I was going to offer you a super-duper watch, but being Swiss, you've got one, eh?' He waited for approval for this joke. Mr Crowne obliged and asked if he might sit down.

'Sure, sure. What can I offer you? I mean before I persuade you to buy something really eye-catching. Wine? Beer? The food's quite good here.'

Settling for a beer and a *pasticcino*, he took his place opposite Fernaldi. 'Here on a visit?' Fernaldi asked.

'Yes, I'm staying out at Castelli Romani.'

*'Cavolo!* Got an audience with Mr Upstairs?'

'No, no, that's not my kind of thing.' The idea of getting an audience with the Pope was quite outside his plans. He gathered from this short exchange that Fernaldi liked to use the latest Roman slang, to show that he was in the swing of everything young and fashionable. 'Mario Zetto suggested I should talk to you,' he explained.

*'Il chiacchierone* himself! What a blabbermouth. But if you buy something, I'll forgive him.'

'He said you might know about a few . . . er . . . loose stones that have come on the market.'

'Loose? How loose? A broken-up necklace?' His interest was immediate. 'Not recently, and despite what Zetto says, I don't know everything.' He paused. 'Stones meaning what? Real goodies?'

'Diamonds.'

'Hmm . . .' He pushed two little pieces of sparkling jewellery forward. 'Something like those?'

'Are those diamonds?'

'Very nearly.' He grinned. 'Man-made. Can't put real stones on shoe ornaments, might get kicked off.'

'These go on shoes?'

'Will do. You watch the sandal-straps of the models this autumn as they strut down the cat-walk – they'll have my sparklers clipped on them.'

'What a great idea!'

'You want to buy these? For your girl?'

Gregory shook his head. 'I'm saving my money until I get a glimpse of the real diamonds I'm after.'

His meat-tartlet and drink came. The waiter poured the beer into the glass, set down his plate, and withdrew.

'Chin-chin,' said Fernaldi, raising his own glass, which contained something rather sticky-looking and brightly tinted. They sipped. He went on: 'Haven't seen or heard of any loose stones such as you're out fishing for. I could probably get you something, though. I know one or two divas who've got stuff they'd like to exchange for moolah.'

Greg shook his head. 'These are matched stones I'm after.'

'Really? Something ritzy, eh? Can't help you there, then. How about buying a little something for a loved one? Male or female, I'm sure I've got something that would be appreciated.'

In the end the prince bought what Fernaldi called a 'hair-tag'. It was intended to be attached to the end of an errant lock, so as to sparkle at about cheek level. What Liz would make of it, he couldn't imagine.

His next stop was the frame-maker. He proved rather difficult to find because there were few people about from whom to inquire the way. The heat was intense; some shops and restaurants were waiting for the comparative cool of the evening to open and many had closed until September.

In the end, he found the shop in the *centro storico* near the Vatican: a total contrast from the kitschy vigour of La Gazza, its front was painted dove-grey. In the window were several examples of the owner's craft – an ornate gilt frame round a reproduction of Watteau, a severe black rectangle of steel holding architectural draughtsmanship, and two or three smaller examples suitable for family photographs.

Above the window was the name: *Alessandro, Fabbricante di Cornice*. An old-fashioned shop bell tinkled as he went in. From the back of the shop came a very old man in shirtsleeves and thick canvas apron.

*'Signore?'*

'Good afternoon. I believe Signora Ardicci telephoned to tell you I would be calling.'

'Ah, Signor Crowne. Yes, of course. Please, come this way.' He gave a little bow of acknowledgement before opening a flap in the counter to let him pass. 'My workroom,' he said, ushering him through a doorway into a quite large space with big windows. A workbench with clamps and vices took up a lot of room, with a surprisingly modern electric saw on a stand at its end. There was a tool-bench and above it a wall of implements. Finished specimens of his work were in large compartments on another wall, loosely shrouded in white paper marked with a name in wax crayon.

They passed through this to a tiny room, scarcely more than a cubicle. The door was open to the yard beyond, but a heavy bead curtain hung in the aperture to keep out the heat. There were a couple of very battered chairs, a folding table set up to hold glasses and bottles, and an ancient fridge in a corner.

'This is my hide-away,' said the frame-maker with a little grin on his wrinkled face. 'My home is upstairs, of course, where my wife insists on order and decency, but here I can be an old tortoise and do as I please.' He waved at the fridge. 'Something cold?'

'Oh, please!'

'Yes, us that have to work in August need to be kept hydrated, yes we do.' He opened the fridge, took out two bottles, and offered one to Greg. It turned out, to his surprise, to be a supermarket own-brand of Coca-Cola.

But it was icy cool in his hands. Alessandro settled himself in one of the chairs, Greg took the other, and they opened their bottles of cold restorative.

'You wish to ask me about the miniature, Signor Crowne. It was a strange task – although over the past fifty years I've made many, many peculiar frames. The whims of my customers, you understand . . .' The creaky old voice was tolerant though regretful. 'I can't afford to turn away business no matter what weird things they ask for. One from deer antlers, I recall, a horrid piece of work but the owner was delighted.'

'Let me guess, it was to frame a photograph of him with the carcase.'

'Aha! I see you know sportsmen! Still, horn is comparatively easy to handle. Some of my younger customers have asked me to make frames in modern materials – Lucite, Perspex, strange tinted metals . . . Those need power tools, although I prefer to work by hand.' He shook his head and sipped from his bottle.

'I understand Signora Ardicci wanted you to use the diamonds from a necklace.'

He rubbed his hand back and forth across the top of his head, making sparse grey hairs stand on end. 'And she wanted the diamonds to *sparkle*. Now, although I am not a jeweller, I know that gemstones will not sparkle unless the light can reach them through their setting. I had to think about it quite a lot. I couldn't make any kind of wooden frame in which to set them.'

'No, I suppose not.'

'In the end, I made an oval mount of thick clear glass, a little bigger than the portrait. The portrait itself is painted on wood, as I expect you know – that was easy to deal with.'

'I haven't seen it, but so I'm told.'

'I have various little cements and adhesives of my own that I can use for awkward work so I had no trouble attaching the painting to the glass. Then I affixed the diamonds in their existing settings around it. Spacing them was quite tricky but of course I drew several diagrams first.' He frowned at Greg, as if he had been told to make everything clear to him and rather doubted as to his success. 'I was anxious about her reactions. But the *signora* was delighted – positively entranced!'

The prince thought this merely showed that Signora Ardicci was really weird.

'She said that it "blazed with a holy light", that it was "radiant", and she paid me a lot more than my estimate. She said that she would receive additional blessings by doing so.'

It was quite clear from the old man's tone that he thought his customer was a religious crank. He waited for Greg's comments.

'I believe the stones were originally held in gold chains?'

'Yes, I returned those to the *signora*,' he said defensively.

'Do you have anyone to help you in your work, Signor Alessandro?'

'My dear sir! Do you think anyone wants to be apprenticed to an old traditionalist like me? No, no, even my sons backed away from this career. One of them is farming in New South Wales, and the other runs a school in Namibia. I barely make enough to keep myself and my wife, I couldn't pay for an assistant. That's why, really, I took on this . . . this . . . I must say *absurd* commission with the diamonds.'

Greg nodded in sympathetic agreement. They sipped their drinks.

'May I ask why the *signora* has hired a private detective to inquire about the framing?' asked Alessandro, sounding quite hurt. '*All* the stones were used in the frame, I sent back *all* the gold chain.'

'I'm not at liberty to tell you,' sighed Greg. 'But I can assure you you're not suspected of anything underhand.'

'Thank God for that!'

They chatted amicably until the bottles were empty. Alessandro showed him out. The bell tinkled as he stepped out into the street, the old man waving him farewell through the glass panel.

The air was as hot as if it came direct from the Sahara. By good luck, he found a taxi near Castel Sant' Angelo. He was driven to Via Vittoria, where a friend from the Accademia di Santa Cecilia was waiting for him. This was Martina, a lady of some seniority, who worked in Programme Planning.

There were no performances in August, so they spent an enjoyable couple of hours in the empty café of the auditorium, catching up with the gossip – who was sleeping with whom, who had finagled a job with which opera company, and a few hints about the Ardiccis.

'He's only half as important as he thinks he is,' was her verdict on Ruggiero. 'But he's got money and you know, here-abouts, money talks. And *she's* crazy about him, don't ask me why.' She shrugged off the idea that he might get the New York position. 'Depends if he's pulling the right strings. He does have support, but there's a lot of competitors for the job and they have money too.'

'She's very religious, I hear.'

'Yes, Greek Orthodox or something?'

'Russian.'

'Oh, of course.' She made a little moue of irritation.

'You haven't heard anything about her special devotion to Saint Olga?'

'No, but she was always a bit odd, wasn't she? Saint Olga? When she sang here, she was always praying to statues and icons and things. I don't know who they were dedicated to.'

Even this great fount of knowledge seemed unable to supply anything useful.

He had dinner in an air-conditioned restaurant in the area close to the Hotel Pastorella. Traffic had diminished, a breeze had sprung up, and he walked along what had once been an ancient Roman way to the turning where he would find his adored one. Life was good. A couple of days more and he'd detach himself from this absurd hunt for a missing miniature.

The hotel was a bijou affair, with a friendly receptionist who smiled when he inquired for Liz. 'Oh, yes, *signore* she's expecting you,' she said, giving him the room number and pointing out the lift.

They hadn't seen each other for almost two months. Their meeting was joyful and took a long, pleasurable time. Afterwards Liz gestured lazily towards a little table by the window.

'There's champagne in that bucket – let's hope the ice hasn't melted.'

Nothing could have marred their mood even if the champagne had been tepid. They drank a little, then decided to refresh themselves with a shower. By the time that was over, the ice had definitely melted.

'So,' Liz demanded as she combed back her wet hair, 'what's new on the Rialto?'

'You may well ask. It's all very edgy and "mustn't get into the newspapers".' He gave her a résumé of his conversations and what he'd been doing during the day.

She heard him out with patience but a little frown was gathering between her brows.

'This gossipy lady-friend of yours at the Academy . . .'

'Yes?'

'Tell me again what she said about Rini.'

'Ah, let me see. Martina said that Rini had always been rather odd, and that agrees with what I recall about her. Not temperamental in a self-centred way, you know, but always worried about her immortal soul.'

'She prayed a lot even then?'

'Yes.'

'What was it your Martina said about that?'

'About what?'

'Praying.'

'Praying? Sweetness, we're not going to have a discussion about religion, are we?'

'No, we're not. I just want to know – Martina said that Rini was always praying.'

'Yes. Her exact words, if I remember correctly, were "She was always praying to statues and icons and things".'

'*That's* the word,' Liz cried. 'You've talked about it as a miniature and a painting, but something nudged my memory. It's an icon.'

He looked unimpressed. 'I suppose it is.'

'An *icon*! Didn't you do any History of Art at that posh school you went to?'

'Well, yes, and very boring it was too. Conducted round art galleries, staring at Rembrandts and Caravaggios—'

'No primitive religious paintings?'

'Oh, I never looked at them if I could help it. Usually someone was being carved up or shot full of arrows. Anyway, I sometimes begged off those tiresome gallery tours by spending time with the music teacher.'

She nodded in acceptance. 'OK, then. You don't know about it. Now *I* went to art college and I know at least something about religious art. In the Orthodox church, in its various forms, small religious paintings are very important. I don't know what might be the story behind the Saint Olga that Rini has, but it could be worth a lot. I mean, a *lot*.'

He studied her expression. 'You're saying . . . that it's not the diamonds . . .?'

'No, not the diamonds. I think it's the icon that they're so worried about.'

# FOUR

Greg hired a taxi to take him back to the Villa Stefani. When they reached the gates, the driver gave a little toot on the horn to gain access. The door of the lodge opened, Ernesto came out to peer into the cab. When he saw the passenger, he gave a nod and turned to go back into the lodge.

'Sorry to be so late, Ernesto,' called Greg, lowering his window.

'No problem.'

'Is there anyone else about?'

'The rule is, early to bed. Signor Ardicci's health.' This was a low grumble as he walked indoors.

There was a slight pause and the gates yawned open. The driver took them up the drive to the front door. Greg got out and paid the driver. As the cab moved away, he turned, expecting to have to use the great brass knocker on the front door. To his surprise, it, too, opened automatically. Ernesto in his little house had apparently pressed the necessary button.

When Greg was inside, he saw a red light on a little panel of switches. He pressed the switch alongside, and the door gently closed.

So the house was electronically protected, as he'd been told. But Ernesto was in charge of the electronics.

Lamps were casting a dim light on the hall and staircase. He could sense the whole house sleeping around him. He went quietly upstairs and to bed.

He'd arranged with Liz that she would come tomorrow in a hired car. He would have the Ardiccis and Floria in the drawing-room so that the matter of the icon's importance could be discussed. He didn't feel confident enough to breach the subject himself.

Yesterday had shown him that Ruggiero and his wife took breakfast upstairs in a leisurely fashion. When he came downstairs he found Cristina wheeling their serving trolley to the kitchens from the back of the hall where, it now emerged, there was a little lift.

He found Floria in the morning room, clad in a dark linen dress of excellent cut, eating Danish pastries and drinking coffee. 'Good morning,' she said. 'If you would like something more substantial, ring for Cristina.'

'No, thank you, this is fine.' He had scarcely taken a seat at the breakfast table when Cristina appeared with a fresh cafetière for him. He poured and drank with appreciation. He never really felt completely awake until he'd had his first cup of coffee.

'You had a long day yesterday. Did you make progress in your inquiries?' Floria asked, but only out of politeness.

'A little, I believe. I'd like to discuss it later with you and Ruggiero and Rini, if I may.'

'Oh, certainly.' She gave an upward jerk of the head. 'They'll be down soon, I expect.'

'Does Rini say morning prayers?'

'Oh, yes, at daybreak, I gather. In thanksgiving for having survived the terrors of the night. And then again after breakfast, to say thank you for the food.' All this was said in a tone of muted spite.

'But to whom does she pray, if the icon isn't there?'

'I have no idea. You must ask her that yourself.' She rose from her chair. 'Excuse me, I must give instructions about today's meals. Shall you be here for lunch?'

'I don't think so. I'll probably be going back to Rome.' She was turning to go when he added, 'I hope you don't mind. I invited a colleague to be here this morning.'

'You're welcome to bring anyone who can help Ruggiero with this stupid problem.' She hurried out.

As he was finishing breakfast, Cristina came in to clear the table. 'Good morning, Cristina,' he said.

'Good morning, *signore*.'

'I hope your husband didn't mind being kept up late, waiting for me.'

She gave a faint smile, which brought to life some vestige of her former good looks. She had a slender figure, masked somewhat by the gathered skirt and plain cotton top she wore. He guessed she had had a hard life before she and her husband were lucky enough to be employed at the villa. There were the marks of past care and misfortune in her face, lines deeply cut into the pale skin.

'Oh, he's used to late hours. Signor Ardicci entertains a lot, evening parties can go on until the early morning.'

'I suppose his guests mostly have to do with his political activities.'

She made a little shrugging movement of the shoulders, not impolite but implying, *How should I know?*

She gathered the dishes up for her little trolley, took off the table cloth, folded it with precision so as to cover her load, then went out with just the slightest of inclinations to signify a polite farewell.

Ruggiero's friends were a subject that hadn't figured largely in Greg's thoughts until now. But the villa was a grandiose site for him to entertain his colleagues or rivals

from the political arena. Could any one of those have taken
the icon?

Possible . . . To possess it might give power – the power of
blackmail, perhaps, in this Catholic country. But only if the
thief had known of the icon's existence. And it seemed to him
that it had been kept very secret. There was a good reason,
of course. Ruggiero's wife from the Russian Orthodox church
was not a helpful adjunct to his political ambitions. He clearly
didn't want it known she was so devoted to her faith that she
prayed to the picture of a Russian saint.

Ruggiero came downstairs as Greg emerged from the
morning room. He was resplendent in riding boots and
breeches. They didn't favour his contours, for he was developing
a slight paunch.

He hailed Greg with eagerness. 'You can see I'm out for a
little exercise!' he said. 'My doctor recommends it. Care to
accompany me?'

They were walking outdoors as they spoke. 'Not this
morning, thank you,' said Greg. 'I thought I'd stroll down
to the village, just to get an idea of what the people are
like.'

'You're thinking that someone from there might have been
the thief? Ah no, Gregory. My family have been here for
generations – we are known and loved by our villagers.'

They approached the stables. Armeno was waiting with the
two horses at the ready, wearing jeans but with a pair of heeled
boots – he was clearly to be Ruggiero's companion on the
morning exercise. He held out the reins of a pretty chestnut
mare. '*Signore* is riding?'

'No, thank you, Armeno. I'm going for a walk.'

Armeno beamed. 'We're all ready then, *signore*,' he said to
his master.

Ruggiero mounted the bay gelding, Armeno swung aboard
the chestnut, and off they went at a gentle walk. Greg set
off on his tour around the grounds, and fairly soon was on
a rise that gave him a view of the track along which the
riders were ambling. Their way was bordered by the undergrowth of the mountainside, clearly beyond the cultivated
extent of the villa.

So how had they managed to leave the terrain? He found
himself a new standpoint which showed him the gardens.

The riders had come out by a track which had an old shoulder-high iron gate, now standing ajar.

So much for electronic protection.

He passed a small farm or two. The village of Tabardi lay something over a kilometre away when approached on foot by the old paths on the mountainside, probably about ten minutes by car allowing for the driveway of the villa and its electronic gates. It had some decent houses, a few shops and bars, and a kiosk catering for tourists. At mid-morning, a little group with backpacks and expensive sunglasses was milling around the kiosk.

Mr Crowne avoided them. At the Riocco Bar, a dozen or so of old men were sitting in the shade of its awning, making a drink last as long as possible while they waited for the amusements offered by tourism. What dreadful clothes! What a display of long naked legs and, on the part of the women, what an exposure of the upper bosom!

Greg bought himself a bottle of apricot juice then wandered out to stand in the shade and watch the visitors. He allowed himself to seem disapproving.

One of the greybeards nodded at him. 'Their upbringing, eh? What kind of parents do they have?'

'Oh, where I come from, we see a lot of that.'

'And where's that?'

'Geneva.'

The smile on the old man's face stiffened a little. Clearly they knew who he was – the guest at the Villa Stefani. They all knew they must mind their manners now.

'How is Signor Ardicci this morning?'

'Quite well, I believe. He's out riding.'

Someone on the edge of the group gave a sniff of derision at the news. No one actually said that they thought Signor Ardicci was a very poor horseman.

For ten minutes Greg tried to make conversation but they were wary. He was glad to give up as a smart little Toyota edged its way along the main street and he saw Liz Blair at the wheel. She drew up at the sight of him, rolled down her window, and called, 'Want a lift, handsome stranger?'

All the old men were at once more friendly. There were murmurs of *'Com'é bella!'* and one old gallant raised his glass to her. When Greg had settled himself beside her she set the car in motion, giving her fans a cheerful farewell wave.

'I should have had you with me when I first got there,' he mourned. 'They would hardly say a word to me.'

'What questions were you asking?'

'Never got that far. It's coming home to me that although Ruggiero thinks of himself as the beloved leader of these folk, they don't like him.'

'Because of the foreign wife, do you think?'

'That's yet to be seen. Well, my angel, are you ready to sound her out about the icon?'

She gave a dubious nod. 'I woke rather late,' she apologized, 'although for very good reasons.' He grinned. She gave him a little admonitory tap on the knee. 'So I haven't had time to do any research. It would have been good if I could have got to a shop selling English books – perhaps near the university – I'd have liked to find something by Professor Wilding. But there, we'll just play it by ear, shall we?'

'I have faith in you.'

Ernesto heard their approach and opened the gates at once. To Greg's surprise, another car was already parked in the drive close to the entrance of the villa.

Cristina let them in. They were shown into the drawing-room, where Rini was looking out of one of the windows. Floria was offering coffee to a tall, black-haired man with a long face made even longer by a short beard. He was dressed in slacks, sandals, and a sort of smock or loose shirt of dark-blue linen.

'Good morning,' Rini said, turning from the window. 'Let me introduce you to my dear friend and adviser, Dr Tamaldov. Yuri, we all speak English for the present. This is Gregory Crowne and his colleague . . .' She waited to allow him to introduce Liz, who shook hands first with their hostess and then with the doctor. She gave Floria a bright smile.

'And this is Signorina Massigna,' Greg supplied, vexed at Rini's omission.

'How do you do?' Floria said in precise English but without warmth. 'Would you like some refreshment?'

'Oh, I would indeed! I got up in rather a rush this morning.' She pretended to sense the smell of coffee. 'A cup of that would be lovely, if there's enough?'

Floria seemed quite offended. 'There will be fresh, of course,' she said. Rising, she went to a table by the door, where she picked up a silver bell to ring for Cristina.

Rini had returned to look out of the window. Tamaldov went to stand behind her, a little way back. He bent towards her to say softly, 'He is quite safe. Come and sit down.'

And with a little touch on her shoulder, he made her turn and come more into the centre of the room.

She gave an embarrassed smile. 'You will think I'm a fool. But I always worry when he's out there, even with Armeno. Horses always seem to me to be so big, so lofty . . .'

'But so easily controlled,' Greg said to comfort her.

'Ah, you're a horseman? It would be so good if you would ride with him! Armeno – well, he rides well but he is such a . . . such a numbskull, if anything went wrong, he wouldn't know what to do!'

'But nothing goes wrong, my dear,' said Tamaldov. 'And you know it does him good.'

'So you say, Yuri! And of course I believe you. But—'

Cristina came in, preventing further lamentations about horse-riding. Greg was trying not to smile as he remembered the slow meander he'd witnessed earlier. Coffee was ordered, with the additional warning from Floria, 'Signore Ardicci will be back soon. Have the hot water ready for his tisane.'

Cristina nodded in silence and withdrew. Greg said, 'I hope you don't mind that I've brought Ms Blair to help me with our inquiries. She has a background of art education.'

Floria raised her eyebrows. Rini seemed perplexed. The doctor smiled at Liz, who smiled back.

'I'm no expert,' she said, 'but I'm told an *objet d'art* has gone missing?'

Rini said at once: 'This was to be kept confidential!'

'I'm sorry,' said Liz, surprised. 'I thought it was only the servants who were not aware—'

'Oh, of course, they know nothing, they'd gossip to the villagers and then it would be out all over Rome.' Rini pulled herself together. 'I'm sorry. Of course if you are a colleague of Gregory's then we must accept that you are made *au fait* with the situation.'

'My dear Rini, be easy in your mind,' Tamaldov said in a deep, very soothing voice. 'Ruggiero will be back soon, safe

and sound.' He smiled around at the others. 'Our good friend
tends to have great worries over her husband, yet she knows
that Saint Olga has him in her protection.'

She managed a smile at his words. 'But does Saint Olga
have power over horses?' she said, trying for lightness.

Cristina brought the fresh coffee and with it a plate of
*biscottini* that Liz recognized as the product of one of Rome's
best confectioners. She was hungry so she pounced on them
with delight.

Rini's head was turned towards the window. She'd heard
the sound of hooves. She rose and went to it, waving a greeting.
Tamaldov nodded to himself. 'Now she will be content,' he
murmured.

Floria, having poured coffee for her guests, rose from her
chair. 'Excuse me,' she said, hurrying out.

Tamaldov gave another little knowing nod. 'She goes to
make a peppermint concoction,' he remarked with a shrug.
'And yet, you know, good health does not come from little
potions and mixtures. It comes from within, from peace of
heart and touch of the Holy Ghost.'

Liz, mouth full of biscuit, coughed and tried not to choke.
She exchanged a startled glance with Greg, who was keeping
a very straight face. Rini smiled affectionately at Tamaldov.

'Yuri has this wonderful gift,' she explained. 'He has helped
Ruggiero so much!'

'You believe in some form of alternative medicine?' Greg
asked. 'The laying on of hands?'

'Oh, no, that is a little too physical for my liking,' said Yuri
Tamaldov in his deep, velvety voice. 'My method is to be in
communication with my patient at deepest level. The soul
opens like a blossom when it is at complete rest, in touch
with another in kindness and compassion.'

'Ruggiero is in such anxiety about his career,' Rini explained.
'The possibility of the ambassadorship never leaves his mind.
And of course, he has always had a delicate digestion, so
anxiety made things worse.'

'Oh, I do understand,' Liz enthused. 'I am a designer, you
know, and sometimes my clients drive me almost mad with
their demands. But I try not to take anything for it even though
some of my friends tell me it makes their lives easier.'

Tamaldov turned his great dark eyes on her with approval.

'You are very wise, Ms Blair. Good health comes from tranquil mind, fresh air, and a little gentle exercise.' He set aside his coffee cup and with a nod towards Rini, got to his feet. He looked tall and imposing, rather younger than Greg had thought at first sight. 'I will go up to Ruggiero just to ensure all is well with him for the day,' he announced.

'*Spasibo, doktor*,' said Rini. She added in explanation as he left: 'He counsels my husband from day to day – any time that Ruggiero is under stress, he will come and spend some time with him. He is so *good*.'

'He's an old friend, then?' Liz asked.

'No, no, I heard of him through contacts from my old life, the world of opera.' Her olive skin had some colour as she went on with enthusiasm. 'I prayed to Saint Olga. I had the border of diamonds made for her portrait, and she rewarded me by putting it into my head to contact some friends in Paris, who sent me Yuri. He had a clinic there but he was so generous as to come to Rome, where he has built up a little consultancy already. But any time that my poor husband is unwell, Yuri will come here to us at the villa.'

Liz felt a little surge of sympathy. Poor soul, married to a man whose career was perhaps his first interest, living in a house some way from the city life she was used to, and perhaps rather disapproved of by his friends . . .

She leaned forward so as to chat with her more confidentially. Greg understood what she was up to, and amused himself by looking at the room's furnishings – the recent work of his grandmother.

Floria came back looking smug. 'Ruggiero enjoyed his pick-me-up,' she said. 'He'll be down in a minute.' She added, addressing Greg: 'He very much wants to hear what luck you have had with your inquiries.'

When Ruggiero joined them, he had changed from his riding outfit into a black silk shirt and black jeans. Liz, seeing him for the first time, couldn't help thinking that the cut of the clothes was a bit too young for him. Tamaldov, in his loose linen tunic and sandals, was a decided contrast.

Rini held out her hands in greeting. 'Did you enjoy your ride, my darling?' she asked.

'Oh, very much. I chat to Armeno and he nods and looks happy, but I think it's the horse he listens to.' Laughing, he

kissed her hands, one after another. He looked expectantly at
Greg, to be introduced to this charming newcomer.

It seemed to her that he held her hand just a little too long.
She smiled prettily, to soften the impact of the very difficult
conversation they'd be having in a few moments. He let go
then took his place beside his wife on the ornate sofa, spreading
himself comfortably.

'Now, my dear Gregory, tell me,' he invited.

The relation didn't take long. Greg omitted the opinions
that Martina had given him, nor did he dwell on his view of
the villa's staff except to say he didn't think of them as suspect.
Ruggiero looked a little surprised when he said he'd chatted
with some of the inhabitants of Tabardi.

'Good heavens, you can't expect any sense from people
like that, Gregory! Their view of the world is limited to what
happens in the village and what they see on television.'

'But Floria mentioned that she hires extra staff as
needed—'

'Not from *there*,' Floria intervened, somewhat offended.
'From a very trustworthy firm in Rome.'

'Ah. If you'll give me the address, I'll go to see them.'

'As you wish. But I assure you they are reliable.'

Rini was clearly disappointed at the report. 'So it seems
we're not much further forward . . .'

Greg glanced at Liz. She gave a slight inclination of the
head to signify she was ready. Greg said: 'In view of my lack
of success over getting any trace of the diamonds, I had a
conversation with Ms Blair. She had a suggestion.'

'Yes,' she agreed. 'Because I was trained as an artist, my
thoughts turned from the diamonds and more towards the icon.'

She slightly emphasized the last word, and there was just
the faintest change in Rini's expression. But she said nothing.

'My opinion on how to go on has been influenced by her
view,' Greg put in.

'I'll tell you what occurred to me,' she said, in a manner
she made somewhat hesitant. 'From time to time I've heard
that religious icons can be very important in the art world, so
it occurred to me that perhaps the thief wanted that, rather
than the gemstones. Of course, if the painting is one by a
modern artist, it might not be worth a very large sum.' She
paused, waiting to be told who had painted the icon.

Rini clasped and unclasped her hands but made no comment.

'There are some quite well-known painters who make replicas, I believe,' said Liz, to give her time to get some words together. 'And there's a market for those. Could we hear something about the provenance of your Saint Olga?'

A long hesitation followed. Greg noted that Floria looked rather pleased at having the subject brought up. Dr Tamaldov seemed to be paying only polite attention. Ruggiero pulled himself upright on the sofa, and took his wife's hand.

She appeared unable to speak. Her mouth trembled, she stared down at her husband's hand covering her own.

Ruggiero took up the conversation. 'You must understand that it upsets Rini to have to talk about the theft. The painting is very dear to her.'

'Of course. But it might help us to get it back if we knew' – a slight pause – 'if we knew its value in cash.'

The word 'cash' seemed to quiver in the room. Tamaldov frowned. 'Ms Blair, I am no expert, but this is a religious object. Rini loves it because she has faith. Perhaps it has no cash value.'

Floria gave a little grunt. 'When it arrived, it came by special carrier. From the way it was protected in its packing, I got the impression it was valuable.'

She coloured at a glance of vexation from Ruggiero. 'Of course it was well packed,' he said. 'It's a work of art.'

'Where did it come from?' Liz inquired innocently. Once more she waited, her attention directed to Rini.

'Ah . . . It came from . . . I have friends from my career in opera . . .'

'Yes?'

'They have connections in the art world.'

'I understand. They acted on your behalf. They're gallery owners?'

'No, no, they just . . . Many followers of the Russian church share my belief in the power of the heavenly mediators. They understood my longing for a portrait of my particular saint. So they found the painting for me.'

'But Signora Ardicci, that still gives us no idea of its worth.'

'It's . . . it's priceless.'

Liz smiled and waited a moment before going on. 'To you,

yes, of course. But to the thief? If he hoped to sell it, what would he get for it?'

Rini's great dark eyes filled with tears. When she spoke, her voice trembled. 'Why do you ask me that? How can I know what price a wicked man would ask?'

'Ms Blair,' Ruggiero intervened, 'this is very distressing to my poor wife—'

'I understand. She values the icon above any money she might have paid for it. But it would help us if we knew how much.'

Tears were trickling down Rini's face now. She dragged out the words through a choked sob. 'I paid the equivalent of fifteen thousand dollars.'

Floria gave a faint gasp of astonishment. Dr Tamaldov frowned. Liz was translating the sum into sterling and coming up with seven and a half thousand pounds.

That was a lot of money. All the same, it wasn't equal to the value of the diamonds. But there had been no clear answer to the question: what was the provenance of the icon?

She was about to resume her questions when Rini got up and hurried from the room. Ruggiero followed, but turned at the door to say, 'This has been too much for her. You must excuse us.' He went out looking worried.

Tamaldov was shaking his head. 'In this house,' he announced in his rich, sonorous voice, 'there are great turmoils of the soul. Rini must listen to her inner guide and ask for peace.' He got up from his chair. 'I must find a quiet spot to pray for her,' he murmured, and went out of the room and out of the house.

'Ha!' said Floria. 'Quite a performance!'

It was unclear whether she meant from Rini or from Tamaldov. Catching the smile on Liz's face, she added, 'The man's a charlatan!' With that as an exit line, she too made her escape.

Liz gave a little shrug. 'I think we'd better make ourselves scarce until the diva has recovered, eh?'

'Let's go for a stroll and come back in half an hour. It might be that Ruggiero will call the whole thing off.'

'And you'd like that, would you, love?'

'I wish I'd never got involved in this business in the first place. I just can't find any sympathy for these people.'

In the hall they paused for a moment, and through an arch they could see Tamaldov standing in the loggia that ran along the back of the house. He was gazing out at the parterre, but whether in prayer, it was difficult to tell.

Outside the sun was very strong but the mountain air was fresh and reviving. Greg led her along the route that Ruggiero had taken him, so that in a few minutes they were at the top of the slope where the old vine cast its shade. Under its branches there was now a wrought-iron table to match the antique old chair.

'Oh, look, there are actual grapes growing!' Liz exclaimed.

'Yes, Ruggiero's going to sample the first of them soon, I gather.'

Liz sat on the chair. He leaned against the table, long legs stretched out.

'What did you make of all that?' he asked.

'I think there's something dodgy about that icon.'

'You mean it's a forgery, or something.'

'Or *something*? I'm beginning to think it's a genuine antique painting, and if she only paid fifteen thousand, it may have been a bargain.'

'What on earth does that mean?'

'It means – I think Rini got some pals of hers to hire a poor skint peasant to get that icon from a local church somewhere in Russia.'

'What!'

'It's stolen, Greg. I'd take a bet on it.'

# FIVE

There was a silence between them. The only sounds were the rustle of the vine leaves and the faint chugging of some agricultural machine in the distance.

'Well . . .' Greg muttered.

She could see he was unwilling to accept her theory. 'Think about it, Greg,' she urged. 'She's *so* upset about it. She takes refuge in tears so as not to tell us anything about how it was acquired. I gather no one has been allowed to see it . . .'

'Floria said she had a glimpse of it. And of course the frame maker, Alessandro.'

'What did he say about it?'

'He said the work had been painted on wood. I gathered he'd had to glue the wood on to clear glass so as to provide a base for the diamond frame.'

'Painted on wood. Well, of course, some modern replicas are probably painted on wood to make them seem authentic. Did your Alessandro say the wood was old?'

'No. We'll ask him.' He paused. 'Are you really saying you think this painting is some ancient treasure stolen from a church?'

'A treasure? Well, perhaps not exactly that. You know, lots of churches have things that have been hanging on their walls or standing in some niche for ages. These things become so commonplace that you disregard them. But then along comes this rich lady asking for an icon of Saint Olga, and you happen to know of one that's covered in dust behind the door of the local chapel, and you just nick it and accept whatever sum is on offer . . .'

'And then that buyer sends it on to someone in the city somewhere who's asking for a portrait of Saint Olga. And in the end . . .'

'In the end, Rini Ardicci pays fifteen thousand dollars for it.'

'But does she know it was stolen?' he asked.

Liz considered this for some moments. 'I think she must guess,' she said at last. 'Don't you think she's – well, she's the kind of person that rather enjoys being in a bit of an uproar? She's feeling guilty at owning a precious thing that belongs in some old church, but she's triumphant that it has helped her beloved Ruggiero's health. "Torn in two by ethical struggle" – great stuff.'

He chuckled unwillingly, then grew serious. 'Listen, *Liebchen*, I've just thought of something. What if this confounded painting *doesn't* come from a church?'

'What? Where else would it come from? Oh – you mean from someone's private collection?' The amusement went out of her face too. 'Oh dear.'

'Yes, "Oh dear". And – even worse – what about this? What if it was stolen from some state museum?'

She grabbed his arm. 'Greg!'

'And Rini suspects that, and is in terror that the KGB or something will come after her and her husband.'

'No, no. Don't say things like that. In any case,' she said, pulling herself together, 'it isn't called the KGB any more.'

'Whatever it's called, it wouldn't be nice to think they were looking for that icon.'

She jumped to her feet. 'Enough of this! We're scaring ourselves to death! Let's go to Rome and speak to the frame-maker. If he says it was painted on modern wood and with acrylic paints, we can breathe easier.'

'But let's ask Floria for the address of her catering firm. We ought to make sure that none of their staff could have found out about the icon. And of course, if that's a possibility, then it's more likely it was taken for the diamonds, don't you think?'

'How do I know? Perhaps there's an Italian waiter who's knowledgeable about Orthodox icons.'

He joined her to go back to the villa. He said mournfully, 'Don't just think about Italian waiters, Liz. Countries that belong to the European Union have lots of other nationals working for them – and now I think of it, some *Greek* waiter might recognize a Russian saint when he sees one.'

In a subdued state, they went back to the house. Armeno, the stableboy, was at work sweeping the front steps. He stood back to let them enter, but Greg paused. 'Do you know where I can find Signorina Massigna?'

Armeno stared at him. The Italian of the visiting *signor* wasn't the same as the dialect he'd been brought up with. Greg said it again, very slowly. This time Armeno recognised the *signorina*'s name and murmured that she was likely to be supervising Sara as she cleaned the bedrooms.

'Upstairs,' he explained, eager to be helpful.

'Thank you, Armeno.'

Greg led the way into the hall. Liz said, 'That one doesn't seem very bright. I suppose he's not a suspect?'

'I wouldn't imagine so. He only seems to think about horses.' In the hall, they paused. 'Perhaps we'd better use the telephone to speak to Floria. I don't think she'd like us to walk in on her during her housekeeping duties.'

'Good Lord, what a household!'

He found a telephone in the drawing-room, but didn't know which button to push for which bedroom. He called Ernesto, who put him through. Floria asked him rather huffily to wait a moment while she came downstairs.

'Everything to do with catering is in my office,' she said when she arrived.

To Greg's surprise she led the way to the back of the house, as if to go into the kitchen. Instead she opened a door just in front of it, to reveal what in an English country house would be called a butler's pantry. It was tiny, but it had been fitted up as a comfortable den: a desk-like shelf with pigeonholes above gave her something like an office, where she kept her correspondence. There was a table with the requirements for making coffee and hot chocolate, and perhaps also the tisanes which were good for Ruggiero's digestion.

She took a folder out of one of the pigeonholes. From it she produced a glossy brochure. She said as she handed it over, 'You'll remember not to let them know that anything has gone missing, Mr Crowne.'

'Of course, *signorina.*'

'Ruggiero regrets very much the outburst of Rini,' she went on. 'She is indisposed, but Ruggiero is hoping that you will bring your colleague Ms Blair to dinner this evening, when all will be well again.'

'Perhaps I'll be able to discuss the provenance of the icon with her, without making her upset,' Liz said very innocently.

Floria fussed about with some papers but Liz noticed that her lips tightened. 'She values it very greatly. She is very anxious to have it back. One would think she would like to tell you anything that helps in that.'

'But you know, opera stars are famous for being temperamental.'

'Hmm,' said Floria. But she refused to be tempted into censure of Rini.

'Thank you for this, *signorina,*' Greg said, tapping the brochure.

They left her in her little domain. As they emerged they caught a glimpse of Cristina in the very modern kitchen, scrubbing vegetables at a stainless steel sink. She glanced round as they came out of Floria's office, but turned back quickly to her work.

'She seems awfully reserved,' Liz remarked, meaning Cristina. 'I noticed she didn't say a word when she brought the coffee. I was going to say thank you but she was gone before I could say a word.'

'She's got her hands rather full, I think,' Greg said. 'The usual household cooking, and I gather Rini likes to eat well. Then there's Floria fussing about giving her orders, and on top of all that she has her husband to look after and I suppose the stableboy too.'

They had traversed the hall and were going out. Ernesto was clipping the herbs in the paved garden, with Armeno gathering up the pieces into a weathered pannier. Armeno looked up and gave them a wide smile. Ernesto ceased his work and walked away, to be ready to open the gates.

'They're really not friendly, except for the horse-boy,' sighed Liz. She added thoughtfully, 'You call Ruggiero by his first name, and he calls you by yours. But I notice you speak to this Floria woman as '*signorina*' and she calls you Mr Crowne.'

He shrugged. 'There you go. Floria doesn't get on first-name terms very easily, I suspect.'

The brochures showed the catering firm to have its offices in a sparkling high-rise building in Rome. Liz drove them there, parking in the underground garage.

The manager in charge of the department for outside catering was an extremely smart young woman. She had brochures in a substantial album, and was surprised but pleased when Greg explained he came on behalf of Signorina Massigna. 'Signorina Massigna is a valued customer,' she said. 'She has recommended our service to you?'

'Not exactly.' Greg spoke in an easy, comfortable tone. 'We were speaking to her this morning and she mentioned the staff who had come to the villa last time she had a dinner party.'

'She had a complaint?' the manager cried in alarm. 'If she had any fault to find, I wish she had let me know personally! As far as I'm aware there were no breakages, no mishaps, when we last served her at the villa.'

'No, nothing of that kind,' he soothed. 'On the contrary, she was telling us how competent and discreet she found your workers.'

She relaxed visibly. 'Oh, that's good to hear. It's only what I expect, you know. We've been in the business thirty years

– my father founded the firm. And we have some workers who've been with us since the very beginning. Let me just look it up.' She turned to her computer and tapped the keyboard. 'Ah yes. Enrico led the waiting staff that night, and Nora was in charge of uniforms – Signorina Massigna likes us to provide our dark-green outfit. And Giulio took care of the kitchen. Four of our employees in all.'

Greg nodded and smiled. She smiled back. Liz was very much on the sidelines, her Italian too poor to follow much of what was being said. She busied herself with turning over some of the items in the album.

'Do you have some event in mind, *signore*? We can cater for almost any celebration.' The manager allowed herself a little side glance at Liz, as if to imply they might be about to announce an engagement, or perhaps even a wedding.

'We're beginning to get started on something,' said Greg. 'Forward planning, you know.'

'I understand completely.'

'Signorina Massigna spoke well of your employees. Those who were at the villa – are they of the group you mentioned, who've been with you a long time?'

'Oh, Nora, yes, she's been with us for ever. Enrico . . .' She smiled fondly. 'He's grown grey-haired in our service. The chef is relatively new – that's Giulio – he's only been with us three years but his father was one of our cooks until he retired. And then the last of that team . . . let me see, that was Serena. Oh yes, she's one of our stalwarts, she joined us eight years ago.' She turned away from her computer screen. 'Signorina Massigna likes us to send mature people. Some of our customers prefer a more youthful team and that, of course, we can supply but all our staff are completely reliable.'

'That sounds great.'

'Let me give you some of our information leaflets. What date did you have in mind?'

'Well . . . perhaps around Christmas?'

'Ah! We have quite a lot of bookings at that time. Perhaps if you make up your mind to go with us, you could let me know soon?'

She sorted out some brochures and handed them to Liz, who said '*Grazie*' as the only contribution she'd been able to make to the entire conversation. She followed that up with *'Buon giorno'* as they left.

'I don't think the catering team had anything to do with the theft,' Greg said as they went down in the lift. 'They sound as solid as the rock of Gibraltar.'

'So now we're off to talk to the picture-framer?'

'That's the plan.'

Signor Alessandro was surprised to see Greg again, but delighted to be introduced to Liz. He ushered them through to the little room at the back, dusted off a chair for Liz, produced cold bottles of fizzy drinks, and sat down with them as if he intended to stay there for the rest of the day.

Greg explained that Liz was an art expert who was deeply interested in the icon he had framed. He then turned to Liz to say in English: 'Isn't that so, dear?'

Liz nodded and smiled. Alessandro beamed. 'Of course I too am interested in such things. Although that was the first one of its kind I have ever had to frame.' He smiled. 'Our saints here are a different tribe.'

'Could you tell us whether the painting was very old, *signore*?'

'Old? Oh, dear me, very old. Ancient, in fact.'

She recognized the word *antico*. 'It was painted on wood, wasn't it?' she said. 'Ask him if it was oak, or pine – what kind of wood.'

Alessandro said the painting was on an oval of oak, dark and clearly very old and even with a few wormholes.

Greg translated this for her. 'It's a heritage piece,' she exclaimed. 'I'm sure it is. Rini should never have bought it!'

'I think you're right. Thank you, *signore*,' he said to Alessandro, who kept them talking until they had finished their drink. Alone in his little shop, he enjoyed having someone to talk to, especially a pretty English lady.

They went in search of lunch. In that perverse way that seems to inspire visitors to a great city, they chose not to eat the local food but went instead to a Japanese restaurant. Here Liz was in her element: she was trying very hard to be a vegetarian, so the menu was a great help. It offered a variety of sushi styled in Italian-Japanese as *verdura-shi*, with mushrooms, peppers, and all kinds of seaweeds.

By the time they'd finished their meal, it was late afternoon.

'I don't know about you,' Liz said, 'but what I would like now is a bit of a siesta in a nice cool place.'

'I second that.'

'It isn't a case of "my place or yours", is it?' she laughed. 'It's got to be the Pastorella.'

So they did indeed take a siesta, but after that there was a little languorous lovemaking, and after that a shower.

'Now if I'm going to have dinner at the villa, I've got to glam up a bit,' she mused. 'Something slinky, I think. And I'll wear your sparkly little hair-tag.'

'You really like it?'

'We–ell . . . I tried it on last night after you'd gone, and I find it hits me on the cheek when I shake my head. But it's rather cute.' She dived into the wardrobe, seeking an all-purpose silk jersey dress that travelled well.

'I'll have to change once we get there,' Greg said.

'Look, sweetie,' she said, coming out with the dress bunched up in her hand, 'it doesn't make sense, you staying up there in the hills and me in the Pastorella. Why don't you move in with me?'

'Well, in fact, I think that's a good solution to something that's bothering me. I'm going to have to have it out with Ruggiero this evening. If that icon belongs in some Russian church, I'm not going to do anything to get it back so that Rini can have it.'

She was holding up the dress and surveying herself in the wardrobe mirror. She said over her shoulder, 'But what about the diamonds?'

'Hmm . . . Yes, what about the diamonds? I really don't know, Liz.'

They drove back to the Villa Stefani around seven o'clock. Ernesto was on the lookout, and the gates slid open. The evening air in Rome had been tepid, dust-filled. Here it was fresh and sweet. As they got out of the car the perfume of lavender, rosemary and lemon thyme blended with the strong scent of pine and poplar.

Ruggiero came hurrying out, in dinner jacket and soft-collared shirt. At sight of Liz in her sleek black dress, he stopped in admiration. '*Ammazza!*' he cried.

'Thank you,' she said, letting him take her hand to lead her indoors.

In the drawing-room lamps were softly resisting the shadows. Rini was seated on one of the ornate sofas, with Dr Tamaldov alongside. Clad in a caftan of brilliant colours, she had taken pains with her make-up but couldn't hide the fact that she was pale. Tamaldov, by contrast, was still in the loose shirt and sandals of the morning, although everyone else had changed. Clearly he had stayed at the house – to comfort Rini, perhaps.

She rose to greet them. 'Good evening,' she said, with a little smile to Greg that seemed to ask pardon for her behaviour earlier.

'Good evening, Rini. Are you well?'

'Thank you, of course, everything is fine.'

Floria, standing near the side table with her hand on the silver bell, gave a little snort of irritation.

Dr Tamaldov offered his hand. 'You find all in tune now with peerless harmony of universe,' he said, but in a light tone that robbed the words of pretentiousness.

Liz, meanwhile, was detaching herself from Ruggiero's grasp so as to say good evening to her hostess. Out of the corner of her eye she could see Floria looked vexed as she shook the little bell. As soon as she could she turned to her so as to alleviate the pain of being so thoughtlessly left out. *What kind of a family is this*, she asked herself, *where the guest has to be the diplomat?*

Cristina came in pushing a little cart with bottles and glasses. 'Come,' said Ruggiero, surging up to Liz again, 'help me serve the drinks.'

Greg saw that both Rini and Floria looked on this arrangement with disapproval and it dawned on him that Ruggiero was something of a ladies' man. Although happily married to a woman who adored him, it seemed he couldn't prevent himself from flirting a little with a pretty girl.

Asked what she would like to drink, Rini opted for Dubonnet. Liz took the glass and went directly with it to her. There she stayed, sitting next to her and leaning forward to chat, partly because she wanted to get to know Rini and partly to get out of the clutches of her husband.

Tamaldov, denied his place on the sofa, moved towards Floria but she avoided conversation with him. Instead she began giving instructions to the maid, who nodded and quickly left.

Greg accepted a little glass of Lillet from his host. 'Might we go somewhere to have a word in private?'

'Oh! Certainly, certainly.' Ruggiero glanced around to see that everyone had a drink then led the way out into the dimness and coolness of the hall. There he paused, looking up a little so as to read the expression on the face of his tall guest. 'Is something wrong?'

'I'm afraid I can't go on with this,' Greg began. Ruggiero gave a little exclamation of concern. 'You see, I went back to the frame-maker again, taking Liz with me, and it seems the missing icon is really very old. I mean, something rare and valuable. Liz is fairly sure it's a sacred relic, and I just don't feel that I . . .' He hesitated. 'It doesn't belong with a private owner,' he ended.

Ruggiero sighed. 'You're saying you think it came from . . . perhaps a church.'

'Rini just won't explain its provenance, Ruggiero. Do you know where it really came from?'

A shrug. 'Where do so many of our antiquities originally come from? Marble statues from Greece, images of Aztec gods from Mexico – museums are full of goods that must have been taken without the consent of the temples where they first stood.'

'Have you asked Rini about it?'

'I spoke to her,' he replied, stifling a sigh. 'When she had recovered a little from her agitation. I sat down with her and we talked. She got it from old friends who live in St Petersburg. That's all she knows.'

'And who were these old friends? Can they be approached to give us more information?'

'Ah . . . Rini says . . . She says they've moved.'

'Moved from St Petersburg? To a new address?'

'She says they . . . er . . . they've emigrated.' A pause. 'She says she doesn't have an address for them now, she's waiting for them to write to her. When one moves to a new country, it takes some time to settle, don't you agree?'

Greg didn't ask, 'And you believe all this?' Instead he waited a moment then said, 'My grandmother asked me to take action on your behalf. I was supposed to help recover some missing gemstones. But I feel I've done all I can in the matter.'

'Greg,' implored Ruggiero, 'don't let me down! If we can't

get the icon back, it's always going to be there somewhere in the political arena, hanging over me like the sword of Damocles, waiting to cause a scandal.'

'That's a political matter. I try never to involve myself in politics.'

'But if my career is ruined because of it, Rini will never forgive herself. You saw how upset she was this morning. Please, don't let that happen to her, to us – we don't deserve to be held up to public disparagement because of my wife's religious beliefs.'

This was said with a distress that seemed totally genuine. Greg didn't know what to say.

'Think it over,' Ruggiero begged. 'You might feel differently about it tomorrow.' He patted Greg on the arm. 'I'll come down early tomorrow, we'll talk it all over at breakfast, you and I.'

He shook his head. 'I'm afraid not. My friend Liz has asked me to stay with her in Rome and I've agreed. So I'll be leaving with her tonight.'

Ruggiero struggled for equanimity. He tried for a roguish smile. 'Ah, who could resist an invitation like that,' he remarked, keeping his voice free of disappointment.

They stood for a moment in indecision. Then Ruggiero led the way back to the drawing-room.

Liz had managed to include Floria in her conversation with Rini. It was on a totally harmless topic, the old grapevine at the top of the garden slope.

'Ruggiero loves the grapes,' Rini was saying. 'Unlike many that were grown for wine, we find they're sweet enough to eat.'

'They're from a very old variety of muscat,' said Floria, to demonstrate how much better she knew the domain than Rini. 'The vineyard was small but in the old days it provided enough grapes for dessert and for a wine that was quite rich, although of course nowadays we'd think it rather rough.'

'Ruggiero's looking forward to the first cluster,' Rini said, smiling fondly. 'I tell him he's sentimental, but Yuri says no, it's good to keep to traditions and besides, grapes are good for you. Aren't they, Yuri?'

Tamaldov agreed. 'You know, there are good wines grown in Russia. Yes, it surprises you to hear that, doesn't it, my dear Floria? But on Black Sea coast, yes, wine is good.' The rich baritone caressed the word 'good', and Liz found herself smiling at him in pleasure.

Dinner was rather an awkward affair. Ruggiero was attentive to his wife, yet from time to time his eye strayed towards his pretty English guest. And the pretty English guest could sense how much that irritated his housekeeper.

Tamaldov helped to keep the conversation going, reminiscing about Paris where, it seemed, he'd lived for a few years before moving to Rome. Rini listened to him, nodding and murmuring agreement when he praised the food and the wines of France. Greg joined in out of mere good manners.

When it came to coffee and liqueurs in the drawing-room, Floria was able to assert herself. 'Now, Ruggiero, you know you mustn't have coffee. You know how it affects your sleep. I told Cristina to have your camomile tea ready and I know you'll be sensible and drink it all.'

'Yes, my dear Floria, yes, I know you think of my health.'

Rini unwisely joined the conversation. 'You will have a liqueur too, won't you, to settle your digestion, dear?'

'Not brandy. You know brandy gives you heartburn,' Floria intervened.

The two women were facing each other, almost like duellists.

'Perhaps,' said Yuri Tamaldov in an effort at peace-making, 'it would be better to abstain from all, don't you think, Ruggiero? Wine with meal is good but more is not perhaps better, and herbal drink may not help.'

'Oh, of course, *you* are an expert, having drunk wine in the best Parisian restaurants and I suppose tea, out of a rusty samovar in Siberia!' cried Floria, driven beyond politeness.

Tamaldov's long face froze in offended surprise. There was a moment of silence, then he rose to his tall height. '*Signorina,*' he said, 'day is ending and so, I believe, is your welcome. I will go.' He swept out of the room in long strides.

'Yuri!' cried Rini. 'No! Wait!'

But by the time she'd reached the door of the room, they could hear Tamaldov's car starting up outside. Next moment it was going down the drive.

Rini turned. 'Oh, how could you!' she wailed, tears brimming in her eyes.

'Tears? That's always your escape, isn't it?' Floria was on her feet now, her head held high. 'Well, weep over him, if you think he's worth it. But you'll learn in time. He's a mountebank!' And with that as her exit line, she marched past Rini and out of the room.

Though there were tears in Rini's eyes, anger dried them. She breathed something in hoarse Russian.

Mr Crowne's knowledge of Russian wasn't extensive, but he had spent many hours in concert halls and opera houses. Words from operas by Russian composers had taught him to understand phrases about murder and death. He thought Rini said: 'One day I'll kill that woman.'

Which was unfortunate.

Because next day, Floria was dead.

# SIX

They had spent the morning in Rome, first at the Museum of Popular Art and Tradition, to which Liz took her sketch book in hopes of inspiration for next spring's fashions. Then they had gone on a stroll along a shady alley by the Tiber, and ended up in an air-conditioned restaurant for a leisurely lunch.

When they returned to the Pastorella, they expected to repeat the programme of the previous day – a siesta and then perhaps some more lively pursuits. But the receptionist gave a little wave at Liz as they entered. 'You have a telephone message, *signorina*. I'll put it through to your room, shall I?'

Upstairs, the instrument was blinking. In some surprise, Liz picked it up. She couldn't imagine who could be calling, for her business contacts would have used her mobile.

It was Rini Ardicci on the line, her voice trembling with tears. 'Ah, Liz, I'm so glad to have reached you! Is Gregory with you? If he is, please, *please* could I speak to him?'

Liz recalled telling Rini where she was staying in Rome, during one of those chatty moments that happen when people have little of importance to say. Stifling a sigh, she offered the telephone to Greg. 'It's Rini,' she murmured. 'Seems very upset.'

He didn't say, *So what's new?* He took the instrument, introduced himself, and was greeted with a flood of incoherent pleading.

'He's in such distress! It's so *bad* for him! Of course we're both devastated – she was perfectly fine yesterday – it's too incredible she's gone! Oh, please, Gregory, please come back and help us!'

'Calm down, Rini. I can't understand what's wrong. Help you with what?'

'With the police! Of course they had to be called – Doctor Genarro is quite right – but Ruggiero was already in such distress and now – now it seems there has to be a forensic inquiry, and he knows the journalists will just tear him to pieces again once they hear of it. Oh, Gregory, please, do come and help us.'

'The doctor called the police. Why did he do that?'

'Because it was a sudden death, of course! That's the law, and I don't at all blame him, although—'

'Rini, who has died?'

'Floria! Floria is dead. We got her upstairs to her room, and I thought she'd be all right after a rest—'

'She had an accident?'

'No, she was just – she was in pain – she said she had a very bad headache, felt she couldn't breathe, she seemed not to be able . . . she came in from the garden, and Sara, the maid, found her staggering on the stairs, and called Ruggiero – and between us we got her to bed.'

'And you called Dr Gennaro?'

'Not then. I told you – I thought I made it clear – we thought it was perhaps a touch of heatstroke – people don't die of heatstroke, or at least – no, no, we thought she'd be better by and by. But – oh Gregory – she died, she died!'

'And it was then you called the doctor.'

'Yes, because Ruggiero thought – you know, it was just something to do with her heart, or something – but Gennaro looked very troubled and asked us to leave the room while he examined her. And then he came out shaking his head and he said – he said he felt there was something unnatural and that he must inform the police. And he did. And they're *here*. And Ruggiero is so distressed . . .' She sobbed. 'Please come, Gregory.'

'But Rini – surely there's someone better you could call – a friend of long standing—'

'I have none!' she cried with unconscious drama. 'In this country, I have made no friends – when I was desperate for help I had to call Yuri to me from Paris. But I can't call on Yuri to help now – he's a stranger here too, and a nobody. But you, Gregory, you are a person that could impress the authorities. And Ruggiero has faith in you.'

Liz was at his elbow, trying to make out what was going on. She whispered, 'Is she having hysterics?'

'Very near,' he replied equally softly, and to Rini he said: 'Just a moment, Rini, let me have a word with Liz.'

He gave a brief summary of the situation.

'She's dead?' Liz cried in astonishment. 'But she was perfectly fit and well last night!'

'It sounds as if she had some sort of collapse. They seem to have called a real doctor – I mean, someone not in the "alternative" medical world – and he wasn't satisfied and had to call the police.'

'Oh dear.'

'That's putting it mildly.' He sighed and studied her face. 'She wants me to go to the villa.'

'Good heavens, why should you be dragged in?'

'Because she says she's got nobody else.' He hesitated. 'I think she may be over-dramatizing, but there's an element of truth – probably the only friends who came to the house were Ruggiero's pals. Most of hers are scattered around the world – St Petersburg, Paris . . .'

'So you think you should go.'

'I don't want to, but . . .'

With resignation, she nodded. 'Mr Softie. OK. Let's just freshen up and then we'll drive there – tell her we'll be there as soon as we can.'

When they reached the gates of Villa Stefani they found Rini waiting beyond them in the full glare of the late afternoon sun. She was haggard, the make-up she'd put on in the morning faded and streaked, all mascara wiped from her eyes by tears. The gates glided open, Liz drove through.

Greg opened the car door. Rini clambered into the back seat and he, feeling he couldn't leave her alone there, sat beside her. Liz drove on at once.

Rini took Greg's arm and pulled it against her. She leaned close. Her body was heavy against him but there was nothing sexual in the contact. 'Oh, I'm so grateful. So grateful! We were feeling so isolated – beleaguered – there are detectives in the house, in the stables, everywhere!'

'What are they doing?'

'They're looking for evidence. Dr Genarro said – he has left now, but before he went he said that – it's so impossible!'

'Said what, Rini?'

'That it seemed that Floria had been poisoned.' She leaned even closer, peering into his face, silently begging for reassurance. 'How can anyone say that? She ate only what we ate last night. Cristina said she had her usual breakfast of Danish pastries and you know, Cristina bakes the pastries herself so how could there be poison? But the police are taking samples from her flour bin and her yeast jar and Gregory – Gregory – they look at us so coldly!'

He patted her with his free hand. 'They have to preserve complete impartiality, Rini. Don't take it as any kind of judgement.'

A police van and two cars were already lined up in front of the villa when they reached it. A uniformed *guardia* stood there on duty. When Rini led the way up the shallow steps he held out an arm to prevent her opening the door. 'Wait,' he commanded. He himself opened the door so as to call inside.

A plainclothes detective appeared. They held a short conversation. The detective said to Rini in an authoritative tone, 'We've finished in the downstairs rooms but you may not go upstairs without permission.' He then eyed Liz and Greg. 'Who are you?'

'These are my friends,' Rini said pleadingly.

'Papers?'

Both Greg and Liz had travelled abroad often enough to know that in times of trouble it was best to have your passport with you. The detective took theirs, waving Rini on into the house as he did so. He eyed Liz as he opened her passport. He seemed not to have any complaints at what he saw. Then he took Greg's, and there was a notable stiffening of his attitude.

'Wait!' he said. He disappeared indoors, leaving the *guardia* gazing at them with heightened interest.

The wait was of several minutes. When he returned, he opened the door wider than before so as to invite them in. 'Inspector Novelli wants to see you.'

In the hall, a middle-aged balding man in a dark suit was speaking on his mobile.

'What's going on?' Liz breathed in Greg's ear.

'We'll find out in a minute. Either he's going to salute me respectfully, or he's going to glare at me and be rude.'

The telephone conversation ended. The inspector turned a very neutral glance on them. 'Well, Your Highness, it seems I'm to treat you with diplomacy.'

'What does that mean, exactly, inspector?'

'I suppose it means I can't actually throw you out.' He offered his hand. Greg shook it.

'This is my colleague, Liz Blair,' he said, ushering her forward.

She gave the inspector one of her sweetest smiles and said in English, 'Pleased to meet you.'

'*Ugualmente*,' said the inspector, thus demonstrating that although he understood English to some extent, he couldn't speak it. He then turned back to Greg, to embark on a long statement of which she couldn't understand a word.

'We're not to touch anything,' he translated. 'We can go into the drawing-room and speak to Ruggiero as what he describes as "friends of good repute" but Ruggiero's lawyer will be here shortly and it's with him that the inspector will discuss any action that may be taken.'

'Gee,' said Liz, pouting a little for the benefit of the inspector. 'Is it all right if we sit on the chairs?'

'Now, now. He's being careful, that's all. Ruggiero's a politician, don't forget. He lost his seat in the Senate in the last election but that doesn't mean he's without friends – or enemies, either. Novelli just wants to steer clear of any pitfalls.'

'I'll drink to that.'

Gregory gave her a little smile of disagreement. 'Floria has just died – of poison, it seems. Let's be careful what we eat or drink here, shall we?'

She managed to stifle any reaction. It hadn't occurred to her that the poisoning – if that's what it was – could affect anyone else.

Ruggiero and his wife were sitting side by side on the sofa

when they entered the drawing-room. Rini was holding one of her husband's hands in both of hers, and gazing at him in anxiety.

For his part, Ruggiero seemed somehow shrunken into himself. He greeted his guests with a heavy sigh.

'You don't look well, Ruggiero,' Greg said. He was surprised that Floria's death had affected him so badly, but kept that to himself.

'I'm all right—'

'No, you are not, my darling!' Rini turned anguished eyes on them. 'He's so sensitive! Floria was dear to him. And to me, because she wanted so much to alleviate the sufferings caused by his delicate digestion. What shall we do without her?'

It was a fine piece of acting. Liz, who had seen the animosity between the two women, almost felt she should applaud.

'What are the police doing?' Greg inquired.

'Ah, they've turned Cristina's kitchen upside down,' Rini cried. 'It's so difficult to manage with everything in a turmoil!'

Ruggiero said, 'So they let you in, Gregory. I must say I'm surprised, because the man in charge, Novelli, he's no friend of mine.'

'You know him?' Greg asked, surprised.

'Oh, not personally. But his boss at the Questura is a friend of one of the men who led a faction against me in the Senate. But there, Rini was right! A man from a family like yours has to be of good standing.' He hesitated a moment then went on. 'I dare say they won't question you too keenly but when they do, I beg you, Gregory, *don't* tell them anything about the missing icon.'

'Why not?' He already knew the answer to this innocent-seeming question, but he wanted to hear it from Ruggiero.

'Oh, don't you see? It would be sure to leak out to the press, and we'd have them dogging our footsteps for weeks to see if they can catch Rini going to an Orthodox group meeting or something of that kind – although of course she never does, because she knows it would be so harmful for me.'

'Of course not, my dearest,' Rini breathed. She looked at Greg with a mixture of pleading and trepidation. 'You won't mention it, will you, Gregory? It can't have anything to do with what killed Floria, and in the end I'm sure, you see, that it will turn out to be something like a heart attack or heat exhaustion. She was sitting out in the sun for quite a long time this morning. I'm sure that's what made her ill.'

'Rini has a right not to be persecuted because of her religion,' Ruggiero declared. 'I'm sure you agree with that.'

'Of course.'

Ruggiero was relieved. He seemed to take it that Gregory had agreed not to mention the icon. Greg had only agreed that Rini should have religious freedom. But he let it go because, in fact, he couldn't really see any reason to mention the icon.

They stayed with the Ardiccis until Inspector Novelli summoned them to be interviewed. He was using Ruggiero's study, a room that hadn't been touched by the redecorating hand of the ex-queen mother of Hirtenstein. He was sitting at Ruggiero's desk. A small tape recorder stood on the blotter next to a notebook.

'Do you mind if I record this?'

'Not at all.'

It was Greg's grandmother who was mentioned first by the inspector, however. 'I understand the Signora von Hirtenstein was here a few days ago, but has left.'

'Yes, she was giving some of the interior a classical look.'

'And you came to help?'

'Not at all.'

'Why did you come?'

'She asked me.'

Novelli eyed him without approval. 'My chief looked you up on our information network. It seems you have a kind of a talent for sorting out problems. Was there a problem in this household over Signorina Massigna?'

'Nothing that I was aware of.' But he heard in his head the sound of Rini's words yesterday: *'One day I'll kill that woman.'*

Should he report that?

The inspector was already on to his next question. 'Signor Ruggiero seems genuinely distressed. Was there anything between those two? Were they having an affair?'

'Good Lord, no!' cried Greg.

Novelli was disappointed. 'You seem very certain.'

'If you're thinking that there was a love triangle, forget it.'

'Hmm. You've eaten here, I believe?'

'Yes, two or three meals.'

'No ill effects?'

'Not at all. I believe Ruggiero has trouble over his food but that's a long-standing dyspepsia.'

'So you don't have an ill opinion of the cook, Cristina.'

'I don't have *any* opinion of Cristina. As far as I can remember, I've only seen her half a dozen times and never heard her utter a word.'

'The others? Ernesto? The maid? Or the stableboy?'

'I've exchanged a few words with the boy about horses. I complimented Sara on her dusting. As for Ernesto, he's nearly as silent as his wife. I really can't help you there, inspector.'

'So you think of this as a normal household?'

'What's normal?' He added, after a momentary pause, 'Ardicci's a politician. To my mind, politicians are never normal.'

The very faintest smile touched the lips of Inspector Novelli. He wrote a few lines on the notebook, presumably to remind himself to look into Ruggiero's political associates. Then he asked: 'Your lady friend doesn't speak Italian?'

'Only the Italian of the fashion world.'

'Oh?'

'She's a designer.'

Novelli turned his eye on Liz. He couldn't help but smile a little at this engaging Englishwoman. 'Is she a close friend of the Ardiccis?'

'Never met them until yesterday.'

'Ah.' He picked up the tape recorder and switched it off. 'That's all then, at least for now.' After a second's hesitation, he added, 'Thank you, sir.' He was remembering to be polite, as instructed. 'You're staying at the Hotel Pastorella, I believe?'

'Yes.'

'I may want to be in touch again.'

'Very well.'

'As for the present, I'd prefer it if you left the villa,' he said, still polite but rather curt. 'Signora Ardicci called you in but I don't see any reason for you to be here, and as this affair has complications – because of Ardicci's political ambitions – I'd like you out of it.'

Greg nodded and they went out. In the drawing-room they found Rini pouring a drink for Ruggiero from the array on a side table. She said in distress: 'I think he has a slight temperature.

He should have cold mineral water but we are not allowed to go to the kitchen, even for ice.'

Her husband seemed a little flushed. 'It's nothing dear. Please don't take everything so hard.' Perhaps the flush was from irritation rather than any physical ailment. 'We're living like gypsies,' he grunted. 'Gypsies in our own house!'

Greg, thinking of the fuss that was made about his food, said: 'You say the kitchen is out of bounds. Have you had anything to eat?'

'Oh, I sorted that out when I telephoned Perriero – my lawyer,' he explained. 'He arranged for some food to be delivered and when he comes' – he glanced at his watch – 'which should be soon, he's bringing our evening meal and some supplies for breakfast.'

'This isn't how Ruggiero should be cared for,' Rini lamented, coming to him with his drink. 'He needs proper meals, a regular regime.' Her distress made her beautiful contralto voice sound cracked and unsteady.

Ruggiero said to Liz in a petulant tone: 'She's worried about not going into mourning for Floria. She hasn't any black clothes, she never wears black.' He was baffled that it should matter so much.

'Oh, dearest, you mustn't concern yourself about my little problems!'

He shrugged, took a sip of his drink. 'This is Cinzano,' he complained.

'It will have to do, darling. There's no lemonade left.' She turned to Liz with an air of apology. 'Of course he's out of sorts, even with me, poor darling. But then men don't understand about clothes. People of this area – they're old-fashioned – they *expect* women to wear black.' She touched herself on her breast. 'But I don't own any black clothes, and I feel I can't go to Rome to shop for them – it would look so . . . uncaring.' Tears brimmed at her eyes as they so often did.

'It's all right, it's all right,' soothed Liz. 'I'll buy you a black dress tomorrow and bring it to you.'

'Oh! How kind! Th–thank you.'

'A hat? Shall you want a hat?'

'I–I don't know. Yes, later – I must go to the funeral, mustn't I? And I look so *dismal* in black!'

'But that's appropriate in the circumstances, Rini. Look,

I'll get you a black skirt and jacket too, and then you can perhaps wear a plain white blouse with it. That will lighten some of the gloomy effect.'

This went on for several more moments while the two men looked on wordlessly. When the difficult questions were solved – what size and which fashion house – Greg was able to say that the inspector had given permission for them to leave in a manner which said he wanted them gone.

Ruggiero roused himself to see them out. Greg stepped back a moment to say quietly to him in English, which he knew Novelli didn't speak, 'You said the inspector isn't friendly, and it's clear you're right.'

'There's nothing I can do about that, I'm afraid.'

'I'd think he'd be quite happy if the press got some information.'

'Thank you. I'll get Perriero to hire some private security to keep out reporters.' They shook hands. 'Goodbye, Gregory. Please keep searching for the sacred relic.'

'Don't you think it would be better to let that go for the moment?'

'No, no, please, Gregory. Please don't desert me now.'

Liz had the car started when he reached her. 'What was all that about?' she said.

'I was just giving a hint about the police inspector.'

'What about him?'

'He's being unnecessarily strict. He's probably had a hint from some political enemy of Ruggiero's.'

'But surely Floria's death hasn't got anything to do with politics!'

'I agree with you. But this is Italy, where they've had a new government almost every year since World War Two. Everything has to do with politics.'

As they drove through the village, they were aware of inquisitive stares from the inhabitants. The earlier passage of the police cars had not gone unnoticed. 'I wonder what they make of it,' Liz mused. 'Do you think Ernesto comes down here for an evening drink? I bet they'll cross-question him.'

'They'll get it out of Armeno,' Greg said. 'He doesn't have quarters at the villa so I imagine he lives in Tabardi. He'd be a lot easier to quiz than Ernesto.'

It was early evening when they drew up at the hotel. 'What's the plan now?' she inquired.

'Well, I have to telephone Grossmutti and tell her what's happened.'

'Oh?' The tone meant, *Do you really have to bother*?

'The Ardiccis are to some extent friends of hers. Or at least, they're valued clients . . .'

'Oh yes.' She added mischievously, 'And of course she still has the ballroom to decorate. She won't want that cancelled.'

'Now, now, don't be unkind. When my honoured forebears were chased out of Hirtenstein she didn't manage to bring the crown jewels with her. She has to earn money and, moreover, if the Ardiccis decide not to have her back to do the ballroom, she still has to get paid for the work she's already done.'

She laughed. 'I see, it's a matter of economic diplomacy. Right, then, I'll tell you what. I'll go now and scout around the shops to see where I might find something to suit Rini's style. Something a bit dramatic and not too self-involved.'

'You mean all of that can be expressed in a dress?'

'*Anything* can be expressed in a dress,' she declared, but with a grin. 'So we'll eat when I get back, shall we? Think of somewhere that offers at least some vegetarian choices.' She held her face up for a kiss then when he'd got out, drove off towards the shopping centres.

Greg went up to their room to speak to his grandmother on the landline. He felt it might be a lengthy conversation.

Her first reaction was disbelief. 'You can't mean it!' she exclaimed. 'Has she had an accident?'

'Well, perhaps. The police are at the villa, because the family doctor called them. He thought there was something suspicious about the death, and the idea now seems to be that Floria had swallowed poison.'

'Swallowed? On purpose, do you mean?'

'Who knows? I gathered that the forensic people thought it could be accidental – something in the food—'

'Now that's absurd! Cristina is an excellent cook.'

'I agree. But samples have been taken of everything in the kitchen. Everything there is either under guard or locked up. Cristina isn't being allowed anywhere near it.'

'Food poisoning? But I believe Floria always orders – I

mean, ordered – from the very best suppliers. Special deliveries came from as far away as Turin, and once, I think, Prague . . .'

'I don't know if the food's really in question – they seem to be acting very officiously, Grossmutti. The inspector in charge of the inquiry asked me very politely to go away, and I'm very glad to obey.'

He heard her blow out her breath in perplexity. 'But what about the diamonds, Gregory?'

He groaned. 'What *about* the diamonds! Did you ever see that stupid thing Rini prayed to?'

'No, never.'

'Well, it turns out it's probably an ancient icon and it could well have been taken from someone or somewhere without the owner's permission.'

'Gregory!'

'Those things are extremely precious, aren't they? They're kept in museums and cathedrals and so on. If they're privately owned, I'd imagine they're with some grand family that had them painted in the distant past – I mean, like the Russian royal family, for instance.'

She was making little sounds of dismay. 'My boy, are you sure about this?'

'I tried to get some information about the icon's provenance from Rini, but – well – to be utterly frank, I think she lied about it. Which leads me to believe the icon really might have been stolen and that she knows it.'

'This is awful, my child.' She gave a great sigh. 'If I had known that, of course I would never have got you involved. I thought it was just the diamonds that were important.'

'There isn't any news of the diamonds,' he said, 'but to tell the truth, I haven't pursued that very far. I got sidetracked.'

'Of course any publicity about Rini and her Russian Orthodox views would be harmful to Ruggiero. I suppose they haven't let the police in on that?'

'No, and I didn't say anything about it either, but I'm not sure whether that was right.'

'My dear boy, it's up to Ruggiero and Rini. But if it became known that this thing has gone missing, one way or another it's not good for his chances of getting the UN ambassador post.'

'Why should we care?'

'We–ell . . .' Nicoletta seemed at a loss. 'I suppose it's silly of me, but I'm feeling terribly sorry for Rini. If she's the cause of harm to her darling Ruggiero, she'll never forgive herself.'

Greg said nothing.

She sensed his reluctance and said, 'All right then, step back from it. After all, Rini has Yuri Tamaldov to hold her hand.'

'Ah.'

'What do you mean, ah?'

'It's rather interesting. She didn't call in Tamaldov when Floria was taken ill this morning. And after Floria died, she called the Ardicci family doctor.'

'What are you saying, Gregory?'

'Who is he? I mean, really? It's like the icon – he seems to have no provenance. He comes from some friends in Paris, so she says, and he does this "New Age" treatment – and I suppose it works, because Ruggiero goes along with it. But Rini didn't seem to want to bring him to the house while the police were there.'

'But . . .'

'But what?'

'He's so *nice*, Gregory.'

He didn't say, *Con men make a point of being 'nice'*. Instead he said: 'Floria called him a charlatan.'

'Floria just didn't take to him.'

'And now Floria is dead.'

# SEVEN

Next morning Mr Crowne awoke to find himself alone. This wasn't unusual. His beloved had this weird habit of going for a morning run.

He studied the ceiling for a while, had a look at the light slanting in at the edge of the shutters, examined the bedside clock, and discovered it was time he got up. A quick look at the outside world showed him that it had rained in the night, but the sunshine was already strong.

He started the little coffee-making machine, then went to get ready for the day.

Liz came in while he was drying himself in the bathroom. He put his head round the door to greet her. Her T-shirt, wet with sweat, clung to her breasts. Her hair was plastered against her scalp. She waved at him, got a bottle of mineral water from the tiny fridge, and drank deeply. Mr Crowne came out with his damp towel wrapped around him.

'It's going to be another scorcher,' she muttered.

'Coffee?'

'You bet.' She wandered into the bathroom, where he felt bound to join her as a good way of helping her recover from the exertions of her run.

Later she was combing back her wet hair. 'It'll normally dry in five minutes,' she commented, smoothing down the straight strands.

'I wish you'd go back to having those little twirly wisps,' he sighed. 'All the girls seem to have straight hair these days.'

'Fashion, my love, fashion.' Her thoughts were elsewhere. 'Now, it's no good trying for haute couture for Rini, because most of the posh shops are closed until September. So I'd better wear something in keeping with the shopping malls – smart but not too smart.' She settled for a pale-blue shift and sandals. 'How do I look?'

'Gorgeous, as ever, my Lizzie. So that's your plan, is it, to go in search of some mourning wear for Rini.'

'Yes. How about you?'

'I'm not going to dress shops – not even for you.' He considered a moment. 'I think I'll try for a chat with Ruggiero's *avvocato* so I'd better wear a suit.'

'Why the lawyer?'

'I thought he might have some background knowledge. You know, when Ruggiero mentioned Russian Orthodox groups, he emphasized that Rini didn't go to any. But as I recall, when she was still singing, one of the complaints against her was that she'd be late for rehearsal because she'd been off in some church.'

'But she has the little corner in her boudoir at the villa—'

'But I have a feeling she probably needs human contact – likes to be praying with others. I could be wrong, but I think Signor Perriero might know.'

Greg sat down with the phone. Inquiries gave him the number. He dialled, was put through, and after a short colloquy, nodded in satisfaction. 'Eleven fifteen, he'll offer me coffee in his office. Seems quite approachable.'

'Can't do any harm,' she agreed. 'Well, shall we meet somewhere around lunchtime?'

They drove off together, kissed goodbye in a parking area at the Piazza del Popolo, and went their separate ways. Greg first dropped in on Mario Zetto in his office, an untidy cubbyhole notable for its pinboard showing flyers for bands and gigs all over the Rome area.

'Ah, *paisano, come va*? Did you buy anything from Signor Scintillio?'

'As a matter of fact, I did. But what I want to know now, Mario, is – do you know anybody more criminal than him? Someone who might actually buy important stolen gemstones?'

'If I do, I'm not going to tell you,' said Mario Zetto in alarm. 'There are lots of shady characters in some of the places I go to, but to tell you the truth, they're more into selling drugs than fencing stolen property.' The journalist leaned back in his swivel chair to stare up at his tall visitor. 'What *are* you up to, Grego?'

'Er . . . A friend of mine has had something taken. I'm just trying to help.'

'Who is she? Anybody I can do a paragraph on?'

'No, this lady doesn't want publicity.'

'Ooh! Someone high-calibre?'

'Depends what you mean by high-calibre.'

'It's not Grandma, is it? I heard she was in Rome, doing some decorating thing. Lost the crown jewels, has she?'

Greg hesitated. 'I'm not saying it's my grandmother, but if it was, and she'd lost something, who's likely to be in the market for it?'

'Mmm. Necklace? Tiara?'

'Let's just say some loose stones.'

'Well, there's a *commissionario* in Vicol' Armadonna who's said to be open to trade in that kind of thing.'

A pawnbroker. Why hadn't he thought of that himself? The word meant "agent" but was short for *commissionario del Monte di Pietà*, the agent for the Mount of Piety, in other words the owner of a pawnshop.

'Thank you, Mario, you're a great fount of knowledge.'

'Well, repay me by letting me have it first if you marry that English girl.'

Greg smiled and waved farewell. Liz was never going to marry him. In the first place, she was too immersed in her love of the fashion world. In the second place, she didn't want to be an ex-royal.

He took a local bus to Vicol' Armadonna, an alley in the Trastevere area. The buildings on either side were high. It was cool in their shade. The sign, so well known throughout the world, showed him a doorway. He walked under the three golden balls and climbed some stairs. He knocked on a door and was bidden entrance.

There was a counter with a glass screen, behind which glass shelves showed various articles on view – watches, rings, cameras. There was an access panel now closed. He knocked on it, and a rather well-dressed young woman with thick black hair and glasses came from a screened area further back.

'Yes?'

'I wonder if you have any fine gemstones for sale?' Greg asked, trying for an expression between anxiety and eagerness.

'Gemstones, yes, we have gemstones. What are you looking for?'

'Er . . . Diamonds?'

'At what value?'

He tried to recall the carat, but it eluded him. He used another method of identifying the missing stones. 'Enough to make a necklace,' he ventured, 'for my fiancée – to wear at the wedding.'

'You mean, *loose* stones?'

'Yes.'

'Hah!' said the saleswoman. 'You'll be lucky!' She glanced back at the screened area. 'Necklaces we have, ready for your bride to wear. Diamond and pearl, diamond and turquoise . . . let me see, what else, diamond and aquamarine?'

'No, thank you. She wanted matched stones, to wear close against the throat – what's that called?'

'A choker?' She shook her head. 'Can't help you. What we've got in stock at the moment, it's a lot fancier than what you're after.'

'Do you know anywhere that might have something like that?'

She looked pained. 'Recommendations we don't do. In any case, what you're after sounds unusual to me. Necklaces, bracelets, rings – plenty of those. Unset stones . . .' She shook her head.

'If you hear of something of that kind, would you let me know? I could make it worth your while.'

She gave him a hard stare through her fashionable glasses, then turned and stalked back to the door in the divider. It opened, and a man in slacks and shirtsleeves appeared. There was enough similarity to suggest they were brother and sister.

They held a colloquy of a few minutes. Then the young woman went in the area beyond the screen and her brother came to the counter.

'What brought you here?' he inquired, quite sedately. 'How did you get our address?'

'Mario Zetto mentioned you.'

'Oh, him.' A pause. 'What's your line? Night club manager? Casino dealer? Or . . .?'

'I'm in music,' Greg said, with perfect truth.

'Really? Are you with a hit band? My sister says you were talking money. Big money?'

'Well, not little money,' he replied, trying for lightness.

'Hmm. Well, see here, we've no loose gemstones and if you want the latest update, we haven't heard of any. But I could put out a few feelers. Where can I get in touch if I hear of anything?'

For a moment Greg was in a quandary. He couldn't give the Hotel Pastorella as his address without involving Liz. For the same reason, he couldn't say the Villa Stefani.

He gave the number of his home office. The office might well be empty, because this was August and his assistant, Amabelle, was the mother of two school children on holiday. But the calls would go through to her house on the outskirts of Geneva.

'Where's that, for heaven's sake?' asked the money-lender on hearing the number.

'Geneva.'

He scowled at him. 'Is this a joke?'

'All right then, *I'll* ring you in a day or two if you'll give me your number.'

After a momentary pause he was handed a card with the single word '*Prestiti*' and a telephone number.

'Thank you. Good morning.'

'Huh,' said the pawnbroker as he left.

Greg was fairly sure that the man's first call would be to find out whether his client was an agent of the Questura.

He walked up the alley to the main thoroughfare and rang Zetto on his mobile. 'Mario, if a man rings you to ask if I'm bona fide, tell him yes.'

'Ah, so it's you, chum. Listen, there's news of some sort of hubbub at the Villa Stefani, and a hint that you've been staying there. True or false?'

'Quite true.'

'Connected with this treasure hunt you seem to be engaged on?'

'No comment.'

'Which means yes, of course. Can I put a bit in my column?'

'If you do, I'll never get you tickets for the Vienna Opera House again.'

'Don't be like that! You know I need an occasional fix of something good to counteract all the rubbish I listen to in bars and clubs.'

'Is it a deal?'

'We–ell – promise me you'll give me *something*.'

'Not now. Later.'

'All right then, it's a deal.'

It was nearly time for his appointment with *Avoccato* Perriero. He found a taxi, luckily with air-conditioning, and was driven there. The premises of the law firm were in startling contrast to those of the *Monte di Pietà*. There was marble on the walls, multicoloured tiling on the floor, a desk of rich wood at which sat a young and pretty girl. On hearing his name, she conducted Greg to a lift, pressed the button for an upper floor, and told him he would be met.

At the first floor, an older woman in what Greg thought might be something very fashionable greeted him with some deference. 'This way.' He was ushered into a room where the bright morning light was veiled by louvred window screens.

An elderly man in a summer suit of navy-blue linen rose at his entrance.

'Mr Crowne,' he said, shaking hands. 'I'm Luca Perriero. Ruggiero says I may treat you with complete confidence. Please, sit.' He led the way to a comfortable sitting area, with easy chairs and a low table. The well-dressed lady hovered. 'Coffee? Something stronger? Something cold?'

Greg said he'd like iced mineral water. 'See to that, Beata, will you? I'll have the same.'

She disappeared into the room next door. The two men settled themselves. The lawyer remarked that he was looking forward to going to the coast for the weekend and hoped that the Roman heat wasn't causing his guest too much trouble. The drinks appeared, Beata withdrew, and Perriero leaned forward.

'You've come about the death of Floria, I suppose. The autopsy has been completed, the results will be available later today.' He sighed. 'God knows what will come of this. Ruggiero's career opportunities were severely narrowed when he insisted on marrying Rini Grushenka – and now this.'

'So Rini's religion really is quite an issue in Italy.'

'My dear sir, it varies from day to day. If the Vatican is in one of its sulks with the Orthodox church, our politicians tread warily. Although we're not always too respectful of the Vatican, when it comes to voting it has an influence. Faithful church-goers don't support candidates who leave the one true path.'

'But Ruggiero hasn't left the path. He's married a woman from a different one, that's all.'

'But the press did its research. They found out she was quite well known for being . . . well . . . very zealous. A bit of a crank, in fact.'

Greg sipped his drink. Then he said, 'Are there any Orthodox services that she goes to?'

'Well . . . I'm no expert. I made a few discreet inquiries when it became clear that it might have some influence on Ruggiero's prospects. I believe there are meetings under the auspices of the Russian Saint Catherine, but I do sincerely hope that Rini has enough sense not to attend them.'

'There are enough people to keep the services going?'

Perriero shrugged. 'There are enough followers of all sorts of cults and religions to keep anything going.' He eyed his visitor with interest. 'Is it an issue where the death of Floria is concerned? Are you suggesting that it was someone from the Russian church who . . . who is responsible for her death?'

Greg was thinking that some fervent believer might have somehow got a hint of the icon's existence. The thief might be someone Rini had met in some religious setting. But that was a connection to the icon, not to Floria. No, Floria's death was clearly an accident. He shook his head and sighed.

Perriero had his own train of thought. He cleared his throat and began, with some hesitation: 'You must allow me, Mr Crowne, to say that I am aware of your real name. I must ask you . . . Are you at Ruggiero's house as an emissary for some monarchist group? Because if that's so, I most earnestly hope Ruggiero is not inclined to support you. Italy doesn't seem to want a return of the former monarchy.'

Greg was totally taken aback. An emissary for the Italian monarchy? 'Not at all,' he said. 'No, no, I try never to involve myself in politics.'

'But Ruggiero is a politician.'

'But his wife was an opera singer. Music is my profession.'

'Ah!' It was an exclamation of great relief. 'Beata said as much. She goes to opera and so on, and said she'd seen the name of your agency on programmes.' He studied Greg. 'Is Rini thinking of going back to the stage? Is that why you're staying with them?'

'She may have that in mind,' Greg replied, not knowing whether it was true or not.

The lawyer murmured something to himself. It might have been, 'If only she would!' Greg understood his feelings. Italian voters might be a lot more forgiving if they could see Ruggiero's wife as an opera star, not a follower of some foreign religion.

'Thank you for seeing me,' he said, rising.

'I gather Ruggiero is expecting to see you some time today?'

'Oh, we had made no actual plans—'

'But if you go to the villa, please tell him to answer his telephone. His party chairman and many of his colleagues have been trying to get in touch, and some of them have contacted me.' He hesitated. 'The fact is, Rini is fielding his calls – I suppose on the grounds that it would be too distressing for him to deal with business matters. I've said this to Rini but . . . where Ruggiero is concerned, she is very protective.'

Greg agreed to pass on the message if he saw Ruggiero. They shook hands, and he left.

Liz was waiting for him at the restaurant. She looked pleased with herself. 'Have you had a good morning?'

'Not really. But I can see you have.'

'I feel I've done well by a friend in need,' she announced, raising her wine glass in a toast to herself. 'Sit down, have a drink. This was recommended by the wine waiter, it's local and rather nice.'

'You bought something suitable, then?'

'Oh, several somethings. I left them with the cloakroom attendant. But they'll need alteration before they'll look good so I've arranged with Rini to go there this afternoon and do some dressmaking.'

'Good heavens!'

'It's all right if you don't want to come.'

'No, no, I think I'll tag along. I've got a message for Ruggiero from his lawyer, and besides I want to hear what the post mortem turned up.' The waiter appeared and poured some wine for him. He glanced at the menu. After ordering he asked, 'You spoke to Rini? How was she?'

'Oh, less tempestuous than you might expect! It seems her darling Ruggiero hasn't had any trouble with his digestion despite all the hoo-ha, and she puts that down to the care she's lavishing on him.'

'Did she mention anything about the investigation?'

'Only that the police are still there. She got a bit upset about that, says they're being victimized, but at least they got some proper food when the legal eagle flew in, and the kitchen has been declared fit for use.'

'I had a chat with the legal eagle, but he couldn't be very helpful. It seems possible there are other followers of the Orthodox church that Rini might be in touch with.'

'Meaning what? Oh, I see. One of them might have known about the icon?'

He shrugged. 'But if they did, so what? Why was that painting stolen? For the icon or for the diamonds? I wish the diamonds were more promising, Liz. I went to see a firm recommended to me by a pal, a pawnshop that he said dealt in black-market goods, and it seemed like a total dead end.'

'No one's offering them for sale?'

'Well, you know, Liz, people who deal in stolen goods aren't going to open up to me. The police could do this a lot better and a lot faster if Ruggiero wasn't so scared about his career.'

'I could ask around among some of my mates in the fashion world, but . . .' She shook her head. 'It would sound so odd, really. Diamonds? I'm known to be in at the rather hard-up end of the catwalk.'

'Well, I left my number so that if the pawnbroker hears of anything, he can get in touch.'

She frowned. 'What number?'

'It's all right, it's my office in Geneva. And when we've had lunch I'm going to ring Amabelle to say she might get a call and to take a message.'

'Ring her now.'

'Sweetheart, Amabelle is only human. She's probably getting her children's lunch at the moment.'

She laughed, and the rather pessimistic mood was lifted. 'We must go to the hotel to change. I'd better wear something dark,' she mused. 'There might be paparazzi hanging about and we don't want to seem to be disrespectful to Floria.' She was wearing a summer dress, he was in his lawyer-visiting suit. 'Should you wear a black tie?' she wondered.

When at last they set off for Villa Stefani, it was mid-afternoon. Greg had changed his tie, Liz had put on a dress of blue denim and shoes with heels.

When they reached the gates of the villa, there were a couple of cars and motorbikes outside. A man in the uniform of a security firm was leaning against the gateposts, keeping an eye on them.

It was he who opened the gates for them after checking their identity. He used a hand-held gadget and made sure no one else got through.

'Where's Ernesto?' Greg wondered.

'Probably being grilled by the cops,' Liz said lightly. But it proved to be true.

A detective let them in when they knocked. In the hall, Cristina was sitting on the marble bench against the wall.

Her face was white and drawn. As she saw Greg was about to speak to her, she turned her head away.

'What's going on?' Liz muttered.

The door of the drawing-room opened to allow Rini to rush to them in greeting. She tried to embrace Liz, but the pretty carrier bags got in the way. 'My dear friends! How truly good of you to come! Please, come in, let me offer you something cool.' She urged them in. 'Ruggiero, here they are. Ah, in times like this, we learn who our friends really are!'

Her husband was looking through some correspondence that had apparently just been delivered. He waved them before dropping them on a table. 'Just been handed on to me by those confounded detectives! What possible reason could they have for withholding my mail? It's sheer spite!'

'I saw Cristina in the hall. What's going on?'

'They've got Ernesto in the study, questioning him. *Ernesto!* What on earth do they want with him?'

'Dearest, it will all prove to be nothing,' Rini soothed. She turned to her guests. 'Now, we have proper supplies of drinks today, what can I offer you?'

They accepted refreshments. Liz nodded at her carrier bags, deposited on a chair. 'I've brought you a dress, Rini, but it's an evening dress.'

'What?'

'There was nothing among the *prêt a porter* day dresses – you're so tall, the skirts would have been unsuitably short. So the dress is ankle length but I'm going to take it up—'

'My dear Liz! I can't ask you to—'

'No, no, that's my trade. I'm in the fashion business. And with the piece I'll cut off the skirt, I'm going to fashion sleeves for the top because it's only got straps. They'll only be short but they'll turn it into a day dress.'

She produced the first of the items she had bought. Rini for once neglected her husband so as to see what was in the carriers. After a discussion between the two, Rini said: 'My darling, Liz and I are going to go upstairs and see to my mourning wear. Now if you need anything, just pick up the telephone and let me know.'

'I'm all right, Rini,' he replied. 'I can find anything I want.'

'Of course, Ruggiero, but please don't over-exert yourself.'

She gave him a kiss on the cheek then led the way out, Liz in her wake with the packages.

Her husband made a tolerant grimace. 'Women!' he sighed.

'How are you, in fact?' Greg asked. 'Surviving under the stress?'

'I really am all right. Rini thinks having almost nothing to eat yesterday was good for me.' He pushed out his lower lip in denial of that. 'Fasting! All the same, if only the worry about Floria could be taken away, I'd say I feel good.'

'I had a chat with Perriero this morning. He says the forensic results will be available today.'

'So I hear but so far they're telling me nothing. But you know, to be subjecting Ernesto to this long interview – he's been in there at least thirty minutes. What can it be about?'

'He's your driver and handyman?'

He nodded. 'Knows about cars and generally keeps things going.'

'And he's an old faithful, I suppose, has been with the family for years?'

'He's a local man,' Ruggiero said in a rather grand manner. 'They're my people. All the staff come from Tabardi or there-abouts.'

'But Floria said that catering for big events was done by a firm in Rome? And didn't Rini say Floria had food sent in from rather distant places?'

'Oh, well, you understand, one can't have country bump-kins serving important guests. But as a general rule we try to hire our workaday neighbours.'

Sounds from outside in the hall announced that something was happening. The door of the drawing-room opened and in walked Inspector Novelli.

'Well,' he remarked. 'That's sorted that out.'

He was in shirt sleeves, sweating a little, but had a self-satisfied air.

'You know the cause of death?' Ruggiero asked, getting up out of his armchair. He was divided between eagerness and apprehension.

'It was an organic phosphate, one of the deadliest forms of poison. Specifically,' Novelli said, stretching it out for effect, 'parathion, which has been discarded by most countries because of its extreme effects.'

'Parathion?' echoed Ruggiero. 'What is it? How did Floria ever come into contact with such a thing?'

'You may well ask! It's an insecticide. You see what comes of hiring an untrained nincompoop to do your gardening?'

'What? What do you mean? Are you – are you talking about Ernesto?'

'He found this insect spray in a bottle in the garage! What on earth were you thinking of, letting such a dangerous chemical stand around on a shelf in the open, where anyone could get at it?'

'I don't understand! What shelf in the garage? I don't know what you're talking about?'

Ruggiero was looking flushed, indignant, and very distressed. Greg felt he had to intervene. 'Excuse me, inspector, but it might be easier if you started at the beginning. And maybe you'd like to sit down and have a drink? What would you like?' He went to the drinks tray, looking ready to serve.

'Er . . . Well . . . I wouldn't mind something long and cool. It's not easy, talking to people who can't seem to put two sensible words together.'

Greg surveyed the available supplies. 'Campari with ice and soda?'

'That'll do.'

Ruggiero had recovered enough to usher the inspector to a seat. Greg made Novelli's drink, then topped up his own and Ruggiero's. He was taking enough time to let everything cool down. They all settled in chairs.

Novelli took a long swallow from his glass then said: 'It seems your man of all work has been spraying your grapevine with something that he found in an old drinks bottle on a shelf in the garage and labelled "*insetticida*". He had no idea what it was but says he thought it must be the right thing because somebody before him had been using it.'

'But how did Floria come into contact with it?' Ruggiero demanded in perplexity.

'The grapes. Ernesto says he snipped a bunch of grapes and put it on a terracotta platter on the table under the vine, intending to wash it later and let you know the first bunch had been harvested.'

'What?'

'The first bunch. He says you told him you liked to have it when it became available.'

'Well, yes. That's true.'

'But your lady housekeeper came out into the garden in the morning, saw the grapes, sat down and ate them. Now that precious first bunch from that grapevine of yours was loaded with parathion. The analysts examined the stomach contents and had difficulty identifying it at first because the product has been withdrawn in this country.'

'Floria ate my grapes?' Ruggiero cried, in a tone of almost childish complaint.

Novelli grinned. 'You had a lucky escape, *signore*. Those grapes killed her.'

# EIGHT

Ruggiero dropped his glass of chilled wine. It splintered against the marble floor. The liquid splashed on his elegant shoes but he seemed unaware.

'W–what?' he gasped.

'Quite a culmination, eh? Ernesto thinks the world has opened up under his feet, and he's falling to perdition!' Novelli was enjoying himself. 'You know, in days gone by, none of these villagers would have learned to read or write, so I expect you think it's a shame times have changed. If he hadn't been able to read that label, Ernesto would never have used the contents of that old bottle on the grapevine.'

'Floria was poisoned by my grapes?' Ruggiero whispered in horror.

'Grapes from that grand old vine, been in the family for years, so I'm told. If it was so precious to you, why did you let a dunderhead like Ernesto take charge of it?'

'Ernesto is p–perfectly capable of . . . I've found him quite reliable . . .' Ruggiero was stammering in confusion. Then his expression hardened. 'Take that grin off your face!' he shouted, stepping up to the inspector and glaring up into his face.

The inspector smiled on him. 'Have a go,' he urged. 'Then I'll arrest you for assaulting the police.'

Greg came between them, backing as he did so, causing Ruggiero to step out of his way. 'Now, now,' he said. 'This isn't the way to deal with Signorina Floria's death. Let's all behave like reasonable people.'

Novelli stood his ground for a moment then seemed to listen to an inner voice that told him he was making a mistake. He turned away, shrugging, and took a sip of his Campari. Ruggiero went back to his chair.

Determined to get the situation away from personal feuding, Greg asked, 'Are you arresting Ernesto?'

'On what charge? So far as I can see, he's made a mistake due to inefficiency in managing the estate. *He's* not to blame if a label on an old lemonade bottle leads him into error.' He paused in thought. 'I'll have to consult the prosecutor's department, but I doubt if they'll want to waste time on charging the poor devil. There'll have to be an inquest, but the magistrate will probably rule death by misadventure.'

'In the meantime, what happens to Ernesto?'

Novelli shrugged. 'Nothing to do with me. Mind you, I'd keep him away from stuff in old bottles stored on dusty shelves, just in case.' He drank what remained in his glass then nodded farewell and strode out of the room.

Ruggiero struggled to his feet. He went to the door of the drawing-room. Clearly, he wanted to make sure this enemy left his house. Greg found a pile of napkins on the drinks table and used one to scoop up the broken glass from the floor.

At the door, Ruggiero was saying, 'Now, now, that's enough! Come in here, Ernesto, and explain yourself.'

Looking over his shoulder, Greg saw Ernesto and Cristina bound together in an embrace of passionate affection and relief. They were quite unconscious of Ruggiero's command. Greg tapped him on the arm.

'Come on, give them a few moments to get over all this.'

Rather unwillingly, Ruggiero returned into the room. 'Poison! What was it called?'

'I'm not sure. Parathion, I think.'

'And that idiot's been spraying it on my grapes?'

'It's not his fault, Ruggiero.'

'He should have asked me to order whatever he needed for the care of my garden. Why on earth should he go poking in corners of my garage for old bottles?'

Ernesto came through the open door, his head bent and his arms crossed in front of himself defensively.

'*Signore*,' he said in a low voice.

Ruggiero stared at him aggressively, arms akimbo. 'Well? What have you to say for yourself?'

The servant's gaze was fixed on his boots. He mumbled something.

'What? What did you say?'

'I would never harm the *signorina*. It was an accident.'

'An accident! A member of my family is killed in the prime of her life and all you say is "It was an accident"?'

'Signorina Floria was always good and fair with us,' Ernesto replied, his voice cracking with distress. 'The last thing in the world that I would ever want is that she should come to harm.'

'Yet you leave fruit tainted with poison lying about—'

'*Signore*, I didn't know it was poisonous! I'm not a gardener – you know my special thing is the cars. I only try to keep the plants tidied up. When I saw the little insects on the leaves, I knew the way to get rid of them was to spray.'

'But why didn't you ask about the stuff you found? You should have—'

'Who should I ask, *signore*?' begged Ernesto.

'Oh, don't make excuses! You've plenty of pals in the village who could have told you.'

'But there was nothing on the bottle but the word insecticide.'

'That's enough! I want you out of this house tomorrow morning! Get out of my sight!'

'*Signore!*'

'Go, go, I can't bear to look at you. You and your wife – *out*!'

Beaten, the servant bowed his head in acknowledgement and went out. Greg, the unwilling witness to the scene, was aghast. He tried to put together some words of mediation, but Ruggiero was stamping about the room in fury.

The door was flung open and in dashed Rini with Liz in her wake.

'The police have gone?' she cried. 'We heard the cars drive off – have they really gone?'

'Oh yes,' her husband flared at her. 'They've satisfied themselves that it was an understandable accident and cleared off!'

'Dearest! Please calm yourself.' She put a gentle hand on his arm. 'You know it's bad for you to get upset—'

'Upset! One of my family dies as a result of criminal negligence—'

'Who, darling? Who has been negligent?'

'That halfwit Ernesto! Finds a bottle in the garage and just uses the stuff and it's only God's mercy that we weren't *all* poisoned.'

'Sit down, Ruggiero, sit down and take some deep breaths. My love, perhaps you should have a little brandy – Liz, please, ring the bell and ask Cristina for—'

'Cristina is in the hall crying her eyes out,' Liz interrupted. 'Didn't you see her as we came downstairs?'

'Crying? Cristina? No, I didn't. Well, never mind, ring the bell and—'

'Rini, I don't think she's in any fit state—'

'Is the brandy in the kitchen?' Greg asked. 'I'll get it.'

Rini was in too much of a fluster to reply. He went out, and there, as Liz had said, was Cristina crying as if heartbroken. Ernesto was hugging her to himself and tears were running down his cheeks. They were too wrapped up in each other to notice as the Ardiccis' guest strode off towards the kitchen area.

At first he thought the wines and spirits might be in the little office used by Floria. But when he tried the handle, he found the door locked. He went into the kitchen, where something with a lovely aroma was simmering in a lidded pot on the stove. A quick inspection of cupboards revealed a little array of fine drink, perhaps for culinary purposes. He poured some Martel into a glass and hurried out.

Ernesto and Cristina were still in the hall, but now they were sitting on the marble bench, heads together, talking in whispers. At the sound of his footsteps Ernesto turned his head to give Greg an imploring glance.

Greg didn't respond. He simply didn't know how. He took the brandy to Rini, who was now kneeling at the side of the chair where her husband was sitting with his head back, glaring at the ceiling. 'I'm all right,' he was muttering. 'Don't fuss, Rini. I have a right to feel bitter about what's happened.'

Rini took the glass. 'Drink a little, dear. It will do you good. To please me. Just a sip.'

He sat up, sipped, then shrugged and gazed about in a more rational manner. 'After all I've done for him,' he grunted. 'Gave him a job, gave him a house, and how does he reward me? By utter carelessness!'

Liz had gathered the course of events during Greg's absence. She murmured, 'I gather Inspector Novelli didn't think him to blame.'

'No, of *course* not! Novelli stood there telling me it was all *my* fault! That's what I get from the likes of him – hatred of anyone who owns property and tries to manage the country's economy in a sensible manner!' He blew out an angry breath, but took the brandy glass from his wife and had a good swallow. 'Ah,' he sighed, 'you can't expect anything better from a man like that.'

'It's all over now, my love. We'll settle down now they've gone, and then we'll mourn for Floria, and put it behind us.'

'Can you really dismiss Ernesto and Cristina so easily?' Liz inquired in a very innocent tone. 'Of course I don't know the Italian employment laws, but can they really be sent away at a moment's notice?'

'Oh, it has to be so,' Rini sighed. 'My poor Ruggiero couldn't bear to have them here a minute longer.'

'How will you manage? Can you get a cook at short notice, Rini?'

'Ahh . . .' She was a little taken aback, but recovered. 'I'll contact the agency that Floria used. They'll send us a cook. The man who comes when we have a dinner party – he's excellent.'

'If he's from Rome, will he want to live in?' Liz asked. 'Or will he be coming from Rome every day?'

'Well, I suppose . . . He might be coming every day. Sara and Armeno come every day, although only from the village.'

'Rather a shame,' Greg said, understanding Liz's campaign and joining it. 'Cristina baked lovely fresh rolls for breakfast, I recall. You won't get them from someone who has to drive up from Rome every morning.'

'We . . . er . . . there's a baker in the village. We can get the morning rolls from him.' She shrugged. 'We'll manage until we get proper replacements.'

'Do Cristina and Ernesto have somewhere to go?' Liz inquired. 'A house in Tabardi, or something?'

'No, I believe they were renting their house,' Rini replied with an inquiring glance at her husband.

'Ha! Poky little hole! They had *nothing* until I gave them their jobs here!'

'So someone else may be in their old place now? They have to find somewhere to live?'

'Oh, someone will take them in.'

'With their belongings – but perhaps the gate-lodge furniture belongs to the estate so they'll just have their clothes and things.' Liz considered this. 'The press boys will simply love that.'

An awful silence fell.

'The press . . .?'

'They're outside the gates, Ruggiero. I saw at least one cameraman when we drove up.' She paused. 'It will make a telling picture, the two of them trudging away with their suitcases.'

Greg was about to say, 'They wouldn't trudge, they'll call a taxi,' but caught back the words. He could see that the idea of a photographer recording the departure of the two servants was causing Ruggiero some trouble.

'You know, when you come to think of it,' Liz continued, 'the gate-lodge has been their home – for how long?'

'Oh, about a year.' Ruggiero was trying to minimize the relationship.

'Not long, I suppose. But is it one of the human rights, the right to your home?'

At the dreaded words, 'human rights', Ruggiero gave a groan of alarm, quickly changed into a cough.

Rini was put out. 'We have our human rights too, after all,' she said. 'You can't expect us to live with people who poisoned our dear Floria.'

'No, of course not. Although, mind you, the kitchen was declared all clear so Cristina was in no way to blame. And all Ernesto really does is open and close the gates, so he wouldn't actually be anywhere near you. I mean, now that you've warned him off doing the garden.'

'Hmm,' said Ruggiero.

'What are you thinking, dearest?' Rini asked.

'I was thinking . . . well . . . you know, it will be so inconvenient for you, my dear, having to cope with all this. After all, you have no experience of housekeeping – Floria did all that for us. It might be . . . well . . . quite some time before we could find suitable replacements for the Stresos.'

'We would do that through an agency, wouldn't we?'

'Yes, but interviewing applicants would take a week or two, perhaps longer. You know, Rini, I think it would make sense to give ourselves time.'

'I don't know how it is here,' Liz supplied, 'but in the UK, a month's notice is quite usual.'

'A month . . . Ye–es . . . I suppose we could put up with having them still here for a month, couldn't we, my angel?'

'It's you I'm thinking of, Ruggiero! Could you bear to have them here?'

'Oh, perhaps I was over-emotional. My feelings for poor Floria overwhelmed me.' A pause to let the depths of his regret for Floria sink in on his hearers. Then: 'But Floria herself wouldn't want us to turn our lives upside down while we grieve. She'd want us to be sensible.'

'Oh yes, Floria was always so sensible.'

'So perhaps . . . I'll have a word with Ernesto, make him see that he has to go but that meanwhile we won't want him anywhere near the house. As to Cristina, I should think she'd be particularly careful with the cooking after all this.' He huffed to himself, then grunted: 'A month's notice, what do you say, Rini?'

'Whatever you think best, dear.'

He stamped out of the room, shouting as he went. 'Ernesto! With me!'

Ernesto could be seen sitting in quiet but intense conversation with his wife. He leapt up, staring in confusion at the master of the house and the group that followed after him.

'I'm going to draft a statement,' Ruggiero announced. 'You'll say that it was your fault that the *signorina* died and that you agree to leave my employment within a month. You'll sign the statement and if you do, you can remain in the lodge but you don't do any gardening. Is that understood?'

'Y–yes, *signore*.'

'If you can find somewhere to go before the month is up, so much the better.' Ruggiero frowned fiercely. 'But I'll pay you and your wife for the entire month, irrespective of when you leave. That's fair, you agree?'

'Yes, *signore*.'

'Very well. Come to my study and we'll write it out. Cristina' – he swept round to glare at her – 'you can go to the kitchen if you want to but for today, we won't have anything cooked there, thank you very much.' The latter words were spoken with heavy irony.

'Yes, *signore*,' murmured Cristina.

Ruggiero stamped off towards his study with Ernesto in his wake. Cristina scurried off towards the kitchen. Rini hesitated for a moment, gazing after her husband in awe, then led the way back to the drawing-room.

'He is so commanding!' she breathed. 'Such a leader of men!'

Neither of her guests felt able to make any response to that. Rini gestured them to chairs then asked: 'From upstairs we heard the police driving away. Do you think the reporters have gone too?'

'It's likely,' Greg said. 'They'd go after the police so as to hear the summarizing statement at headquarters.'

'Because, you know, if they've gone,' Rini went on, 'it might be a good thing if Ruggiero and I went out to dinner. To show that our name has been cleared, that Floria's death was a complete accident and nothing to do with marriage problems.' She fussed with her dark hair as she said it, embarrassed yet determined.

Liz was nodding, although Greg felt less convinced. 'You could check with the security man at the gates,' he suggested. 'He had some sort of personal radio.'

'Oh, but the microphone connected to that is in Ruggiero's study. I wouldn't want to interrupt him while he's dealing with Ernesto.' Now she was at a loss.

'I could go down to the gates and have a look.'

'No, no, I couldn't ask you to do that – no, but perhaps you would be so good as to send Armeno?'

'Armeno's here?'

'Oh, of course – nothing would keep him from his beloved horses. I'm sure he's in the stables.'

'All right, I'll find him.' He half-turned to leave, but hesitated. 'Rini, may I ask you something?'

'Of course. Anything.'

'Have you ever gone to services of the Russian Orthodox Church without telling Ruggiero?'

The great dark eyes flashed with momentary indignation. Then a flush of red came over her olive skin. She bent her head. Her lips quivered. 'Why do you ask that?'

'Because Ruggiero's lawyer, Maestro Perriero, implied that you have.'

'N–no . . . Never!' Then tears trembled at her lashes and she said brokenly, 'Never in Rome.'

'In Venice, perhaps? Or Parma?'

'Well . . .'

'What did you do? Invent a reason for going on a little trip . . .'

'You are so quick to catch a hint! I went for a weekend to Venice to hear a friend sing Palestrina. In a Catholic church. And then . . .'

'Then you went on to a service elsewhere.'

'I did.' The admission was in the tone of complete honesty. 'But it couldn't do any harm. No one knew me there.'

'Are you sure?'

'Oh, yes, yes, I took the greatest care. I travelled there by train – you know, nobody would ever think of seeing me travelling on a train, and I wore dark glasses and covered my hair with a scarf, and spoke to hardly anyone.'

'There's no way you could have been found out? Because there is the possibility that the icon was stolen by a fellow-worshipper of your church.'

'No, how could anyone know? Please, Gregory, please – don't say that I in any way brought all this trouble upon my husband! I couldn't bear it!'

'You didn't speak to anyone? Confide in anyone?'

She drew back, startled. 'Confide? What do you mean, confide?'

'I don't know, Rini. Why was it so important to go to a Russian service?'

'I . . . I . . .' She was searching for words. 'Gregory, you understand that even the most loving partners . . . Sometimes there is a little . . . uncertainty . . .'

Greg sighed. 'You went to speak to a priest.'

'Ye–es. But he couldn't know who I was. I spoke to him as a simple housewife.'

'And what did you speak to him about?'

'The first time . . . that was . . . oh, so long ago . . . almost three years . . . I was wrong to suspect it, but I felt . . . I felt that Ruggiero might be unfaithful to me.' She choked back tears.

'The first time? So how often did you do this?'

'Only once more.'

'Before or since you bought the icon.'

'The second time . . . That was when I was so worried about Ruggiero's career, when the elections were taking place. I already had my image of Saint Olga, and of course I prayed to her, yet even so . . . I was worried. So I went to Florence, where I had heard there was to be a private gathering, and I spoke to *Otyets Stralosgov* about my anxieties, and he in his piety told me to trust in Almighty God.' Tears gathered on her eyelashes. 'But it was not to be, and my Ruggiero lost his place in the government.'

Greg was steadfastly refusing to take pity on her emotion. 'So, in speaking to the priest, did you mention that you had already prayed to Saint Olga?'

'No! No!' But then she shivered, and shook her head. 'Yes, I said I had prayed to her. But I never mentioned my icon. No, I never would speak of that to anyone, for it is very personal to me, but once it was stolen . . . *Then* I had to let you know what had happened, but you alone and your revered grandmother, you are the only people outside our family who know.' She had clasped her hands in appeal, and was half holding them out towards Greg. 'Am I to blame? Have I harmed my Ruggiero?'

Liz intervened, seeing that Rini was working herself up to great tempests of tears. 'Of course you're not to blame, Rini. Greg is only following up every possibility, he's not suggesting you've done anything wrong.' She went to her and coaxingly laid a hand on her arm. 'Come along, you and I will go upstairs,' she suggested, 'because I've got to finish the hem on that dress if you want to go out to dinner.'

Rini gave a sob and a laugh. 'Oh! How sweet you are, Liz dear! And how far-seeing! I wouldn't have thought of what to wear tonight. Yes, yes, let's go upstairs and see to it – you're so very kind, such a good friend!'

They departed on their separate tasks, Greg rather unwillingly letting his questions go unfinished. He went out through a back door, passing Cristina in the kitchen. She was conscientiously emptying the something that had been cooking into a bowl for safe-keeping. She bobbed a little acknowledgement of his presence as he went past but kept her eyes averted.

Armeno was sitting in a corner of the stall of the chestnut mare, gazing at her fondly and softly singing a pop song. '*Di blu dipinto di blu, felice di stare lasu . . .*' He sprang up as Greg appeared, blushing. '*Signore?*'

'Armeno, would you walk down to the gates and see if there are any reporters there?'

'*Signore?*'

'Walk down to the gates. Look out to see if there are any strangers waiting there.'

'Strangers?' Armeno looked scared. 'I'm not to talk to strangers, Mama says.'

'Don't talk to them. Just look, and then come back and tell me.'

'What am I to tell you, *signore*?'

'Tell me if there are any people there that you don't know.'

'Shall I count?'

'Yes, please,' Greg said, because it seemed safe to agree to that.

'I can count well. I can read too, if you would like me to do that.'

'I don't think there will be anything to read at the gate, Armeno.'

'I can read the label on the soap packet. It's a special soap for the saddles – for the leather. The saddles are made of special leather. Ernesto showed me how to spell out what's on the label.'

'That's very good.'

'Yes, Ernesto is good. He takes care of the cars; I take care of the horses.'

'You do it very well.'

'Oh, but not as good as Ernesto. Ernesto can *write* labels as well as read them. He likes things neat and tidy. It's a pity the police took away the bottle with the label but the police are important, they do things that are important.'

'That's true, Armeno. So will you go to the gates and then come back and tell me what you see?'

'I'll see the man in the uniform.' Armeno was brushing strands of hay from his trouser legs. 'But he's not a policeman.'

'No, never mind the man in the uniform. Just tell me about anyone else.'

'Yes, *signore*. Thank you.' He set off, shoulders squared, head held high, on a mission.

Greg looked at the mare, who was dreaming in the late afternoon heat. 'He's a good friend to you, isn't he?' Greg inquired, but the mare made no reply.

Cristina was waiting outside the back door as he returned to the villa. She made no acknowledgement as he went indoors but stood in patience, waiting for her husband to be allowed to leave.

There was no one in the drawing-room. Greg sat down, wishing himself elsewhere. By and by there were sounds from the hall, then in came Ruggiero looking cross yet pleased with himself.

'Well, that's one problem dealt with. I've sent them off with a clear view of the future,' he remarked, rubbing his hands. He poured himself a cold drink, drank deeply, then settled himself in an armchair. 'Where are the ladies?'

'Upstairs, finishing off a dress.'

'Good heavens – surely that could wait?'

'No, I think I should warn you – Rini wants you to go out to dinner this evening to show you've been cleared of any fault in the matter of Floria's death.'

'What?' He half rose from his chair, then sank back. 'Oh. Well . . . It might not be a bad idea.' He looked at Greg. 'What do you think?'

'I don't know. I'm not good at that kind of thing.'

'I suppose it's time to get out of the house. We've been cooped up here for two days now.' He felt for the remote to switch on the television set. 'Let's see what they're saying on the news bulletins.'

Channel One was showing pictures of troubles in the Middle East. He switched around but in the end came back to the first news channel to find a police officer with a lot of gold braid concluding an announcement about the '*Processo Ardicci*'. He declared that the matter would be wrapped up according to the usual regulations concerning accidental death.

'Ha!' crowed Ruggiero. 'I don't know who he is but at least he read it without trying to slant it against me! So that's an end of that, thank God.'

Greg nodded agreement. He wished Ruggiero would also say that there was an end of the search for the icon. That had receded in importance while he'd been coming to terms with recent happenings.

While he was trying to think of a way of asking if they could regard the icon as gone for good, there came a very faint tap on the door of the drawing-room. Ruggiero frowned, but made no move. Greg went to the door.

When he opened it he found Armeno trembling on the threshold. The boy's face was a picture of fear and dismay. 'Signore,' he began. 'Signore . . . Ernesto says he's leaving!'

Greg nodded. 'But not at once,' he said, trying to soothe away the shocked expression. 'He'll be here for another month.'

Armeno gave a shake of the head. 'That's not very long, is it? Four weeks, that makes a month. By that time the bushes will need pruning again – and who will do that?'

'Someone else will do it, Armeno. Don't worry about it.'

Armeno pushed out his lower lip. 'Ernesto always said he would leave one day. When he'd finished his task. But the hedges are never finished with, are they? I don't think Ernesto should go.' He drew back as he heard his own words. 'But of course I mustn't say that. Mama says I must always know my place.'

'And Mama always knows best, Armeno,' Greg agreed. 'Now, you remember why I sent you to the gates?'

'What? Oh, yes, signore. Forgive me. Yes, I went to the gates – there's only the man in the grey uniform. Of course Ernesto and Cristina will be there now – I met them as I was coming back. So that's three people.'

'Thank you, Armeno.'

The boy gave a tremulous smile and moved, but glanced around in alarm at finding himself within the aristocratic splendour of the hall. 'I may go?'

'Of course. And thank you again.'

'What was all that?' Ruggiero asked as Greg turned back into the room.

'Armeno reports that there are no reporters hanging around.'

'Ha! Armeno wouldn't know a reporter if he had the name hanging round his neck.'

'No, but he says there's no one at the gates except the security guard.'

'Oh, I see – that means Rini and I can go out without being pestered. Well, that's an improvement, at least. What I think I'll do,' Ruggiero mused, 'is alert my party chairman that we're going out this evening. I'll ask him to alert the publicity department – might get a few friendly comments in tomorrow's papers.' He rose from his chair, hesitating. 'I'll do that in the study, if you don't mind being left on your own, Gregory.'

But before he could leave, in came his wife, her arms outspread, her face alight with pleasure. 'Look, darling!' She twirled.

Behind her came Liz Blair. 'Our model Rini is wearing a black silk *après-six* dress with cap sleeves and a scoop neck-line,' she announced. 'With it she might wear a black velvet jacket for a formal occasion.'

'Isn't it chic?' Rini cried. 'Ruggiero, don't you think she's just the *cleverest* girl? And so tomorrow I can go into the city wearing this and buy another thing or two in black, because with this warm weather I can't manage with just one change of clothes.'

'You look beautiful, my angel,' Ruggiero said. 'But then you always do.'

Liz was beaming. 'Not bad for an off-the-peg frock with a tacked up hem,' she remarked. 'But of course its success depends on the wearer.'

'You are too good! What friends we have found, my Ruggiero.'

'True, true – you've stood by us, like two guardian angels. And now, Gregory, now that the stupid mistake about Floria has been cleared up, you will go on with the task of finding the missing icon, won't you? The press may have their eye on me for a little while yet so please be very discreet.'

'I don't know whether I'm really doing much good, Ruggiero.'

'Don't say that! You must see that if a word gets out about that—' He checked himself. It was clear that he'd been about to say, 'About that damned thing' but had caught it back just in time.

Rini rushed to him and put her arms around him. 'Dear heart, I know how weary and frustrated you are about it! I know it's my fault! Forgive me, forgive me!'

He submitted to being hugged and kissed on the cheek.
'It's all right,' he managed to say, but rather gracelessly.

After another kiss, she let him go. 'All this stress has been
too much for you. Cooped up indoors, your enemies sniping
at you – my poor darling, I ought to be taking better care of
you.'

'No, no . . .'

'Greg, dear good friend, you'll help, won't you?' She swept
round on him with a gesture of appeal. 'He needs to get out,
to get some fresh air – so tomorrow, you will take him riding,
yes?'

There was nothing to do but agree.

'There! It's just what you need, Ruggiero – a riding
companion who can chat with you while you breathe in the
mountain air.'

'Well, yes . . . A lot better than that idiot boy!'

So it was arranged.

Greg and Liz took their leave. She was silent as she drove
first down the drive then paused for the gates, but once out
on the road she said: 'What on earth does she see in him?
It's a mystery!'

Greg didn't reply at once. Then he remarked: 'It's equally
a mystery to me why he ever got entangled with her. She's
certainly not an asset to him.'

'Oh! That's a bit harsh, Greg!'

'You think so?'

'She loves him. I should think very few people could be
as devoted as that.'

He shrugged. 'Somehow she's enlisted your sympathy. You
were a bit too quick, taking her away just when I might have
coaxed something from her about her co-religionists.'

'But she was getting really upset.'

'Perhaps that was because she had a guilty conscience.'

'No, no, she said explicitly she hadn't talked to anyone
except a priest at the church services.'

'But what, exactly, did she say to him?'

'Nothing much, I feel sure.' But her tone was beginning to
lack certainty.

'She told him she'd prayed to Saint Olga. I don't really
know much about saints, Liz, but I looked her up. She doesn't
sound as if she'd be the most popular person to say your

prayers to, in my opinion – she seemed to go in for a lot of unpleasant ways of killing people before she got converted.'

'No!'

'Yes. And I'd think anyone who'd picked her as patron saint would be interesting to a modern-day priest. What if Father Stralosgov pricked up his ears when he heard that? It could be that the priest . . . I don't know . . . Do they get notices about icons that have gone missing from churches and museums?'

'Oh, that's stretching things a bit, Greg. He was helping her with her anxiety over Ruggiero's election prospects, that's all.'

'That's what she wanted us to think.'

'You don't believe her?'

'Do you?'

It was a question she couldn't quite answer.

# NINE

Since no set time had been arranged for the Sunday morning's riding, it was by no means early when they drove to the Villa Stefani. Greg had spent most of the previous evening catching up with messages on his office phone and then dealing with one or two of the problems listed. Liz had contacted a couple of her fashion colleagues, with a view to helping Rini with her urgent need for a supply of mourning clothes.

On their arrival they found another security man on duty at the gates. However, there were no reporters or cameramen: it seemed the interest in the Ardiccis had waned. Ernesto could be glimpsed sweeping one of the garden paths. Cristina was presumably in the kitchen at the villa.

A somewhat battered Renault was already parked in the drive, showing that Dr Tamaldov was here. He had been absent all through the police inquiries but now that the police had gone, it seemed Rini had called him to her side again.

Armeno was on watch near the front steps.

'The *signore* tells me you're going riding with him,' he

said, with a sketchy bow. His tone implied he was hoping for the answer 'No'. When Greg agreed that he would indeed be the master's riding partner, Armeno stifled a sigh but said: 'Brigante is ready for you, *signore*.' Brigante, Greg guessed, was the bay gelding. The gentle chestnut mare could hardly be called 'Bandit'. When he asked Armeno, he was told she answered to Tippi.

Ruggiero was waiting in the drawing-room, booted and spurred and altogether much more horseman-like than Greg in his jeans and shirt. Rini was trying to persuade him to wear sunglasses. 'The light is very strong, dear,' she was murmuring.

Tamaldov greeted them with warmth, and Liz found herself responding to that warm, velvety voice.

'So,' he said, 'you go out together, like Cossack on horseback, to survey our little world from mountain-top.'

Ruggiero gave an embarrassed laugh. 'I'm supposed to ride every day,' he said in explanation to Liz, at whom he was casting glances of admiration. 'It's said to be good for the liver. But of course while I was in the senate, I couldn't always manage to fit it in.'

'Dr Genarro – you know, our family doctor? – he recommends it,' said Rini, 'and Yuri also says it's good.'

'Yes, yes, all exercise in pure fresh air is beneficial. And relaxation of mind, human companionship – all good things, so I wish you a pleasant ride, my friends.'

Thus blessed by his approval, they made their plans for the morning. Tamaldov had to go back to see clients at his little clinic. Rini was driving Liz to Rome, where she would be taken to the busy district around Campo dei Fiori. Here a dressmaker had agreed to have at least one dress made by Sunday evening and another by mid-afternoon Monday.

They planned to have lunch in the neighbourhood, at a restaurant where Liz knew she would find vegetarian dishes. Rini was looking forward to it: 'I've never shopped or eaten in such a bohemian area of Rome before,' she announced with a giggle.

Liz exchanged a smile with Greg. Rini had shown little light-heartedness in the last few days.

Ruggiero took Greg to the stables, where Armeno was standing by offering equipment – hats and riding crops. Ruggiero needed a little help to mount Tippi, tactfully supplied by Armeno.

He was in the lead when they set off at little more than an amble but they joined company once they started on the mountain track. This was so that they could chat – Ruggiero had made a point of how dull Armeno had been as a conversationalist.

Ruggiero seemed to want to talk about Liz. 'Have you and Liz been together for a long time?' he inquired.

'Quite a while.'

'It seems a strange friendship. She's in the cut-throat world of fashion and you're – well, you're who you are.'

'We don't find it strange,' said His Highness with a certain coldness. Then he turned the subject to the recent election, which Ruggiero embraced with personal fervour. He had a tale of spite and skulduggery to unfold.

Even in these cool upper levels, the day was already very warm. Once they left the shade of the domain's tall poplars, they felt the strength of the sun's rays as they threaded their way among birch trees along stony yet well-beaten paths. They were ascending gently. The horses knew the way without direction even when they came to a fork in the track.

'All this is your land too?' Greg inquired.

'Oh yes. My great-grandfather had vines on the southern slopes, but the grape-stock was rather poor so he gave up growing wine. The rest,' he gestured around him with his riding-crop, 'he used for hunting – shooting, I should rather say, although I believe there were wild boar here up until the nineteen hundreds.'

There was a flutter of wings ahead. 'Woodpigeon,' murmured Greg. 'They're always the first to react to any disturbance.'

'Cristina can make a very nice terrine with pigeon,' Ruggiero remarked, 'but the sparrow-hawks get a lot of them.'

Greg pictured the low, dashing flight of the bird as it hunted its frightened prey. They could be glimpsed around his home at Bredoux, the old farm outside Geneva where his father now taught equestrianship. It reminded him he ought to telephone this evening; it was wise to keep his family up to date with his activities here, otherwise his formidable grandmother might ring to lecture him.

They rode on, the pace leisurely, the ascent taking them up where the birch trees grew more sparse. Their place was taken by thorn bushes and stunted larch intermixed with sturdy butterbur. Although the gurgling of a stream could be heard now and again, the soil was clearly poor, with stones and rocks plentiful among the thicket.

Now the path was wending its way like a ribbon beaten out of the side of the mountain. The riders had to go in single file, with Ruggiero leading the way. On one side was the upward slope, cloaked with its cover of thorn and tall, vigorous weed. The down-slope was now much steeper, although clothed in thick, parched undergrowth.

The views had become more extensive as the trees thinned out. A sparkle in the distance suggested Lake Albano. A faint suggestion of haze in the brilliant sky was the sign of Rome's ring road, some twelve kilometres away.

Ruggiero's thoughts were on Rome, and its inner world of rank and influence. 'My party chief arranged for some journalists to be around when Rini and I left the restaurant last night,' he remarked. 'Too late for today's gossip columns but Mercanti says there should be something tomorrow.'

'You went into Rome for dinner?'

'Oh, yes, we went to Tullio's. They know me there.' Although Ruggiero was ahead on the track, Greg could sense the proud smile that went with the words. To be recognized by the *maître d'hôtel* at such a famous place meant a great deal to Ruggiero.

Something skimmed across the path in front of Tippi's head, then crashed into the scrub on the farther side. Ruggiero's mount flinched then reared. She came down wrong-footed on the stony surface. She lurched to the left, towards the outward incline.

Ruggiero gave a cry of terror as he was flung sideways in the saddle. The mare had been frightened by the arrow-like passage of the object. Now there was this strange off-balanced weight on her back. She tossed her head in protest, gathering herself to buck it off.

As for the reins, Ruggiero had lost them. They were trailing loose.

Greg closed the few yards between them. He managed to get close enough without thrusting the mare over. Leaning hard forward, he grabbed the reins. He shortened them, trying for the headstall. His own mount, Brigante, wondered what on earth he was up to. He jerked and tossed, half-deciding to join his stablemate in her escape manoeuvres.

A short command and a tug on his own reins made Brigante quiet at once. He stood as still as he could, pressed close to the mare, with thorn bushes stabbing at his flanks.

Greg leaned over. Tippi tried to avoid his grasp. '*Stand!*' he said. She gave a shivering twitch then, obedient, eased to nervous rest.

Ruggiero, now leaning forward and clutching at her mane, sat up. He was white with terror. As he had been swept to and fro by Tippi, he had glimpsed the fall waiting for him on the mountainside.

Greg handed him his reins. He took them uncertainly. The two horses fidgeted about for a moment or two, scared, anxious, uncomfortable among prickles and barbs, but trained to behave. The mare soon quietened completely, a gentle soul except when she was frightened. Brigante snorted and shook his head in indignation, then was still.

'My God! That was a near thing! She nearly had me off!' The tone was harsh, edged with panic.

'Quiet, Ruggiero, quiet. Don't startle her again.'

Ruggiero made a great effort, and found refuge in anger. 'Those damned sparrow-hawks! One of them nearly made me shoot my foot off, when I was out with my gun! Flew past like a rocket!' He was wiping his forehead with the silk kerchief from around his neck. His colour was coming back.

'That was a bird?' Greg asked, surprised.

'Of course, what else?' He tucked the kerchief into his shirt pocket, patted it a time or two, and conjured up a smile. 'Well, thank you, friend, you probably saved me from a broken neck!' He turned the mare. 'Time to go back. I need a drink after that.'

They made their way very soberly back to the villa, the horses picking their way among the pebbles and snickering once or twice as if to say, 'This is no easy matter, travelling on this tricky mountainside.'

Armeno stifled an exclamation of dismay when he saw thorns sticking into the sides of his beloved charges. '*Tesorina, piccina mia . . .*,' he crooned as he led the mare in to be groomed.

Luckily Rini was still out shopping in Rome, otherwise the

sight of her husband looking strained and with a sweaty kerchief peeking out of his pocket would have induced hysteria. Sara, the housemaid, was mopping the hall floor and scarcely looked up as she got out of their way.

'Is Cristina here?' Greg asked her.

'Yes, *signore*, in the kitchen.'

'Ask her to bring brandy to the drawing-room, and then black coffee.'

'Yes, *signore*.' No inquiry as to what had happened, although now that she looked at them, she must see that the *padrone* had had some sort of accident. She scuttled away.

Ruggiero flung himself into an armchair. Safely home, he seemed to be letting himself experience the fright he'd been thrown into again. 'God,' he groaned, 'that's the last time I'm getting on a horse! Good exercise? It's likely to give me a heart attack!'

'That isn't going to happen again, Ruggiero—'

'I won't give it a chance. I'm selling the horses. I never really liked riding – my father made me take it up but why the devil should I live my life to please a dead man?'

Cristina came in with the brandy, glasses, and soda. She set down the tray then waited to see if she was to pour. 'That's all for the moment, thank you, Cristina,' Greg said. 'Coffee now, and bring plenty of sugar.' He was warding off any chance of after-effects from the accident.

He gave his host a good three fingers of Martel. Ruggiero swallowed it in one gulp and asked for more.

'No, no, wait for the coffee.'

'What, are you a doctor now?' Ruggiero growled.

'All right, have another and knock yourself silly,' retorted Greg in irritation. 'You must know that alcohol isn't the best treatment for shock.'

'What makes *you* an expert?'

Regular training each year with the regiment to which as a Swiss citizen he was assigned, that was what. He didn't say it aloud; instead he took Ruggiero's glass and set it back on the tray. Ruggiero glared, but his resources were too weak to let him put up a fight. He relaxed back into the chair cushions, and was still half-reclining when Cristina came with the coffee.

'*Signore* is ill?' she murmured to Greg.

'A slight accident. Nothing to worry about.'

She nodded acceptance, poured coffee into two cups and silently withdrew.

By and by Ruggiero recovered. He said: 'Let's not make too much of this to the womenfolk, eh? Rini will throw a fit if she hears there was a mishap. Luckily she never talks to Armeno.'

Greg recalled how restlessly she'd fidgeted by the window on the morning he arrived while Ruggiero was out with Armeno. He nodded agreement. The thought of Armeno gave him a momentary pang. Poor lad, what would he do if his master really got rid of the horses?

While Ruggiero went upstairs to change, Greg poured himself a second cup of coffee, switched on the television, and watched car racing from Istanbul's Park Circuit.

Later they had a leisurely al fresco lunch on the shady side of the house. They were eating Cristina's *meringa di limone* when Rini and Liz came out to find them.

'I'll have something very smart to wear if we go out again this evening,' Rini announced in smiling triumph. 'Liz has introduced me to this wonderful woman, Ruggiero – she can make even a mourning dress look high fashion. Oh, what are you eating? It looks delicious!'

'Doesn't it? I could do with some of that!'

'I think there's plenty left,' Greg said, having watched Cristina carry indoors the remains of the meringue. 'Didn't you find a good place to eat, then?'

'Oh, yes, very *folkloristico*,' Rini said, but without enthusiasm.

'I'm sorry,' Liz apologized. 'Last time I was there, I think it must have been a different chef.'

'I forgive you, my dear, because you solved my problem about clothes.' She flourished a hand in the air and twirled as if showing off a dress. 'So I'll go and order you a large helping of dessert.'

'Too kind!' cooed Liz. It occurred to Greg that perhaps they'd had a little too much wine with their disappointing meal.

Accounts of their morning's shopping took up the last part of the meal, but at last Rini asked the inevitable question.

'Did you have an enjoyable ride, my darling?'

Ruggiero smiled, frowned, then half shook his head. 'That

path up by one of the bends needs attention. Hasn't been done for years. I think I'll give up riding until it's been re-surfaced.'

It was an expert lie. It satisfied Rini without arousing any anxiety. Greg said nothing.

He was eager to leave the villa. He was finding that he could only take Ruggiero in small doses. As soon as it was possible, he and Liz set out for Rome.

They were about halfway there when Greg's mobile rang. He looked, and saw the caller was his grandmother. He groaned, hesitated, and said, 'It's Grossmutti. Do you mind if I take it?'

She looked steadfastly through the windscreen at the road on which she was driving. 'Not at all,' she said calmly.

'So there you are at last,' exclaimed Nicoletta when he connected. 'You must have been locked up in the villa all day – I know the signal's bad there. Where are you now?'

'On the S7 heading for Rome.'

'Oh, good. Then you can meet me in about half an hour, I should think.'

'Meet you?' At his startled exclamation, Liz gave him a sharp glance. 'Where are *you*, then?'

'I'm at the Lanterna, in the Via Scrignolo – do you know it?'

'The Lanterna – that's a hotel?'

'Of course it's a hotel.' There followed minute instructions on how to find it.

'So I'll expect you in . . . let's say about an hour. That will be just in time for a nice evening drink.'

'Grossmutti, what on earth are you doing here?'

'I've got something to tell you about Dr Tamaldov.'

'Couldn't you tell me on the telephone?'

'No, no, it's too delicate for the telephone. I've done a little research, my boy.'

'Well . . . Thank you.'

'If you're on the *autostrada* it's time to stop talking on the phone. À *bientôt!*' And with that she rang off.

Greg drew in a slow breath. Liz inquired: 'She's here?' Her tone was icy. The ex-queen mother of Hirtenstein was no friend of hers.

'I'm afraid so.'

'What's she doing here?'

'Heaven knows. She says she wants to talk about Tamaldov. I'm commanded to go to her hotel to hear all about it.'

She was silent a moment then said, 'Well, of course, if she's got anything useful to tell, you have to go.'

'Yes.'

'Don't tell her I'm here.'

'No.'

Suddenly the comic side of the situation got the better of her. She began to giggle. 'I think a lot of women have mother-in-law trouble, What's the name for my problem?'

'Armageddon?' he suggested.

She gave her attention to the traffic. Sunday was moving towards evening, picnickers were heading home. Then she said, 'Where's this hotel? I'll drop you off there.'

'No, set me down and I'll get a taxi.'

'Nonsense.'

So when they got into the city he relayed his grandmother's directions and she found the place without much trouble. It was an old building, a mini-palazzo with tall balconied windows and an ornate but worn entrance. 'Bye for now,' she said as he got out. 'Try to come back in one piece.'

The receptionist caught the name almost before Greg had finished uttering it. 'Ah, yes, Madame Hirtenstein is in the bar, *signore,* just on your right beyond the arch.'

He made his way there. His grandmother, in pale-green silk and pearls, was sitting in a corner seat reading a magazine. She gave him her hand to kiss, as she often did when they were in public; she liked formality.

'My dear, why do you wear clothes that make you look like a tourist?' she scolded.

'I find them comfortable. When did you get here, Grossmutti?'

'I came by train. Very convenient, straight in at the Termini by three o'clock. I got a return ticket so as to go back to Geneva in the morning.'

'But why did you feel you had to come?'

She smiled to herself. 'Let's order our drinks. I must say, I feel in need of some refreshment.' She waved a hand, and as if by magic a waiter almost at once appeared at her side. 'I should like Cinzano with *limonata* and lots of ice, and you, my dear?'

'I'll have a *birra tedesca*, please.'

The waiter hurried off. Greg gave his grandmother a hard stare. 'Come on, now, Grossmutti – what is this about Tamaldov?'

She looked serious. 'I think he might have taken the icon, Gregory.'

'What?' True, he'd wondered a little about Tamaldov – but he seemed so ingenuous, so unworldly. 'What on earth makes you think that?'

She spoke with a hint of pride. 'Well, you know, I have my contacts in the world of diplomacy. Old friends, people who still keep in touch from the old days.' Former lovers, perhaps, her grandson thought as she paused. In the days when she'd been the young queen of Hirtenstein, she'd never been very faithful to her husband.

'And does the world of diplomacy know something about Dr Tamaldov?'

'I asked a friend to make inquiries for me, someone who's still got contacts in high places in Moscow. And the result is this, my boy. Yuri Tamaldov isn't a doctor at all. His name is not on the Russian medical register.'

'Oh. Well. You know, he's one of the alternative medical types—'

'There's more. Tamaldov was chased out of St Petersburg a couple of years ago for some sort of fraud, and has been lying low in Paris ever since.'

It gave him pause. 'That's rather . . . unexpected.'

'What I gather is this. He's by no means a . . . what's the expression? A big-time thief. And he's put out feelers once or twice about getting back to St Petersburg, so they say.'

'And from what we infer . . .?'

'I gave it some thought, Gregory. Don't you think he might have taken the icon so as to offer to return it to its rightful place and curry favour with the authorities?'

Their drinks came. The waiter poured Greg's lager into a chilled glass. He took a long swallow, thinking over what she had said.

'But it's a big coincidence, isn't it? That he should be on hand to get back a stolen icon.'

'Not entirely. See here, if Rini asked friends in St Petersburg to get her an icon, they might not have been exactly . . .

well . . . law-abiding. Tamaldov might know them if he was on that sort of wave-length, so he could have heard of it. And somehow wheedled his way into the villa, by getting friends in Paris to recommend him.'

'Ah. Yes, I suppose it's possible.'

'Well, have you found any other and more satisfactory suspect?'

'I'm afraid not.'

She gave a little smile of triumph and sipped her Cinzano. 'So what will you do now?'

'That's a good question. I've no idea.'

'You could confront Tamaldov.'

'I don't think so. There's no real evidence, Grossmutti.'

She was a little offended. Having to offer proof hadn't occurred to her. 'Well, ask if the Rome police have anything against him.'

He shook his head. 'We at the Villa Stefani are not on very good terms with the Rome police.' He gave her an outline of the investigation into Floria's death and the bad feeling that reigned there during the proceedings.

'So she died of poison? Poor Floria – what an ignominious end.' She sighed, then smiled wickedly. 'I wouldn't have put it past Rini to do something like that, but it's certain the poison was on the grapes?'

'Oh yes, Ernesto was in tears about it. It's certainly the insect spray that killed her.'

'When is the funeral? Perhaps I ought to stay on and attend it.'

'The body hasn't been released yet – red tape, you know. Nothing's been arranged about the funeral so far.'

'Well, good – I didn't really like her enough to make a return trip. In fact, if there was any poisoning to be done at the Villa Stefani, I always rather thought Floria would be the one doing it.'

'Grossmutti!'

'Oh, come on, you must know she hated Rini, and what with her little tisanes and potions, it might have been quite a temptation to drop something in Rini's coffee.'

'You make it all sound like something to do with the Borgias!'

'Ambition, jealousy, revenge – those were the incentives of the Borgias, and those emotions are still around, my lad!'

Greg was glancing at the clock on the wall. She said: 'You're in a hurry? I was going to offer you dinner.'

'Thank you, madame, but I have to be elsewhere soon.'

'Oh, I understand. You want to hurry off to your inamorata and pass on all the information about Tamaldov.'

He was stricken utterly speechless.

She laughed. 'You thought I didn't know she was here? I saw her drive up and let you out at the door. I was watching for you out of the window, Gregory.'

Talk about Armageddon! He braced himself for the battle. 'Liz and I have been together again since last year,' he said, waiting for an outburst of criticism.

To his astonishment she shrugged. 'I gathered as much. Your father murmured a word or two, about having met her for a few minutes and thinking she was quite amiable.' Her expression was troubled. 'Your dear father has never been good at concealing anything. I think he's been trying to win me over.'

He knew better than to ask if his father had succeeded. The ex-queen mother didn't give in so easily And for years now she had been determined to dislike Liz.

'So,' she said, 'I thought I'd just prove to you that I can be as good as she is at finding out things. Don't you think I've done well?'

'Very well indeed. Thank you, Grossmutti.'

'Oh, drink up and be off! I know you want to.'

He obeyed, and when they said goodbye kissed her on the cheek with something of the old affection.

He wondered what Liz would say when he told her they now had a helper in the search for the missing icon.

# TEN

Liz was inclined to be unconvinced when she heard what Greg had to say.

'Yuri Tamaldov is a crook?' she cried. 'Don't be silly.'

'That's what Grossmutti has been told.'

'Huh!' said Liz.

'*Mein Englein*, don't dismiss it just because it's my grand-mother's opinion. She's not always wrong.'

Liz had been of the opposite opinion. Nicoletta had been wrong in thinking Liz was a fortune-hunter. She'd also been wrong in making a public scene in a grand hotel last year so that Liz had walked out on Greg.

'She can't be right about Yuri. He's so nice,' she pleaded.

'But don't you see, if he's a con man, it's part of his act to be nice.' He was a little jealous. He'd seen how Liz warmed to the so-called doctor from the first. She'd been glad to see him again when they got to the villa this morning. 'It's the voice,' he said to himself. That velvety bass voice was almost irresistible.

They discussed it intermittently as they changed to go out to dinner. They were sitting in the patio of a nearby restaurant beginning on their first course when at last Liz gave in.

'So if your grandmother's right, what should we do?'

'She suggested we ask the local police about him. But you know how they behaved at the villa – they made it clear they didn't like Ruggiero or anybody who might be a relative or friend of his.'

'But if Yuri really did take the icon . . .?'

Greg chased a piece of melon around his plate before answering.

'If he took it, don't you think it's probably gone by now? He'd get in touch with the Russian authorities and they'd put it safely back where it belongs.'

'How exactly could he take it?' she wondered. 'He didn't know where it was kept.' She was still defending him.

'He had access to their suite, Liz. I saw him go up to Ruggiero's room to give him a session of calming therapy.'

'Oh, come on – that doesn't necessarily mean he went delving about in Rini's boudoir! I mean, I've been up there doing my dressmaking stint, so I know the layout. The boudoir opens out of the little anteroom – if Ruggiero was waiting in the bedroom for Yuri to come up and do the magic-hands thing, he'd think it very odd if he heard the door of the boudoir opening. Wouldn't he have bounced out and asked him what he was up to?'

'I agree it's not very likely.'

They were silent for a while. The main course was brought.

Liz said: 'If he's really a fraudster, we ought to tell the Ardiccis.'

'Yes.'

'It'll break Rini's heart.'

'If only there was some way to verify Grossmutti's information . . .'

'We could ask around.'

'Around where?'

'Where he works. The clinic. If he's really got a clinic, then he ought to have patients. We could ask them.'

'Liz, how do we know the names and addresses of his patients?'

'Ah.' That was a decided problem.

They addressed themselves to the *gnocchetti al ragu*. 'Do you have your laptop here with you?' Greg asked.

'Yes. Why? Oh, you think he might have a web page?'

'It's possible, but if it's in Russian it won't be much help.'

'Don't tell me you don't speak Russian! I thought you were fluent in everything, including Pekinese!'

'My love, sometimes I only know enough to handle performers or conductors or how to ask for directions to the theatre. I could actually sing you bits of *Boris Godunov* in Russian, but I'm not sure what they mean.'

She laughed. 'That's no help! Let's just hope we get an Italian page – I know you're OK with that.'

When they got back to their hotel room Liz got the laptop out of the wardrobe. There was a slight problem finding the website: '*clinica*' was too general a term, '*clinica di terapia allementicala*' was no better, but in the end 'Clinica Tamaldov' brought them a bright screen with doves in flight over a column of text – luckily, in Italian.

'Find serenity in the clinic where Dr Tamaldov offers relaxation and release from stress . . . Healing without chemical intervention . . .' Greg translated. 'A lot about contact of the mind, peaceful journeying to . . . what? Oh, a new understanding of one's inner being.'

'Never mind all that,' scolded Liz. 'Is there anything about patients he's treated?'

'No, but really, I don't think he'd give details like that. But there's his telephone number, so let's ring and see what we get.'

The telephone rang six times before Tamaldov's rich voice spoke in its attractively accented Italian. 'This is Dr Yuri Tamaldov at the Clinic of Tranquil Inspiration at 41 Via Bardolo in Testaccio. Appointments can be arranged by email or by telephone. The clinic is open from six till ten on the evenings of Tuesday and Thursday and also on Saturday by prior arrangement. Please leave your message after the tone.'

Greg noted down the main points then gave the gist to Liz. 'Hmm . . . We don't want to hang about until Tuesday, do we?'

'It would be better if we could see him tomorrow.'

'Yes.' She paused in thought. 'What are we going to say to him?'

'Have you got Rini Ardicci's icon?' Greg suggested.

'Hardly.' She was frowning. 'We know where he hangs out. What good has that done?'

'I don't know. Do you think he lives there? The limitation of the consultation hours seems to imply something like that.'

'You mean he does the treatment in one of his rooms . . . let's say in his living-room, so he has to clear it up in advance?'

'It's possible. Testaccio's a working-class area – accommodation around there isn't very grand.'

They talked it over for a while but came to no helpful solution. It seemed a good idea to go to bed and forget about it all.

Next morning Liz came back from her early-morning run in a state of exhilaration.

'I've solved the problem of what to do about Dr Tamaldov!' she announced with a delighted throwing out of her arms.

'You have?' Greg, as usual, was still coming to terms with the start of the day, and only halfway through his first cup of coffee. He tried to engage his long face into an expression of interest.

'Sleepy-head,' she scolded, dropping a kiss on his hair as she headed for the bathroom.

When she emerged in her bathrobe, he had wakened up enough to pay attention. She towelled her hair vigorously for a moment then emerged from the folds to explain. 'We must say we're tremendously interested in his clinic and want to pay a visit, and when we get there we must snoop around and get a look at things.'

He raised his eyebrows. 'That's your plan? How exactly can we snoop when he's showing us around his clinic?'

'Well, one of us must get away – ask to use the bathroom, for instance – and look in a few cupboards and things.'

'I see. And what did we say yesterday about Tamaldov snooping in Rini's bedroom? That it's not an easy thing to do when there's someone else around, I seem to remember.'

'Oh, there's two of us. One of us distracts Yuri's attention while the other snoops.'

He grinned.

'It's perfectly feasible!'

'No it isn't. All this bouncing around on early morning pavements – it's jumbled your brains.'

She came to poke him in the chest with a forefinger. 'Well, *you* think of something better.'

'Let me have another cup of coffee and I'll see what I can come up with.'

She went to return the towel and bathrobe to the bathroom. When she came back into the bedroom she began to survey the items in the wardrobe. They were few: she had already worn almost all of them. 'I ought to buy a couple of things . . .'

'Shopping.' He considered for a moment. 'Now that's an idea.'

'What is?'

'How would you like to go shopping for books about relaxation therapy?'

'I'd rather shop for something else to wear.'

'But you don't say that to your friend Yuri. You tell him you're tremendously interested in his clinic—'

'That was *my* idea!'

'Yes, but you say you'd like to study the whole concept, and would he help you choose some helpful books.'

Now she turned to give him her full attention. 'And then what?'

'He meets you in the Piazza della Repubblica and you keep him there for an hour or two looking at books while I do the snooping.'

'That sounds sort of doable. Except for one thing. How are you going to get into the clinic if he's not there to let you in?'

'There'll be someone there – to take messages and so forth.'

'I don't think so, chum. If I remember that recorded message correctly, he said the clinic's only open in the evenings Tuesdays and Thursdays. I'd take a bet he hadn't got a receptionist or anything like that. He can't afford one.'

'Then I'll pick the lock.'

She grinned. 'You're experienced in lock picking?'

'Not exactly. But it's probably an old building, so there isn't likely to be a difficult lock. I think I could manage it with one of the appliances on my trusty Swiss army knife.'

'You don't own a Swiss army knife.'

'I can buy one.'

'Greg, be sensible!'

'All right, let me have my shower and I'll see if I can come up with something better.'

When at last they went down to the little breakfast room he had something like a plan to offer. 'We go there together and we ask him to go out with us to choose some books. I'll come out of the apartment last and I'll leave the door slightly ajar. Then I'll think of some reason to leave you with him and go back to the apartment.'

'As simple as that, eh?'

'Well, if it's a spring lock, there's usually a little knob that prevents the lock from engaging.'

'And how about if it's an ancient Roman thing and he has to use a key to lock up?'

He sighed. 'Then I'll have to hypnotize him and leave him standing in a trance while I search his home.'

She went off into a fit of giggles. He shook his head at her but couldn't come up with anything useful. When she recovered, she said: 'Look, let's just play it by ear. We'll go to see him and get an idea of the set-up. I mean, for all we know he's got a live-in girlfriend who'd let you in if you went back alone. Or he may leave his key under his doormat when he goes out. Or there's a kindly neighbour who has his spare key and would let us in.'

'Perhaps it's a bad idea in the first place, this snooping idea.'

But that made her stubborn. 'I'm not going to think Yuri's a crook just because your grandma says so, Greg. She's put him under a cloud and if she's right we have to do something about it. And the only way to be sure whether he's a robber is to take a look at his hideout.'

'Well . . .'

She got her mobile out of her handbag, glanced at the notes
Greg had written from the website, and pressed buttons. Almost
immediately Tamaldov's voice answered speaking Russian.

'Tanya, *s'dobrym utrom*! *Gde*—'

'Yuri,' Liz interrupted, 'it's me, Liz Blair – you remember?'

He was surprised but pleased. 'How could I forget? Miss
Blair, good morning, you are well, I hope?'

'Very well, thank you. I've been thinking about you quite
a lot.'

'Indeed? Nothing could be more pleasing! What can I do
for you?'

'I was going to ask if I could come to see you,' she said
in a hesitant voice. 'You know, I'm in the fashion business,
and it's such a rat race . . .'

'Oh, that I can believe. And you – always tense, always
striving to be best—'

'Exactly! You understand so well! Yuri, could I come and
just have you explain it all to me – because you know, I *am*
very busy and if your method means taking up hours every
day with meditation or anything—'

'Oh, no, no, my method is very simple, Miss Blair—'

'Please call me Liz – I always think of you as Yuri, you
see.'

'You must let me tell you how it is easy to alter your way
of life so that life force flows easily through your heart and
soul. Come, please come and let me explain.'

'I was going to ask if I might come today, but you're
expecting someone – a patient, perhaps . . .'

'No, not at all. I thought you were Tanya ringing to say
"Alter the time" but no, it was you so I have to go out as
arranged – I visit some patients in their home but that is only
short visit. I make suggestion. Why not come now, Liz? My
lady who cleans, she will let you in, and in an hour or so, I
will be back and we can have tea and long talk. Is this a good
idea?'

'Wonderful!' she cried. 'I can be there in about fifteen
minutes – I looked you up on the internet so I know where
to find you.'

'Good, good. I will be gone but you will find brochures to
look at, magazines to read – also I will leave music playing

in my consulting room, music is good for relaxation. So until later, then, Liz?'

'Until later.'

Greg had been listening to her end of the conversation in a mixture of amusement and mystification. As she disconnected he said, 'What? What happened?'

'You won't need to use your hypnotic powers,' she said, gurgling with laughter. 'He's going out but his cleaning lady will let me in to wait for him. I mean, let us in.'

'Oh, *Dieu merci*! That's a lot easier.' But then he held up a hand. 'Listen, Liz – let's think this through a bit further. What if, just *what if* we actually find the icon hidden in Yuri Tamaldov's apartment?'

'Oh!' She was taken aback. 'I never thought of that.'

'Neither did I until now.'

'If we find the icon, we put it in my handbag and hurry away.'

'But Liz – then what?'

'We give it to Rini Ardicci.'

'But Rini Ardicci may have no right to own it. It probably belongs in a glass case in a museum.'

'But that's not our concern, Greg. We want to get it back to her so that no scandal can damage Ruggiero's chances of that job in New York.'

'But I don't care about Ruggiero's chances of the job in New York.'

'Well, neither do I, to tell the truth . . .' She made an impatient gesture. 'No more buts. Let's see if he has the icon and then we can decide what to do.'

They took a taxi to Via Bardolo. The address proved to be a tenement building of considerable age. A small wooden plaque announced that Clinic Tamaldov was on the first floor. They went up a stone staircase to find the door ajar, and a plump lady in an apron waiting for them outside. 'Please go in,' she said in Italian. 'Dottore Tamaldov will be back in an hour or so.'

In they went. The little vestibule had a side table bearing information leaflets, magazines, and a statuette of a man in flowing robes. There was a chair to make it serve as a waiting-room. Beyond that was the consulting room, exquisitely neat, furnished with a couple of wickerwork chairs and a chaise longue laden with cushions in soft colours. There were tall windows, but the light was masked by louvred shutters. The sound system was softly playing flute music.

'Mozart,' said Greg. 'Good choice.'

'Music to search by. Come on, let's get to work.'

There was nothing of any interest in the consulting room. The room next door was a bedroom, with bookshelves, a chest of drawers, a small desk bearing a closed laptop, and a curtained alcove that contained clothes. Beyond that was a tiny passageway with two doors, one the entry to the kitchen and on the opposite side the shower room.

'My word, he's hard up,' murmured Liz.

'He's a Russian exile in Rome,' Greg remarked. 'His patients are probably all fellow exiles. Not many of those, I imagine.'

'Poor chap. Honestly, Greg, I'm beginning to feel guilty about this.'

'But don't forget, sweetheart, he's not really a doctor. This is all false pretences.'

'Ye–es.' She sighed. 'I'll take the bathroom and kitchen, because the titles on the books seem to be all in Russian or Italian.' Off she went.

Greg addressed himself first to the laptop. Never adept with computers, he was immediately baffled by the fact that the screen showed Russian. He tried a few of the icons showing on the desktop, one of which was the traditional staff of Mercury, the symbol of medicine. He clicked, but got a file in Cyrillic letters. With a sigh he closed the laptop, and tried the desk drawers.

The top drawer held stationery and an alphabetical address book. The alphabet, alas, was once again Russian, but he tried each cipher and found addresses in French and Italian as well as Cyrillic. Mostly women, and none seemed helpful. He tried the next drawer.

This held cardboard folders. One was labelled with a word that he was able to translate: *Den'gi* – Money. A swift glance showed bank statements and receipts. The next was 'Letters'. This he opened.

The contents were mostly greeting cards and the kind of little note on fancy paper that women send on special occasions. Easter messages, birthday messages, and at last a manila envelope with the word '*Kontora*' – 'Official'. He opened the envelope to slide out the papers.

They were letters typed or computer-produced. There were logos at the top of some of the sheets, very authoritative. The addresses of the senders were in St Petersburg, Moscow and Volgograd. He was unable to make much of the text. He recognized the words for 'not satisfactory' and for 'government', and felt that '*cartina*' might mean 'picture'. But he couldn't see the word 'icon', which he presumed would be more or less the same in Russian.

He put everything back in its place then tried the last remaining drawer. He half hoped he would find the icon there. But it contained discs for the music centre.

He turned his attention to the chest of drawers. This held Tamaldov's T-shirts and underwear. He felt in among the clothes but the icon wasn't hidden among them. The curtained wardrobe showed three of the loose tunic-like tops that were Tamaldov's usual wear, cotton-poplin slacks, a city suit, a rather worn evening jacket and trousers, four tailored shirts, a pair of corduroys, a mackintosh, and an umbrella leaning in the corner. On the floor were various kinds of footwear: open sandals, a pair of rain-boots and ordinary city shoes.

The room held almost nothing more except the bookshelves. He cast his eye over them thinking perhaps an icon in a slim box could be hidden among them but they were mostly paperbacks – Gurdjieff, Kalil Gibran, Tolstoy, Santayana, other names he didn't recognize but guessed to be writers on spiritual subjects.

He tried opening the shutters a little to see if there were any alcoves or niches that he'd missed, but there was nowhere to hide anything unless it was under the floorboards – and they seemed intact.

Liz came into the room. 'I've looked in his cooking pots, of which he has two, and in his cornflakes packet and among the clean towels in the bathroom, and everywhere else I could think of, but he doesn't have the icon.'

They gazed at each other in something like relief. No icon. They didn't have to decide what to do with it.

'I found some official correspondence,' Greg said. 'People in authority have been in touch with him, but as it's all in Russian I could make nothing of it. Except that in one letter they didn't seem to be very pleased with him. And I gather he's been engaged in something or other which might have been to do with a picture.'

'A picture. As in portrait, perhaps – a portrait of Saint Olga?'

'She was never mentioned. I don't know, Lizzie. Have we proved anything?'

'That he's in contact with somebody official?'

'But that might just be about being allowed home to St Petersburg. And the "picture" might be for his passport.'

They went into the consulting room. Liz sat down in one of the wicker chairs. 'You'd better take off,' she said. 'I'm supposed to be here on my own, longing to know his views on changing my lifestyle.'

He stooped for a goodbye kiss. 'If he takes you to lunch, try to pay the bill,' he suggested. 'I don't think he's got more than about a hundred euros to his name.' He was surprised to find himself feeling almost charitable towards the man.

Liz sat thinking she ought to give up the idea of the meeting with Yuri. Now that she'd seen how he lived, it seemed wrong to take advantage of him. Yet Greg's grandmother had taken the trouble to ask for information and the result was to label Yuri a con man.

The flute music came to an end and in its place was a tune played on some sort of stringed instrument – a balalaika, perhaps? No, it was more harp-like. Soft, dreamy, very relaxing. She found herself on the point of nodding off, and was brought back to attention by the sound of footsteps on the stone staircase.

In came Yuri Tamaldov, in a loose smock, chinos and open-toed sandals. 'Miss Blair! Have I kept you waiting? I hope no. Please, let me make you tea – and look, I bought some *biscotti*.'

'That would be lovely,' she agreed. She followed him to the kitchenette and helped by undoing the biscuit packet. 'You've been with one of your clients?'

'Ah yes. Very sad case – a young widow, you see. After only a short marriage, she does not know how to live on without him. Ah well . . . And you, Miss Blair, how are you?'

'You must call me Liz.'

'Liz . . . Strange name, very short. And you make designs for dresses, and find in this there is pressure, too much, yes?'

He poured hot water into two glasses and to her surprise dropped a tea bag in each. She'd expected . . . well, not exactly a samovar, but something more Russian. However, she found it quite Russian enough when she learned she was expected to drink it without milk.

They settled themselves in the consulting room. 'You lead a very simple life,' she said, glancing about. 'Do you get homesick for Russia?'

He sighed. 'Too long away from home. Paris, yes, I love Paris, and Rome I am settled a little by now, yet always I think of St Petersburg.'

'Rome's too hot in this weather,' she complained. 'You long for the snow, do you?'

'Ah . . . You know, I find it very strange to live in a land where even in winter it never snows.'

'Perhaps one day you'll go back?'

He gave a shrug, looking downcast. 'If I can, if I can. I have been a little . . . what is it in English . . .? In French it is "*méchant*".'

'Naughty. Oh, you're in disgrace with someone?'

'But that will become all right, if all goes well.'

'Is it about your work? I thought the regime was more tolerant towards religion these days.'

'No, no, I am not religious – nothing to do with that. But it is easy to be in trouble in my homeland, you know, and not so easy to make it better.' He clapped his hands together. 'Now let us talk about your work, your career. Tell me what is right and what is wrong with it.'

She spent ten minutes inventing problems to lay before him. They finished the tea, she suggested they might go out to buy some books that would help her find her way to a more holistic view, and out they went.

Greg, meanwhile, had had a call from Amabelle in the little office in Geneva. 'I had a man ring me from Rome,' she reported. 'He said he had something you might like to take a look at. I said I'd pass the message on at once.'

'Thank you, Amabelle. Anything to do with ordinary business?'

'Pierre Demarre says he can't stay in the hotel I booked for him because it's full of noisy rugby supporters even though it's handy for the concert hall.' They spent some time dealing

with minor problems to do with concerts or recitals, then he
set off to the pawnshop to look at its offering.

His hopes were dashed as soon as it was produced. It was
a *rivière* of graduated diamonds, rather fine but not at all what
he'd been hoping for. After an unfriendly conversation with
the pawnbroker he was out on the street when once again his
mobile rang.

It was Rini, almost in tears. 'Gregory. I'm so sorry to
trouble you with it but I have no one else to turn to. Gregory,
please come and talk to Ruggiero. I can't make him listen
to me.'

'What's happened, Rini?'

'He's sold the horses! The buyers are coming with a van
to take them away and when he told Armeno—' She broke
off, sobs overtaking her. 'Gregory – Armeno *attacked* him!'

# ELEVEN

The taxi driver had read about the *imbroglio Ardicci* and
wanted to get some insider gossip from Greg. But Greg
acted the part of the ignorant foreigner so in the end
the conversation died.

When they reached the villa, Ernesto opened the gates. He
gave a little bow in greeting but nothing was said. Rini was
looking out for him and ran to welcome him.

'Oh, my dear and good friend! Please come in and talk to
Ruggiero. He wants to fire Armeno at once. And I know you
and Liz said . . . You said it would look bad . . . But he says
this is different, the boy tried to *hit* him!'

Ruggiero was in the drawing-room and had clearly taken
more than one drink.

'Hello, so you've come to tell me how to manage my affairs,
have you? Lemme tell you, my mind's made up! Nobody
raises his hand to me, nobody!'

'I'm very sorry about this, Ruggiero. Did you get hurt?'

'Hurt? Me? Wha'dyou take me for? Can't d'fend myself
against a stupid kid? No, I walloped him a good one and he's
off in the stable now, blubbering like a five-year-old.'

'Dearest, you must realize that it's Armeno who got injured—'

'Damn right he did! And so will anybody else who tries it on with me, and I don't care if't *does* get in the papers.' He took a swig at the glass he was nursing. Greg could see it was nearly empty and the contents looked like brandy. 'Dunno why Rini had to call you in, Gregory – whaddayou care if I hit one of my servants, eh? Deserves it, doesn't he?'

'That may be so, Ruggiero,' Gregory said, drawing up a chair close to his. He leaned forward. 'But you know, it's not going to look good.'

'Don't care! Don't care! I'm inna right!'

'To some extent—'

'To what extent? They're my horses. Aren't they? And one of 'em nearly threw me! I've got a right to sell 'em if I want to, haven't I? And this little half-witted village boy tells me I mustn't do it! Must not! What sorta language is that to use with the master of the house, eh?'

'Armeno's a child, really,' Greg suggested. 'He's – how old? – perhaps sixteen? But he's got the mind of an eight- or nine-year-old. Go easy on him, Ruggiero.'

'I'll fire him if I want to. Anyway . . . what's he gonna do around here once the horses are gone? Tell me that.'

'It's a big place. It needs someone to keep it looking good.'

'Now don't tell me he can do the gard'ning once Ernesto's gone, 'cos he can't. Sweep and pick up the litter, tha's all he could do.' He drank off the remains of the brandy. 'Fine bunch of servants, eh? One poisons my cousin-in-law and now Armeno wants to punch me in the face. No, no, I can't allow any of that.'

Greg was silent.

Ruggiero was trying to struggle to his feet but found it too much trouble. He held out his glass to his wife.

'Ruggiero, dear heart, don't you think you've had enough?' she ventured.

'Never you mind. I can hold my liquor. Have one with me, Gregory.'

'Not just now, thank you. And if the press are going to descend on you, don't you think you'd better try to sober up a bit?'

'Press are gonna descend? Who says so?'

'Well, they will, won't they? Once they hear you've hit one of your servants.'

'How're they gonna know? Eh?'

'Armeno will tell them when he goes home. Which means any minute if you really intend to throw him out now. It's only just lunchtime. It will be on the evening news.'

Ruggiero relaxed back into his chair. He frowned at Greg. 'You said all this sorta thing when I wanted to fire Ernesto.'

'Yes, and it's still true. It's getting to be quite a list, isn't it? First you have a suspicious death in the house, then you turn out two of your staff without notice, now you hit the stableboy.'

'You – you make it sound as if it's all *my* fault! I haven't done anything wrong!'

'Hitting a sixteen-year-old boy isn't exactly right, though, is it?'

'But he was gonna hit *me*! He came at me.'

'He was angry?'

'He was – I dunno – he gave a sort of cry and threw himself at me.'

'And hit you?'

'N–no – I didn't let him – I got my punch in first.' He grinned in a sort of fuddled pride. 'That let him know who was the boss! Started to cry! Great big baby!'

'There you are. You've said it yourself. You're a big, fully-grown man and he's a kid in his teens and not right in the head. How do you think it will be treated by newsmen who dislike you?'

'Argh!' It was a roar of frustration.

At that moment a rumble of tyres could be heard from the side of the house. 'That's the horse van,' groaned Ruggiero. He tried to get to his feet. 'I better go an' supervise or he'll attack the driver too.'

'No, no!' Rini cried, clutching his arm. He swayed under the impetus.

'I'll go,' said Greg, and immediately went out.

The van was slowly easing itself into the stable yard. Greg hurried past it into the stable. Armeno was standing with his arm looped over the neck of the mare. 'It's all right, Tippi,' he was whispering. 'I won't let them take you.'

The van stopped, the driver and his mate jumped out, and

the business of getting down the ramp was begun. Armeno buried his face in Tippi's mane and began to sob. Attack was clearly the last thing on his mind.

Greg went out. The older of the two men was giving directions. Greg addressed him. 'Listen, the stable lad's very upset about all this. Where are the horses going? Anywhere near?'

'No, the firm's in Lombardy, and we only act as an agency. Buy the horses, have the vet run an eye over them, and sell them on.' It was said with a shrug, but there was some sympathy in his tone. 'We've got several inquiries for a good lady's mount so the mare probably won't stay with us long.'

'Would you tell the boy they're going together to a good home?' Greg asked, producing a high value euro note.

'Ah, well . . . Why not?' The money vanished into a pocket. The ramp was fixed. The driver sauntered into the stable, his mate behind him. 'Now then, young fellow, it's time to say goodbye to your friends. But don't worry, they're going to stay with a nice lady who'll take good care of them.'

'A lady?'

'Yes, she's got a daughter called Rosa who'll really like the mare.'

'Her name's Tippi.'

'Right, then let's get her into her special limousine.' But Armeno couldn't manage the slightest smile at this joke. He stood aside white-faced while the horses were led out of the stable one by one. Tippi jibbed at the ramp but went up it after some coaxing. Brigante walked up as if he did it every day. They were closed in, the men got into the cab, the engine started, and the transporter lumbered off.

'No!' shouted Armeno, running out of the stable and after the van. For a moment it looked as if he might catch up so as to grab the chains hanging at the back, but the driver put on a spurt once they were out of the stable entry. Armeno stumbled and fell on the paving stones.

He lay there, face hidden in his folded arms, weeping. Greg went and eased him upright. Tears streamed down the boy's cheeks, where on the left side an intense red mark showed up. He mopped the tears with the backs of his hands.

'Come on, now, let's go back and tidy up their tack,' said Greg.

Armeno obeyed. There was really little to do because the

boy kept the place in perfect order. 'Have you got anything to drink? I'd like something to quench my thirst,' Greg suggested.

Armeno produced some bottles of supermarket cola from a cupboard – lukewarm, but the drink was only an excuse to talk. Armeno had recovered quite well from his crying fit, but the red mark was glowing more vividly on his cheekbone.

'Does your face hurt?' Greg asked.

The boy touched the mark with his fingertips, almost as if he'd forgotten its existence.

'It's all right,' he muttered.

'Now that the horses are gone, what happens?' Greg asked.

'I don't care. He told me I had to go too. I don't care, I don't care!'

'What will you do?'

Armeno shrugged. 'My mama will find me some other work,' he mumbled. 'I won't tell her what he called me when I told him he mustn't sell the horses.'

'What did he call you?'

Armeno blushed. 'It's a bad word. I'm not allowed to say it.'

'So did you hit him?'

'Me?' There was utter astonishment in his voice.

'You didn't hit him?'

The boy ran his hands through his untidy hair. '*Hit* the *signore*? No, of course not.'

'But he hit you?'

'Yes.' He touched the side of his face again. 'It hurt.'

'But why did he hit you? What happened?'

Armeno screwed his eyes shut in an attempt at memory. 'He said the van was coming, and I said I wouldn't let the horses go, and he said . . . well, what he said, and I . . . I think I *did* try to grab him . . . the front of his shirt maybe . . . It all happened so fast.'

Greg sighed inwardly. A few seconds of emotion on either side, and now the boy was being turned away.

'It was all a mistake, Armeno. Perhaps if I explain to Signor Ardicci, he'll change his mind about firing you.'

'No,' the boy said with unexpected decision. 'I don't want to stay. What would I do? I don't do the garden. Ernesto does the garden. And Ernesto's got to leave, he told me, so I don't want to stay. Not without Ernesto.'

'You might get on well with Ernesto's replacement.'

'No. Ernesto was helping me. He taught me to read writing.'

'To read what?'

'Writing.' He made signs in the air to show cursive script. 'I could read printed letters before. He was teaching me to write the joined-up things. That's hard. But you need it for gardening, for writing labels on things.' He hugged his cola bottle and traced on its label with his fingers, making simple curling motions that were a long way from actual letters.

His employment chances seemed slim. Perhaps the villagers would rally round for him. Greg debated giving him money but decided that it would be better if Ardicci sent some to his mother.

He helped the boy gather his few personal belongings. They put them into a carrier bag. They shook hands. 'Goodbye, *signore*,' said Armeno. 'I'll tell Mama you were nice to me.'

'Thank you,' Greg said.

He watched him walk away. He put the empty bottles in the trash bin then he sat down on a hay bale to call Liz.

When she replied, it was clear she was in a shopping mall. 'Hi! I've just bought a really sweet dress, and what's more it was a bargain in the sales.'

'Glad to hear it. Liz, I'm at the villa.' He explained what had happened. She exclaimed in dismay at the news. 'Yes, never a dull moment,' he said. 'You'll have to come and fetch me. I don't know what happened about lunch at the house, Ruggiero was so drunk he couldn't have held a knife and fork. I expect Rini will offer me something but I've had enough of the Ardiccis for today.'

'Okey-doke. I'll be as quick as I can but I've got to go back to the hotel for the car.'

'I'll come down to the gate – don't drive in.'

He had no intention of going back into the house to wait. He wanted as little contact with the Ardiccis as good manners would allow. He went round by the side entry and walked on through the garden, where the herbs filled the afternoon air with scent. He made his way to the gate that led to the upland path.

The sun was warm but there was shade under the birch

trees. He picked his way without much attention until it dawned on him he was following the route to the spot where the horses had shied yesterday. He walked on, hearing only a distant murmur of traffic on the main road, the rustle of leaves, the sound of a tiny brook. After some time he saw the bruised and damaged bushes where Tippi had nearly gone over.

The angle of light was just so poised that he saw what he thought was a line of flight across the tops of the thorn bushes. He walked up the path until he came opposite. He stood staring at it.

A bird had flown across and crashed into the bushes?

He picked his way down the slope, taking care for the soil was dry and loose. He looked for feathers, but found none. That was odd. The tops of the bushes were damaged, so something had thrashed across them. Surely a bird's wings would have left a feather or two.

There was a stone lying just beyond the last sign of injury to the foliage. A slim, flat, black stone, about the size of the palm of his hand. It was the kind of stone that children like to skim across the surface of a lake.

He stood staring at it.

He tried to reconstruct the incident. He hadn't actually seen the thing that flew past. When Ruggiero said it was a bird, he accepted it. Something very fast in flight. A swallow, perhaps? But swallows generally kept to open skies, and when they flew low it was over water, to catch insects.

Could some naughty or careless child have thrown this stone? The estate's upland territory was open to anyone who cared to make the trek up the slopes. The Alban Hills attracted many visitors – antiquarians wanting to look at the old Roman fortresses, hikers, tourists. Any of those, or their children, might have skimmed the stone across the maquis just because it was the right shape to travel swiftly.

Or could it have been done on purpose?

Ruggiero had nearly been taken down the slope by Tippi's curvetting. He could have broken his neck.

It had become clear to Greg that the man was not popular. He'd lost his seat in the last election. His wife was something of a handicap. He was angling for the post of ambassador to the United Nations in New York. Could some political rival for the post have sent someone to cause an accident – to kill or at least incapacitate Ruggiero?

He cast his mind back to the things that had been said about Ruggiero by the villagers. They had spoken about him with derision – but then he was rich, and so they were likely to be envious and unkind. Would any of those have come up here with the intention of harming Ruggiero?

He put the stone in the pocket of his linen jacket. As he walked back towards the villa he tried to think what, if anything, he should do. Warn Ruggiero? But of what? A stone? Could he prove that the stone had actually been thrown and not just reached the spot by the gentle downhill force of gravity? As to the damage to the bushes . . . He couldn't understand it.

He decided not to mention it. If Ruggiero had enemies, he must fend for himself.

When he got back to the Villa Stefani, the front door was open. Duty bound to say goodbye, he walked in. Rini came at once to the drawing-room door. 'Ah, Gregory my dear, I've absolutely neglected you! Come in. I'll ask Cristina to bring you something on a tray – we skipped lunch, Ruggiero didn't feel up to it.'

'No, no thank you, Rini,' he said. 'Liz will be here to fetch me in a moment. We'll get a bite to eat on our way back to Rome.'

'I'm so sorry – I was just so worried about Ruggiero – he's lying down now.'

*No doubt*, thought Greg. *And developing a bad hangover.*

'The horses are safely gone,' he reported. 'I had a chat with Armeno. He says he didn't hit your husband—'

'But—'

'I'm inclined to believe him,' he went on, ignoring the interruption. 'He's not the aggressive type. He's gone home to his mother, and I think you can take it that he's not going to cause trouble of any kind. He just isn't the type to do that, and I daresay his mother wouldn't want to put him in difficulties.'

'Oh. Well, that's good. Ruggiero will be so relieved.'

'Can you persuade him to send some money to Armeno's mother by way of compensation?'

'Compensation for what?' she cried in indignation. 'For attacking my husband?'

'Compensation for instant dismissal, Rini. And for losing something very dear to him.'

'Dear to him?'

'His horses. He deserves at least a few hundred euros for what he's lost.'

'We–ell . . . I don't know if it will be agreeable to Ruggiero . . . I'll mention it.'

'Thank you. And now if you don't mind, I'll hurry away. I said I'd meet Liz down by the gates.'

'I understand. Give her my love and thank you a million times for coming to our help again, Gregory dear.' She gave him a kiss on the cheek as farewell.

When Liz drove up, she found him waiting for her outside the grounds, leaning on one of the ornate marble gateposts with his arms folded. He got in. She hugged him briefly then set off down the road.

'How are things back at the ranch?' she inquired.

'Ruggiero's in bed getting over a drinking bout, Rini is fussing over him, I suggested Armeno should get a little bit of cash, and I'm glad to be leaving.'

'I never met Armeno but I'm sorry he's got the sack. That's three servants they've lost in as many days, isn't it?' She shook her head. '"To lose one servant, Mr Worthing, may be regarded as a misfortune; to lose three looks like carelessness".'

He managed a grin. 'That's good. Who said that?'

'Oscar Wilde, more or less. Now I suppose the only one who'll be staying is that timid housemaid. Poor Rini.'

He said nothing to that. After a moment he asked, 'Did you buy any books?'

She pointed at the glove compartment. He opened it to find a copy of *Questions and Answers* by Krishna Murti. Flipping it open, he read: 'Truth is a pathless land, and you cannot approach it by any path whatsoever . . .'

'A little light reading,' he remarked.

'Yes, isn't it? It didn't cost much. And Yuri says it will teach me to look beneath the deceptive surface of success.' She gave a little shrug. 'He talks a lot, but you know . . . it sounds sort of rehearsed. As if it's something . . . not exactly phoney but . . . Oh, I don't know! But of course he's got that gorgeous voice.'

'So you're not going to adopt him as your guru?'

'No, but he's important, isn't he. If he's a fake maharishi, we ought to tell Rini.'

'Rini's got problems enough at the moment.'

She heard the distaste in his voice, but couldn't let it go. 'Greg, if it wasn't important, why did we get ourselves into his flat this morning? Your grandmother told you he wasn't a doctor, that he was out of favour with the government back home. It's true he didn't seem to have the icon, but did he take it and send it back to Russia?'

He made himself turn his mind to the events of the morning, for a time totally eclipsed by the events of the afternoon.

'No,' he said slowly. 'I think if he's got the icon he'd insist on getting his passport back and then take it home person-ally. It's a big bargaining point – he wouldn't throw it away, I'm sure.'

'So you don't think he's got it?'

'Probably not.'

'So what's he up to?'

After a long pause he said: 'I think we'll just have to ask him.'

# TWELVE

The confrontation took place next day. Liz rang Tamaldov to make the appointment but in fact it was Greg who went to the clinic. He said to her: 'You like him too much. If things turn out tough, you won't want to turn him in to the cops.'

'We–ell . . .' She couldn't deny it.

Tamaldov opened the door to him, at first with a welcoming smile and then with disappointment.

'Miss Blair is not with you.'

'Not at the moment.'

'Come in, come in, we will wait for her, then, and have cool drink, no?'

He led the way to his consulting room. He waved at a chair. 'Sit down, I will fetch drinks. You prefer juice or mineral water?'

Greg chose mineral water. Tamaldov came back with bottles
and glasses. 'Miss Blair was pleased with her book?'

'Ah . . . Well, so far she hasn't had much time to look into
it.' The drinks were poured, they sipped. Greg took a breath.

'Mr Tamaldov, my grandmother – you met her, I think,
while she was doing the new décor?'

'Madame von Hirtenstein – yes – a very special lady.'

'She has made some inquiries. And she informs me, Mr
Tamaldov, that you have no medical qualifications.'

Tamaldov started, so that the contents of his glass spilled
over the lip. He gave an exclamation in Russian.

'She says that you've been in trouble with the Russian
police.'

'*Kakh govorityeh li vi?*' He sprang up. He seemed to reach
for English words out of the air. 'How dare you say that!'

'I think it's true. My grandmother contacted people who
were able to ask questions in the right quarters. And they told
her you are not a doctor at all.'

They stared at each other. Tamaldov slowly sat down again.
He set his glass on the floor then rubbed his palms together.

'I thought she liked me,' he said, blowing out a breath.

'Oh, I expect she did. But she's lived a long time and is
perhaps somewhat cynical.'

'Well,' said Tamaldov, with a slight grimace of exasperation, 'she is wrong. I *am* a doctor.'

'No.'

'Yes. A doctor of philosophy. I obtained my degree at the
University of St Petersburg. If she sends someone to ask, the
registrar will tell her it is so.'

Greg was momentarily taken aback. Then he said: 'But you
give the impression that you have medical qualifications. You
offer treatments.'

'But I give no prescriptions, use no drugs. My website – you
have seen it? – states that there is no chemical intervention.'

'But you are treating Ruggiero. Rini called you in because
she wanted you to heal him.'

'Yes, and I do heal him,' Tamaldov said, jutting his chin.
'When he is under stress, which often happens, his digestive
system reacts. And I can calm that – ask Ruggiero, he will
tell you that he feels better when I treat him.'

'That's auto-suggestion.'

'Whatever it is, it works – can you deny it?'

Greg had the feeling he was losing this contest. 'If I were to tell Rini that you have no medical qualification, what do you think she'd say?'

That stopped Tamaldov. He gaped at his opponent. After a moment he said, 'Why should you do that?'

'Because she asked me to help find her icon of Saint Olga. And I think you know something about it.'

The dark eyes opened wide in alarm. 'No! You are wrong!'

'My grandmother is saying you're in trouble with the authorities. It seems likely that you could curry favour if you took the icon and sent it back to them.'

Tamaldov jumped to his feet. The water bottle fell over, spilling its contents over the floor. He paid it no heed. He muttered to himself in Russian then threw out his hands in a gesture of appeal.

'Please, I beg, don't say anything to Rini on this subject. No, it will be so difficult for me if you do!'

'But if you're involved in the theft—'

'No, no! I knew nothing of the icon until it went missing.'

'Oh, come on! You must have known she was praying to a special saint.'

'Yes, why not? It is a consolation, no? But it was of no interest to me – I am not religious, and so she never discussed such a thing with me. But when it was stolen – ah, she was so distressed! Almost hysterical! And I happened to be there when she discovered it was gone, and she could not keep her distress hidden, so I heard all about it. But that was the first time – the first I ever heard of it. I assure you, Gregory – please – don't say to her that I am involved in any way with the icon.'

His anxiety was genuine. Greg studied him, then said: 'You didn't take it, perhaps. But you've been in touch with officialdom about it.'

'What?'

'It's true, isn't it?'

Tamaldov took a pace or two about his consulting room. He stood with his head bowed for a moment.

'You are very perceptive. What is the word in English? Shrewd, I think. You have been guessing, and to some extent you have guessed correctly.' He hesitated. 'I have written to the Department of Religious Heritage about the missing icon . . . And I have had a hint that if I can find it and return it to them, it might be . . . helpful.'

'You'd be allowed to go home.'

'Yes.' He came back to his seat, and leaning forward said: 'Please say nothing of this to Rini. I have been ordered to be very discreet. You see, it is not good for the Department to have it known that a sacred icon has gone missing. It speaks badly of their guardianship.'

'You mean I shouldn't tell her that you're hoping to get hold of her beloved Saint Olga and send it back?' Greg asked with heavy sarcasm.

'I ask myself, as a philosopher, what right has she to keep it?' said Tamaldov with a prideful lift of his head. 'I care nothing for the religious side of the matter. I think of the painting as a work of art, in the tradition of the Russian people—'

'No, you don't, you think of it as a bargaining point.'

'Well . . .' He gave a sigh. 'We will not argue. But let me beg you not to speak to Rini of this. What good would it do? The icon is missing, we all want it recovered to a safe place. I am trying to put out feelers among the Russian community to see if anyone knows about it.'

'You mean among your so-called patients.'

'My clients. I am a life counsellor. And through my clients, of whom I admit there are not as many as I could wish, I can contact others from my homeland. Don't you agree that it must be a Russian who stole the icon?'

'For its religious importance? Or for the diamonds?'

Tamaldov hunched his shoulders at the word 'diamonds'. 'You know,' he ventured, 'there is a criminal element among the exiles from my country. The news bulletins call it the Russian Mafia.'

'And you're in contact with that?' Greg asked in immediate concern.

'Only distantly. Oh, don't worry, my friend, I'm not myself part of that – they think me too unimportant and I find them too cold-blooded. But yes, some of the ladies who ask for my help with their problems are, shall we say, minor employees of the organization.'

'And have you learned anything from them?'

'Not so far, alas. But you must understand that if I am to keep the officials in Moscow happy, I must try every avenue. And that means I try to get some hint of what the underworld is doing, and also I keep in touch with Rini herself, the owner of the portrait. If you tell her anything of my problem, she shows me the door. And I lose any chance of pleasing the Department of Religious Heritage.'

Greg shook his head. 'Your problems with the authorities are no concern of mine. And even to get back her icon, I'm certain Rini wouldn't want to have anything to do with a bunch of Russian criminals. She's got to be told what you're up to.'

'You are going to say to her that I am not honest?'

'I've got to tell her at least that you're not medically qualified. I don't think she has the slightest idea of that.'

'Please don't do it.'

'I'm afraid I must.'

'Then . . . Then, let me do it myself. Let me speak to her and put my side of the matter. That is only fair.'

One of the talents of a con man is that he can usually charm his way out of trouble. Let Tamaldov tell his tale alone, thought Greg, and he might very well leave out all the parts that showed him in a bad light.

'We'll go together and I'll correct any omissions.'

'Oh.' He sat back in his chair. The wickerwork creaked as he moved restlessly. Then he said with puzzled irritation: 'You are of a kind I cannot understand – too conscientious. I suppose I must agree to your suggestion. Shall we go now? I must be back in Rome by six, I have a clinic this evening.'

Rini, when consulted by telephone, was welcoming and almost kittenish. 'Yes, do come, you can give me your opinion on my hats!'

'Hats?' Tamaldov exclaimed.

'Hats?' Greg, listening at his elbow, echoed in surprise.

'Oh yes, Liz has been to the shopping mall and brought me a little selection. For the funeral, you see. And we disagree about which suits me best, so now you can have a vote.'

The two men looked at each other in dismay. But then they went out to the back courtyard of the building, to Tamaldov's car, and in silence set off for the villa.

At the lodge gates, Ernesto was attentively on duty, but still disinclined to be responsive to any remark. At the house, Liz came out to welcome them.

True enough, the sofa in the drawing-room had five hats lined along it, all black. Rini, in one of her new black dresses, was standing back from them, looking critical. 'It must have a wide brim,' she told them as they came in. 'The sun will be strong, and my skin does not do well under the sun. What do you think, Yuri?'

Tamaldov hunched his shoulders. 'They are all very smart, Rini.'

Liz picked up a hat about the size of a saucer, but with a cloud of veiling and several black satin roses. 'This is the one. You have such beautiful hair, you ought to show it off.'

'What do you think, Gregory?' Rini appealed.

'I refuse to say anything on the grounds that I might incriminate myself.'

'What does Ruggiero think?' Yuri asked.

'Oh, he hasn't seen them. He was "summoned" to party headquarters to hear how he's to handle the funeral and so on.' She gave a frown of exasperation but the hats reclaimed her attention. 'Come,' she commanded her fashion adviser, 'let's take them up to my bedroom where I can try them on and see them in the three-sided mirror. My dears,' she turned to the men, 'you must make yourselves some drinks and ring for Cristina – she has cold snacks ready, and if you wish you can tell her to take it out to the table in the garden.'

Off she hurried, three of the hats in her arms, with Liz bringing up the rear and carrying the others. Over her shoulder she gave a laughing glance at Greg. 'I shouldn't hurry over lunch,' she called. 'As well as the hats, we're going to look through Floria's things to send them to the charity shops.'

Tamaldov was already ringing for Cristina. 'I'm hungry,' he confessed, 'and Cristina's such a good cook . . .'

The two men decided to stay indoors in the cool of the house. They had little to say to each other. Tamaldov switched on the television then took his place at the little table Cristina set up, to watch a sports programme while he ate. Greg had found the morning paper.

They had finished their lunch and were becoming embarrassingly impatient when there was a slight hubbub upstairs

– cries of surprise and hurried footsteps. Then Liz came flying down the staircase.

'Greg! Greg, come and look at this!'

He dashed out in alarm. She caught him by the arm to hurry him towards the stairs. 'In Floria's room! We were going through her things – quick, Rini's in a terrible state!'

He went up after her, three stairs at a time, and passed her at the door of Floria's bedroom. Rini Ardicci was standing with an opened leather suitcase at her feet. In her hands she held something loosely wrapped in a silk stole. She held it out. The silk fell away.

There was a glitter of fiery brilliance. Out of the silk emerged a small oval object, the sun striking flashes from its rim. In its brightness it was difficult to distinguish the dark features of the saint.

From the doorway Yuri Tamaldov gave a gasp. 'It was here all the time?'

'And look,' whispered Liz, picking something out of the suitcase.

It was a portrait photograph of Rini Ardicci. And someone had scratched out her eyes.

# THIRTEEN

Rini swayed on her feet. The icon slipped from her grasp. The two men made a dive to help. Even at that moment of crisis, Greg noted, Yuri grabbed for the icon. Greg caught Rini in his arms and held her up. After a moment her eyes regained their focus. He helped her to the bed. She allowed herself to relax on to it.

'We should send for her doctor,' said Liz.

'No.' The voice was a mere thread. 'I'm all right.'

'You've had a shock.'

'Yes. Yes, but . . . I . . . I am recovering. Give me a moment.'

Yuri had set aside the icon and was clasping and unclasping his hands, murmuring in Russian – could it be a prayer? Rini's glance drifted towards him. Her hand moved as if to gesture to him. He came to the bedside, took both of her hands in his. He spoke to her in his deep, rich voice, conjuring up some magical force that would uphold her even in these circumstances.

After a few moments she said: 'Let me sit up.' Liz helped her up. 'In my boudoir – there's a carafe – if I could have a sip of water?'

Liz dashed away.

Rini sat up. She gazed about her. 'I am lying on her bed,' she said in astonishment. 'She hated me, and I am lying on her bed!'

Liz hurried in with a glass of water. The men moved away so that she could offer it to Rini. Greg took up position alongside the little table on which Yuri had placed the icon – just to be on the safe side.

Yuri said: 'I think you should leave us. She needs a moment or two to come to terms with all this.'

'Very well.' Greg wrapped the silk scarf around the icon, and led the way out with Liz close on his heels. They went sedately down the stairs. In the hall he said, 'What ought we to do with this?'

'It ought to go in a safe. Do you think there is one?'

'Probably in Ruggiero's study.' They went there, but if there was a safe it wasn't in evidence. 'We ought to telephone him.' But then he remembered: Ruggiero was at a meeting with his political advisers. He had no idea where that might be, nor did he have Ruggiero's mobile number.

After some scrutiny of the furniture, he locked the icon in a cupboard and put the key in his jacket pocket. Liz watched him. 'What now?' she asked.

'Let's ask Cristina to make some tea or coffee for Rini.'

'Oh yes, a hot drink with lots of sugar – that's supposed to be good for a fainting fit.' She led the way along to the kitchen area.

Cristina was taking things out of the dishwasher. 'Could you make a drink for the *signora*?' Greg asked. 'Whatever she likes best – tea or coffee. And take it upstairs to the bedroom of Signorina Floria.'

Cristina looked up. Her expression was startled. 'The *signora* is in the room of Signorina Floria?' The tone implied that this was an unheard of thing.

Greg merely nodded. He and Liz went out of the kitchen

and as they did so, they passed the door of the little room
Floria had used as an office. Pausing, Greg tried the handle.
It was still locked. It had been locked since the police were
in the house.

When they reached the drawing-room they weren't quite
sure what to do next. 'Should we leave?' Liz wondered.

He considered that but shook his head. 'I want a word with
Tamaldov. We came here so that he could confess to Rini that
he's not a medical doctor, and I want to make sure he does.'

'Oh, not today, Greg! She's had enough distress for today.'

'Well . . . yes, I suppose so. But I want to remind him about
it.' He went on to report the discussion of the morning. Liz
heard him out with patience mingled with regret.

'We were thinking he was the thief who took the icon, or
was in some way involved in that. And we were wrong, Greg.'

He sighed. 'Completely. On the wrong track from the outset.'

'Floria,' she murmured. Then, after a moment, 'No one
would have thought of suspecting her. What could have been
her motive?'

'"*La haine est un tonique, elle fait vivre, elle inspire la
vengeance*".'

'All I got out of that was the last bit, because it's the same
in English – vengeance.'

'"Hatred is a tonic . . . it inspires vengeance". Balzac says
that somewhere.'

'Oh! You think Floria hated Rini that much?'

He gave a little shrug. 'I think she expected to marry
Ruggiero when his first wife died. But no, he fell in love with
this foreigner, this religious crank who caused him so many
problems in his career. And who also imported this so-called
doctor – Floria sensed Tamaldov was a fake, she said so openly.
Yet *he* was able to be of help to Ruggiero, whereas Floria
with all her tisanes and potions never cured his ailment.'

'So she took the icon for revenge. And watched, I suppose,
while they did all the wrong things as they tried to get it back.'

'Yes.' He was trying to cope with the revelation, trying to
fit it back into context. After a moment he said: 'And Floria
died.'

'But . . . but . . . There's no connection, Greg, surely?'

'Not that I can see. If she was poisoned on purpose, what
did it achieve? It didn't recover the icon . . .'

'And besides, it was an *accident*. Ernesto admitted it.'

'Yes.'

Liz looked at him. He seemed totally perplexed. 'Of course, I suppose no one searched the house when the icon disappeared,' she remarked. 'Because the police were never called in, and to start looking in the servants' quarters might have made them gossip among themselves. The last thing Ruggiero wants is any kind of gossip.'

'When Grossmutti talked about it, she said she felt that she herself might be under suspicion – but that was just her high-mindedness. I'm sure the Ardiccis thought the icon was taken by either a thief or a troublemaker. They never suspected anyone in the house.'

Sounds from upstairs made them turn towards the hall. A moment later Rini came down the staircase, Yuri Tamaldov giving her slight support by touching an elbow.

'Shouldn't you be resting?' Liz exclaimed.

Rini walked past her into the drawing-room. She sat in an armchair and looked around. 'This is much more congenial,' she said. 'I couldn't remain in *her* room.'

Liz picked up a cushion, intending to put it so that Rini could rest her head. Rini looked up at her with a faint smile. 'You are such a good friend,' she said, 'but truly I am re-covered.' She gave a little shrug of the shoulders. 'You know, in the world of the theatre, there can be all kinds of dramas – and so I am strong enough to survive even that awful sight.'

'We felt we ought to take care of the icon,' Greg said, 'so I put it in a cupboard in Ruggiero's study – the one with labelled document files.' He held out the key. Rini took it, and with a nod of gratitude placed it on the table by her chair. 'We thought of telephoning Ruggiero,' he went on, 'but we didn't know what number to call.'

'No, nor do I,' she sighed. 'Some office in Rome. I can give you the number of his mobile but reception up here is not good.' She sighed. 'In any case, dear people, it is news that can wait – it is good news and yet it is bad news, and I dread to think what my poor love will say when he hears.'

'Was he . . . very fond of Floria?' Liz ventured.

Tamaldov, hovering near Rini, gave a gusty sigh. 'Who could be fond of a woman like that?' he said in melancholy tones. 'There was always something very disapproving, very tense, in her nature.'

'She could never forgive you because you were curing Ruggiero,' Rini said. 'And that made her hate me even more. She didn't feel needed any longer.' She hesitated, then added, 'I sometimes think she made him ill with her tisanes and her potions. As a sort of punishment for undervaluing her.'

Tamaldov exclaimed at her words, turning to Liz as if to ask her for confirmation. But she was startled too. It was Greg who spoke first.

'What makes you say this? Is it just a feeling, or is there some basis to it?'

'Well . . . Very often, when she gave him one of her herbal infusions, he would feel unwell. But then you see, often it was after a very good meal, and he sometimes eats too much, my darling Ruggiero . . .' She sighed and smiled, tears brimming on her lids. 'But yes, I sometimes thought my husband was not always made better by the drinks she gave him.'

'Perhaps it would be a good idea to look at the herbs she used? Just to make sure?' Greg suggested in an uncertain tone.

'By all means,' said Rini, leaning back and closing her eyes. 'Her little office is locked.'

'Oh yes. The police demanded we lock up everything after they checked for poisons. And of course we have never thought to unlock it.' She waved a hand. 'The key is in Ruggiero's study – in fact, the keys for all the rooms are on the inside of the door to the cupboard where you have put my icon.'

Greg took the key to the cupboard off the table. His glance told Liz he wanted her to come with him. They found a row of labelled keys on the inside of one of the cupboard's double doors. *Ufficio domestico* was the key they needed. They went to the back of the hall, where he unlocked the door to the tiny office.

There was the shelf-like desk with its computer, cardboard file boxes for receipts and invoices, a telephone, a Venetian glass jar holding pencils and pens, and over it all a fine mist of dust. A window high up on the outer wall let in rays of light through ancient louvres. Here there was no muted purr of air conditioning; the room was cool because of the thickness of the walls.

Against the outer wall there were old stone shelves. On the

top rank were ranged ancient ledgers bound in leather. On the lower shelves were little jars and bottles. Some opaque, some clear glass. They were all labelled in a neat script.

'Primrose leaves,' Greg announced, reading and translating, 'juniper berries, peppermint, willow, valerian—' He broke off. 'Valerian? Isn't that dangerous?'

'Search me,' said Liz.

'I thought you'd know about things like this.'

'What makes you think so?'

'Well, you're a vegetarian.'

She laughed. 'Only an aspiring vegetarian. What you need is a botanist, or at least a keen gardener.'

'Grossmutti knows a bit about gardening,' he said after a moment's thought. 'She looks after the plants around Bredoux, such as they are.'

'Give her a call.'

He was surprised. 'You don't mind?'

'Good heavens, no. She's already done a bit of sleuthing, hasn't she? Let's keep her onside.'

He got out his mobile, but the response was weak. 'Let's go outside.'

They went out by a back door, to the shady side with the table for al fresco eating. They sat down, he tried the Bredoux number and after a few moments heard his grandmother's voice.

'Is that you, Gregory?'

'How are you, Grossmutti?'

'Well enough. How goes to the battle at Villa Stefani?'

'You're not going to believe this,' he said, and gave her a brief summary of what had happened.

'Floria? Really? Well . . .' A long pause. 'In a way I'm not surprised. But then I never liked her much. If Ruggiero had ever asked my advice, I'd have told him to settle his late wife's cousin a long way off.'

'You've known him a long time?'

'Not personally. He's been talked about by people I know, that's all.'

'Talked about in what way? Anything about his enemies?'

'No, no He's always been a bit of a ladies' man, of course. Years ago, there was a bit of a scandal – his son Paolo died in a drugs-related accident, I believe, but it was all hushed

up. After that Ruggiero concentrated his main efforts on politics and his ambitions have been centred on them for a good
long time – at least that's what I gather.'

'Well, listen, Grossmutti – when Rini saw what Floria had
done to her photograph, she was really shattered. And she
said something about . . . well . . . I don't know whether it
really has any importance, but she said she wondered if Floria
was making Ruggiero ill with her potions and remedies – as
a sort of revenge for marrying Rini.'

There was a silence while Nicoletta considered this. Then
she said: 'Those thimble glasses of cordial . . . And cups of
herbal tea when he came in from his morning ride . . .'

'What do you think?'

'It *could* be so.'

'We've been having a look at the little bottles and jars in
her cubby-hole next to the kitchen. The trouble is, what's good
and what's harmful?'

'What sort of things have you found?'

'Bits of flowers. Quite a few dried leaves and berries. The
leaves are mostly withered and crumbly. "Valerian" is on one
of the bottles – that sounds sort of familiar – is it dangerous?'

There was a slight pause while she considered. 'No, no, I
think it's generally used as a gentle sort of herbal sedative.'

'The berries . . . well, they're . . . For instance, one lot is
labelled "Juniperus". Another says "Vaccinium" – now that
has a worrying sound – what on earth is it?'

'Mmm. Juniper berries are used in flavouring gin so I
suppose they were for what Floria used to call a "*digestif*".
But Vaccinium – I don't know what that is.' He heard her
muttering to herself as she tried to identify the plant. 'No, but
you're beginning to bother me. Dried berries – some things
that grow in or around the garden are really dangerous.
Nightshade has berries. Mountain laurel has berries that can
make you ill.'

'What's she saying?' Liz demanded, straining to hear
Nicoletta's voice.

He covered the mobile with his palm. 'She says the things
in Floria's collection are worrying.' He turned back to the
mobile. 'What do you think, Grossmutti?'

'I think you should take the collection to an expert, my
child.'

'But . . . you know . . . I'm not really involved any more, am I? I was asked to help find the icon, and the icon has found itself, so why should I do anything about Floria's herbs?'

'Don't be silly,' she scolded. 'If she was making Ruggiero ill with her concoctions, then Ruggiero's doctor ought to be told so that he can check him to make sure he's not been permanently harmed.'

'I suppose so.'

'Do as I tell you, Gregory.'

'Very well, madame,' he said. Much as he would have preferred to walk away from the Ardiccis and their problems, he knew his grandmother was right. Besides, when she spoke in that tone of voice, he generally obeyed.

Rather to his surprise, Liz was totally in agreement with his grandmother. 'Rini would cry her eyes out if Floria's done any damage to her beloved Ruggiero. We have to find out about that stuff.'

Greg didn't know any botanists. But after some discussion he agreed to call some of those whom Liz called the Musical Mafia, which took him nearly an hour. His friend from the Academy of St Cecilia, Martina, said she would ask Dr Legneno, a retired school teacher. They then went indoors to ask Rini if she agreed to having Floria's collection of herbs taken away for examination.

'My dears – of course – if you think that is a good thing to do?'

'Rini dear,' said Liz, 'if there is anything harmful there, we ought to know. Because, don't you agree, Ruggiero's doctor – Dr Gennaro? – ought to be told about it?'

'Oh! Oh, yes, certainly – please, take them to your expert – how kind of you to be so worried on our account.'

Tamaldov listened to this in consternation. 'You are seriously considering the idea that Signorina Floria would actually injure Ruggiero?'

'He was often quite unwell,' Rini declared. 'And I took so much care in choosing food that I thought would do him good . . . Oh, Yuri, who knows what was in those drinks and mixtures she gave him? We must make sure!'

He took one of her hands and pressed it between his own. 'Calmness, my dear friend. Composure. Breathe deeply, and find a place where your mind can review the facts and give them balance. You have been through confusion and dismay but have borne it bravely, so now once again, look within, look deeply, and find tranquillity.' The velvety voice went on, gradually growing softer and then changing to the Russian tongue, so that Rini laid her head back against the cushions of the sofa, and closed her eyes.

Letting go of her hand, Tamaldov turned to Liz. 'I must get back to Rome,' he murmured. 'I have a client coming at six. Will you stay with her?'

'Of course.'

He leaned over Rini. 'I have to go now, *polruga*,' he murmured, 'but you are with Liz and Gregory, and you feel safe and happy, don't you?'

She opened her eyes, smiling weakly. 'Yes, of course. Thank you, Yuri, you are always so kind to me.'

He kissed her on the cheek, then nodded farewell to the others. Greg followed him into the hall. 'Did you tell her about your interest in the icon?'

Tamaldov looked shocked. 'Good heavens, is your heart made of stone? How could I speak of such things when she is in such distress? No, voice of my conscience! That is for another time.'

He stalked out, closing the heavy outer door with unnecessary firmness. Greg shrugged, then went in search of a cardboard box in which to carry the herbs.

Cristina was at work in the kitchen, preparing vegetables. When asked for a box she looked surprised but went to the utility room, returning with a flattened cardboard carton. 'Will this do?'

'Thank you, that's fine.' He went to Floria's office, wrapped the bottles and jars in sheets of typing paper, then stacked them in the box. That done, he went back to the drawing-room after locking up the office again.

Ruggiero came home as the heat of the day was beginning to wane. He drew up outside with a slamming of the brakes and a banging of the car door. Guessing that the meeting with the political bosses had not gone well, Greg hurried out to meet him.

'Listen, Ruggiero—'

'Sorry, Gregory, I need a drink!' He was about to brush past him but Greg caught him by the arm.

'Don't go storming in like this. Rini has had a terrible shock.'

'Oh, she's always having some sort of drama—'

'No, I mean it – she found the icon.'

That stopped Ruggiero dead in his tracks. 'What?'

'In Floria's room.'

'*What?*'

'Liz and I have been doing what we could, and Tamaldov was here, so she's recovered a bit. But she needs to be comforted and taken care of. You understand?'

'What the devil are you telling me?'

'You should hear it from Rini. She needs to talk about it, talk it through so that she can come to terms with it.'

'Well, of course, I'll talk to her—'

'But gently does it, Ruggiero. Tender loving care, as the saying goes.' With this inadequate advice, Greg let him continue on his way into the drawing-room.

Rini had heard his arrival and his voice in the hall. She was on her feet, holding out her hands. 'Dearest! Oh, my dearest, I have longed for you to be with me.' She threw herself into his arms, and he – at last understanding he had to play his part in her recovery – hugged her against himself and murmured gentle words against her cheek.

Liz rose quietly from her chair, skirted round the loving couple, and tiptoed out of the room with Greg. They let themselves out of the villa without being hindered, got into the car, and drove away.

'Now, where is this botanical authority?'

He read out the address he had taken down when Martina called earlier. It proved to be an apartment taking up the entire first floor of what had once been a very grand house not far from the Piazza Pia. An ancient bell-pull set something clanging inside, there was a great clatter of footsteps, and the door was opened by a boy of about ten.

He stared up at the prince, wordless. Greg bent down to say in Italian, 'I believe Signor Legneno is expecting me – my name is Gregory Crowne.'

'Mama!' cried the boy in alarm, retreating to the safety of about four other children, grouped behind him.

From somewhere within the apartment a young woman appeared, dressed in jeans and a T-shirt protected with a plastic apron bearing the logo 'Save the Whales!'

'Signor Crowne? Please come in. Don Legneno has said you would be calling.' She turned, shooing the children away in front of her with the wooden spoon she carried. *'Nonno! Nonno! L'uomo in riguardo dell'erbaggio!'* She smiled apology. *'Mi scusi* – I am make the supper.'

From the back of the flat came an old man in shirt and linen trousers. He extended his hand, offering a voluminous welcome in Italian that seemed to include an invitation to the meal. Greg was smiling and shaking his head.

Liz stood by, knowing she would be excluded from this conversation, because Mama – perhaps the only English speaker – had returned to her cooking. Two of the children had remained, to admire this pretty young lady with the fair skin and hazel eyes.

After a short exchange, Greg offered the box of jars and pots. Signor Legneno gestured at one of the children, who immediately stepped forward to carry it. Another short passage of conversation, and they were bowing and shaking hands in farewell. The remaining child ushered them to the door, smiling and calling *'Ciao!'* as they went downstairs.

'He says he'll have a look at them this evening and tomorrow morning. He can probably give us an opinion by about noon tomorrow and I'm to ring first to make sure.'

It had been a long, perplexing day. They went wearily back to the Pastorella, to shower and change and then to find a quiet place for dinner.

They slept late, and after breakfast the first task was to ring Villa Stefani. Ruggiero answered, his voice grim and irritated. 'She's well, yes, well enough. Recovering,' he said in response to Liz's inquiry about Rini. There was scant sympathy in his tone.

'Did she tell you we had taken some containers of herbs, to have them examined?'

'Some such thing. What on earth is she talking about? Floria would never have tried to poison me. Really, sometimes, she—' He broke off. 'Ha! It's the artistic temperament, no?'

'Will it be all right if Greg and I come to the villa later today?'

'By all means!' he exclaimed, clearly glad to have someone come and mitigate his problems. 'Rini would be glad to see you, as always.' He went off-line, and could be heard calling to his wife.

Rini picked up. 'Oh, Liz dearest, have you taken those dreadful plants to your expert? What does he say? I always warned my darling that Floria wasn't to be trusted, you know, but he was so firm in his belief in her – so unsuspecting, so open-hearted!'

Liz murmured something that might have been agreement, and Rini surged on. Nearly half an hour later Liz was able to end the conversation. 'I need a drink!' she announced. So they went out so that she could have one and a chance to recover.

When Greg telephoned Don Legneno, he was told that the examination had been completed and that he could come to hear the result as soon as he wished. Liz drove him there, but elected to go off on her own while he talked to the old teacher. 'I can't be any use, so I'll just nip back to a fruit stall I noticed. I'll get something thirst-quenching and come back in about half an hour, okay?'

This time the door of the apartment was opened by a grown-up, a young man who introduced himself as Ettore Legneno. 'My grandfather is in his room, let me show you the way,' he said in heavily accented English. As he went, he added over his shoulder, 'It was a great pleasure to him, to be asked to do this service. He teached botany and biology for many years, but of course is now retired and has not many opportunity to use his science.'

They came to a door in a little passage off the main entry. He tapped, opened the door, and ushered Greg into a cluttered room where pride of place was taken up by a table bearing a microscope. A computer with its printer stood on a bench under the shuttered window. Italian text books were piled nearby.

'Good morning,' said Don Legneno in eager Italian. 'I have greatly enjoyed looking at the samples you brought. I've produced a report for you,' he picked up a sheet of paper from the printer, 'and if you wish I'll go through it with you, but in fact, *signore*, there is nothing of great interest except perhaps this.'

He delved into the cardboard carton and came up with the little jar labelled 'Vaccinium'. Its contents were dried berries, insignificant and now very shrivelled.

'Vaccinium is a very general name,' said Don Legneno in the tones of a lecturer. 'These prove to be *Vaccinium myrtillus*

– what we call *mirtillo*. You have seen them, perhaps, if you take country walks?'

Indeed he had. Growing in woods, a tangle of bright-green twigs with black berries in the autumn. He had eaten them sometimes as a boy during his wanderings with his friends around Bredoux.

'I know them. They're rather sharp to the taste.'

'Exactly. Quite common, and I imagine used as a herbal tonic, although I am not a herbalist.'

'Not harmful,' suggested Greg.

'Not at all, unless you were to eat a couple of kilos. But just a moment, *signore*!' He uncapped the jar and with tweezers selected a berry and drew it out. 'What do you think of this one?'

It was slightly smaller than the other berries but otherwise unnoticeable. Greg shrugged and admitted it meant nothing to him.

'This is not *Vaccinium*. This is *Ligustrum vulgaris*.' He waited, expectant. Greg shook his head. 'You don't know it? *Ligustro?*'

That he knew. He said it in his head in English. 'Privet.'

The old man smiled. 'I see you recognize the name. A common plant used in garden hedging. This is a berry of *Ligustrum vulgaris*. And it is quite injurious, *signore*. Children have died from eating these berries. I used to warn my students not to eat them.'

Greg was silent, trying to take it in.

'In this little jar,' Legneno went on, in his lecturing tone, 'there are approximately forty berries of *Vaccinium myrtillus* and fifteen berries of *Ligustrum vulgaris*. The person who collected them is presumably an enthusiast for herbal remedies. The other jars bear witness to that. But he or she is extremely careless. If these berries are mixed and administered in some way – perhaps baked in a little cake, or steeped to make a drink – they could cause considerable pain in the digestive system.'

'You said . . . you said they could kill a child?'

'Yes, it has happened.'

'Could they kill an adult?'

'Well, I think not. Not unless taken in quite large quantities. The contents of this jar, if they were all *ligustro*, could make an adult quite ill. But what troubles me, *signore*, is how they come to be mixed up in this way. A herbalist should know not to pick any berries from the *ligustro* border.'

Yes, thought Greg. Floria should have known better.

Or perhaps she wanted to punish Ruggiero, as Rini had suggested, for preferring another woman. Punish but not kill.

Twice in one household, a connection with poison. An accidental death, and the slow impairment of a man's health. It was the strangest coincidence that he had ever encountered in his life.

And as a general rule, Mr Crowne tended not to believe too much in coincidences.

# FOURTEEN

L iz had a small carrier bag of oranges on the back seat. They left the car in a supermarket car park then found a shady square with a fountain playing. They sat on the edge of the fountain's rim, dabbling their fingers to clean them as they ate the fruit.

Liz listened with dismay to what Greg had to say.

'Don Legneno looked it up in a book and showed me. It said the berries could cause vomiting, diarrhoea, and coldness of the body. Death could follow – but that was in children.'

'Not in adults?'

'Not so far as the records show. But Ruggiero could have been made to feel quite ill if he was dosed with a drink made from a mixture of those berries.'

'The *Vaccinium* one doesn't do any harm?'

'No, that's just "*mirtillo*" – I don't know what it is in English – myrtle-berry?'

'Never heard of 'em. What's it like?'

He gave her a description. Liz too had memories of childhood explorations of local woods and farms. 'Sound like bilberries,' she said. 'Or, where I come from, whinberries, that grow on the moors. So they're harmless, and Floria mixed them with another berry that could make Ruggiero ill.'

'It seems so.'

'That's weird.' She ate a piece of orange, licking her lips to collect all the juice. He leaned forward to kiss her. She tasted of citrus fruit – a new sensation.

She said: 'I only knew Floria briefly, but I got the impression that she was deeply attached to Ruggiero – protective, not aggressive.'

'It seems that was just pretence.'

They sat for a time in silence, watching the traffic slowing for the turn around the square, watching pedestrians come into its welcome shade and breathe a sigh of relief.

Greg said: 'There are two distinct cases of poison connected with the villa.'

'Yes.'

'Does that seem . . . strange to you?'

'Well, one lot was something that had been stored away and was used accidentally and the other was used on purpose.' She hesitated. 'Now you make me say it out loud, it does make me feel peculiar.'

'As if it's unlikely.'

'More than unlikely. Greg – there couldn't be any connection, could there?'

'How? I don't see how. Unless . . .'

'What?'

'The poisons were found in a place where someone could have put them there.'

'Someone put the old bottle of poison in the garage so that Ernesto would find it and use it?'

He frowned. 'That seems to depend on chance. First of all that Ernesto would find it. And then that he would use it.'

'But perhaps . . . I don't know . . . could someone have suggested to him that he should use it?'

Greg stared at her. 'I don't suppose the police ever asked him that question.'

'Do you think it's possible that Ernesto was prompted to use it?'

'Well . . . Ruggiero has enemies.'

'Enemies that might like to see someone die in his family – because it could cause a scandal?'

'I don't know.'

She arranged little pieces of peel along the fountain's rim, like characters waiting to be summoned. 'So someone slinks into the garage and sets the insecticide on the shelf. Then he chats with Ernesto about grape-growing, says, "There's some nifty stuff left by the last gardener, it's in the garage", and Ernesto falls into the trap. So it has to be someone familiar with the villa, or at least the grounds.'

'That seems possible.'

She flicked one of her pieces of orange peel on to the ground. 'But Floria's medicines?'

'Well . . . That too is possible.'

'The same person who put the stuff in the garage? I mean . . . It's not hard to stroll into an outhouse, but getting into Floria's office?'

They looked at each other. Then almost simultaneously they shook their heads.

'That's just not on, Greg,' she said, thumping her fist on the marble rim.

'I agree. But the first one – that somebody put something harmful into the garage – that's feasible.'

'It all sounds very Machiavellian. You say Ruggiero has enemies – is he important enough for a plot like that?'

Greg thought about it. 'Perhaps not in the larger political sense. But let's say someone else desperately wants that job at the UN. He – or she – might want to kill him off.'

'Or just make him ill enough so that he's unfit for the post. Hence the tinkering with the stuff in Floria's little herb collection. Because of course' – she picked up a large piece of peel and waved it at him – 'a rival with the qualifications for New York might well be a seemingly friendly visitor to the villa.'

'Yes, at a dinner party? Wandering off to step outside for a breath of air and popping into Floria's office . . .?'

'But Greg – someone as clever as that – wouldn't they get hold of the jar with the privet berries once Floria died, and dispose of it?'

He took the orange peel from her and set it back firmly on the marble rim. 'But they couldn't. Floria's office has been locked up ever since she died. You and I are the first people to go into that room.'

She sighed, accepting his point. Then she said, 'Are we just making up scary stories?'

'The simplest idea about Floria is the most likely. Floria

was poisoning Ruggiero *just a little* – to pay him back for loving Rini.'

'Maybe,' she said. But she sounded unconvinced. She ate the last segment of her orange then said with a sigh, 'You know, I don't really know enough about Ruggiero and his household. First of all we think they've been the victims of a serious theft, then it turns out that the confounded icon never even left the house and it was a member of the family that took it. Then Ernesto is in big trouble about the insecticide and Ruggiero deals out punishment like Attila the Hun. I mean, Greg, he thought he could just *dispose* of poor Ernesto!'

'He's certainly never caught up with modern management theory.'

'And then you know, Ernesto's reaction – he and Cristina were in absolute floods of tears. As if the world was coming to an end.'

'Well, as you pointed out, they were losing their home.'

'Yes, but they could have put up a defence – after all, it *was* an accident about the insecticide. They just seemed to go to pieces.' She was gathering up the scraps of peel and putting them in the carrier bag. 'There was a sort of . . . atmosphere . . . undercurrent . . . I don't know what.' Then she giggled. 'Maybe they were just being Italian! You know us Brits think Italians are very operatic!'

They disposed of the carrier bag in a waste basket then set off to retrieve the car. 'What are we going to do now?' she asked.

'I suppose we ought to take back Floria's herbs. And perhaps on the way we might stop off in Tabardi and see how poor Armeno is getting on.'

She gave him a hug. 'You're really bothered about the poor kid.'

He took the opportunity to return the hug and give her a kiss. A passer-by murmured, '*Alla grande*!' as he skirted round them.

'What did he say?' she asked.

'He approved.'

'Me too.'

When they reached the village of Tabardi, it dawned on them that they'd forgotten that great Italian custom – the long lunch break. Tabardi was closing up to avoid the heat of the afternoon sun. There were few vehicles in the car park and only one old gentleman outside the inn, asleep with a newspaper over his face.

In the square, two young men in motorbike gear were studying a map. The ice cream kiosk was still active, with a little group trying to decide between hazelnut or chocolate. The pizza outlet at the side of the bakery was in process of closing up.

They headed towards it, as being the easiest to approach. The assistant, giving them a hesitant glance, stopped wiping down his counter and waited.

'Good afternoon,' Greg began in very polite Italian. 'I wonder if you could tell me how to find Armeno Federa?'

A pause. The assistant began to wipe busily. 'Who?'

'Armeno, who worked for Signor Ardicci in the stable.'

The man was clearly thinking hard. He had never seen Greg before, but had probably heard about the foreigners who were driving back and forth to the Villa Stefani.

Folding his washcloth, he placed it on a shelf behind him. 'One moment,' he said. He disappeared from the serving area into the bakery.

'He's gone to ask the boss if he should tell us anything,' Liz suggested.

'Very likely. I expect the whole village knows Armeno was in some sort of trouble, and nobody wants to get mixed up in it.'

The assistant appeared again, this time without his white cap and his apron. 'This way, *signore*, *signorina*,' he said, with a bow and a sweep of the hand.

They went through the shop and into the bakery itself. The place was still very warm from the morning's work. The smell of good bread and of rich sauces for the pizza hung heavy in the air. He led them on to the back of the premises, to a stone-floored area for the cleaning of the baking equipment.

Here a small, tired-looking woman was untying an apron to reveal her sombre black cotton dress – widow's weeds. She wiped her hands and held out one in greeting.

'*Signore*,' she said in a husky voice. 'You are the gentleman who has been so kind to my Armeno. Thank you, sir. I am Armeno's mother, Pia Federa.'

He shook her hand. 'This is my friend and colleague,

Signorina Blair.' Liz, hearing her name, shook hands too.
Signora Federa looked at her with interest and perhaps
some envy, for she was a picture in her slim jeans and jade-
green top.

'How is Armeno?' asked Greg.

She gave a weary but expressive shrug. 'Unhappy. He slept
not at all last night. But the horses are gone – he understands
that. And so of course the *signore* would have no further use
for Armeno.' She nodded, as if to assert to herself that those
were the facts. But then she added, 'Yet there was no need
to turn him away absolutely at once.'

Greg was having some slight trouble in following her words.
She spoke a different kind of Italian from the one he was used
to speaking in Switzerland, a village version with less attention to the consonants.

He said: 'Signor Ardicci claims that Armeno attacked him.'

She exclaimed in denial, and so did the assistant from the
pizza stall. Clearly the idea that Armeno would attack anyone,
let alone the local landowner, was nonsense.

'That stony-hearted oaf!' the man cried. 'It's often the way
with him, give somebody a job for a month or two and then
– oho, goodbye! And no little handout to make up for suddenly
getting the boot.'

'Now, now, Filippo, it's no use talking like that – and don't
let me hear you saying it to Armeno because he's miserable
enough as it is.' She sighed, and turned to hang up her apron.
'If you'd like to come with me, *signore*, I know Armeno would
love to see you. It's just a few steps up the hill. Until later,
Filippo.' She took down a black and pink shawl from a peg,
draped it over her greying hair, and led the way.

They went out by a back door, through a courtyard, and
out another door to a little paved track between small two-
storey houses all painted with whitewash. Pia Federa led the
way rather slowly. Liz thought she was very tired, and rather
regretted that they were troubling her when she ought to be
looking forward to an hour or two's rest.

She opened a door calling, 'Armeno, it's Mama! Are you
asleep?' She turned, inviting them into a narrow passage and
saying in apology, 'He spent the morning cleaning out the
Santa Elena fountain – the council will pay him for the work.'

She led the way into the main room of the house, the parlour, where fine old chairs with horse-hair seats and a walnut table hinted at better days. There were the sounds of movement upstairs, and a moment later Armeno appeared, rubbing his eyes. He was clad in shirt and jeans, barefoot and with his hair on end. He gasped when he was able to focus on the visitors. '*Signore!*'

'How are you, Armeno?'

The boy was caught in embarrassment. 'Oh . . . I'm just waking up . . .' And now he was staring at Liz in amazement.

She held out her hand. 'Armeno,' she said, calling upon her slight vocabulary, 'I'm Liz.'

'Liz . . .' He tried it for sound. 'Liz . . .' Then, minding his manners, 'How do you do, *signorina*?'

She smiled. He gazed at her, and it was clear that seeing this pretty foreigner almost made up for all he'd been through in the last couple of days.

'Please, sit down. What can I offer you?' said Signora Federa.

'Oh . . . nothing, thank you. We just stopped to ask after Armeno.'

'I've been working at the fountain,' Armeno announced. 'You know, people throw money in. I collected it. There were more than twenty coins, and that's not as many as some other times. I don't know how much it was. Benno said it was nearly fifty euros.'

'And Benno will take the money to the council office, won't he?' coaxed his mother.

'Yes, and we must always be careful with the money, because it's *village* money, it doesn't belong to anyone who finds it.' He looked proudly at Greg as he reported this.

'Quite right,' Greg agreed.

'Dearie, go upstairs and put on your shoes,' said Pia.

'Yes, Mama.'

Off he went, with a smile of apology to Liz. She smiled back.

'You see, *signore*,' said Pia, 'there's not a bit of harm in him. He would never "attack" anyone.'

'No, that's what I thought.'

'You are a friend of Signor Ardicci. Could you ask him to take Armeno back?'

'I'm afraid not. This isn't a good time for Signor Ardicci.'

'No, that's true,' she said, but with an utter lack of sympathy. 'Signorina Floria died.'

'Yes, it was a great shock.'

'And we hear Ernesto is blamed for it,' she went on.

'Yes, that was the verdict.'

'I find that very strange, sir. Ernesto is a very steady sort of man.'

'But not a very experienced gardener.'

'What makes you say so?' she asked in some surprise. 'He may not have any diplomas from a college but he knows his way around a garden.'

Armeno appeared, hair somewhat tidier and wearing shoes. 'Ernesto clipped the little plants in the signor's garden and I collected up the clippings,' he ventured, joining the conversation.

'Yes, and when he lived here in the village he used to grow wonderful tomatoes,' agreed Pia.

'Mama grows tomatoes – don't you, Mama? In big pots.'

'We all have our little plots where we grow what we can,' she explained to the visitors. 'And you help me, don't you, Armeno?'

Armeno was off on a conversational tack of his own. 'The house where Ernesto used to live has a proper garden. Giovanni Prevadi has it now, but he doesn't take such good care of the grapes.' His expression grew troubled. 'Ernesto is leaving Villa Stefani too. Will he get his house back?'

'No, dear, Giovanni has it now.'

'Where will Ernesto go? And Cristina? Will they come back to Tabardi?'

'Perhaps. We just have to wait and see.'

'I hope they come back. Then Ernesto can teach me more writing.' He made curving signs in the air. 'For labels and things.'

Greg watched him then said thoughtfully, 'There are no labels on the plants in the villa's garden, Armeno. What were the labels for?'

Armeno shrugged. 'Ernesto needed them. For things.'

Liz had been sitting patiently through all this, but now squirmed a little on the very upright chair. Greg glanced at her in apology. 'We ought to be on our way,' he remarked. 'It's good to see you, Armeno, and to hear you've been at work.'

'Thank you, *signore*.' A moment's hesitation. 'Have you heard from the nice lady who bought Tippi?' he asked in a trembling voice.

'Not yet. Perhaps in a day or two.'

'Oh yes. That would be good.'

They began a move to the passage. Signora Federa said, 'Thank you for coming to see him. It will keep him happy for the rest of the day.'

'Goodbye, then, *signora*.'

'Goodbye.' The two women shook hands. Armeno opened the outside door and stood by importantly to see them out. Greg lingered, to put a handful of euro notes under the vase of flowers on the table before coming out of the room.

As they walked back down the alley, Greg said, 'I was told by Ruggiero that Ernesto didn't know anything about gardening, that he was really hired to look after the cars.'

'Yes?'

'Signora Federa said he had a garden when he lived here. She implied that he was a decent gardener.'

'Really?' Her tone implied, *Why are you telling me this?*

'Well . . . It's been taken for granted that he is a bit of an ignoramus and when he found this old bottle of insecticide he just used it. Would an experienced gardener do that?'

She considered. 'He might. After all, the bottle was labelled "Insecticide", wasn't it?'

'Was it?'

She stopped and frowned at him. 'I just said it was.'

'Armeno's just been telling me again about how Ernesto was teaching him to write. And what were the two of them writing?'

'What were they writing?' she asked, as expected.

'Labels.'

They stood in the narrow lane, silence all around them except for the humming of insects and the momentary cooing of a sleepy dove. She was looking into his face, trying to catch up with his train of thought.

'Explain,' she said at last.

'Well, what if the bottle had a label saying "Poison" or "Parathion" or some other sort of warning. So he takes off that label and puts on another saying "Insecticide" and he gets Armeno to write it so that no one can ever identify the writing.'

'No, Greg!'

'Then he sprays the grapes, and he lets Floria eat them.'

'No, no! Don't say that, Greg – that's absolutely horrible!'

'And he gets Cristina to slip the poisonous berries in among Floria's harmless collection.'

'But Floria doesn't use the stuff in her little bottles for *herself*—'

'No, but he might think that she usually tastes her tisanes before serving them up.' He paused, shaking his head in bafflement. 'But then the only problem is . . . Why on earth would Ernesto want to kill off Floria?'

# FIFTEEN

As they drove the few kilometres to the Villa Stefani, their minds were taken up by what they had been discussing.

'Are we going to tell Ruggiero?' asked Liz, sounding very unwilling.

Greg took his time before replying. 'If we tell Ruggiero he'll go after Ernesto with a gun.'

'Do you think so? To me he didn't seem very fond of Floria.'

'Well . . . Not being fond of her is quite different from not caring what happened to her. His sense of family is probably very strong. He talks about the family traditions . . . that sort of thing.'

'But that's just to make himself appear important.'

'And caring about his cousin also makes him seem important.'

'She was only a sort of second cousin twice removed.'

'The cousin of his first wife. His "dearly loved" house-keeper. He could be on the telephone to the police before we've finished saying our second sentence.'

'Do you mean,' she asked, 'that we *shouldn't* tell him?'

'If we had proof . . .'

'It's the job of the police to find the proof.'

He shook his head. 'Just think about it. Imagine how willing Inspector Novelli would be to do anything for

Ruggiero Ardicci! Ruggiero will report it, but who knows how long it might be until there's any action?'

She was silent a moment, then sighed. 'I don't know what to think. Don't we owe it to them to inform them? That we think Ernesto knew what he was doing when he sprayed those grapes with poison?'

'What was his motive, Liz? You don't go around poisoning people without a reason! If I could think of a reason I'd be ready to talk about all this to Ruggiero. But for the moment, I'm at a complete loss.'

'Could we . . .' She hesitated. 'Could we confront Ernesto?'

'*Should* we confront Ernesto? I don't fancy that. Who knows how he'd react? We don't understand him. We see him open the gates, but we scarcely say a word to him.'

'But that's who he is, just Ernesto Streso, the man who looks after the gates.'

'He's the man who taught Armeno to read and write so he could make the label for the poison bottle.'

'We don't know that. That's just what we're supposing.'

'You don't agree about that? Well, let's make a list.' He began counting on his fingers. 'First, he's not a numbskull about gardening, you heard Signora Federa. He must have known that something left covered in dust on a garage shelf could be harmful. Second, he gets Armeno to write the new label so that he, Ernesto, could never be suspected of writing it. You think we've got that all wrong?'

'I . . . I'm not sure.'

'Third, the poisonous berries among Floria's herbs – you're not sure about those?'

She made no reply to that. She stared out of the windscreen, though her mind was on something other than traffic.

They drove on in silence for some minutes. Then Greg said: 'Liz, listen. I've just thought of something. I'm beginning to think that it was Ernesto who threw that stone.'

'What stone? What are you talking about?'

'I didn't tell you about that . . . Well, you remember I went out riding with Ruggiero a couple of days ago?'

She nodded, half wishing to turn so as to study him but knowing she had to watch the road.

'We went up the mountain paths and when we were quite high up, something flew in front of the little mare Ruggiero was riding. She was scared, went jerking about on the path and could easily have gone over the slope.'

'What?' she cried anxiously. 'Why didn't you tell me?'

'Well, at first it seemed that it was a bird that went by. But I went walking up there afterwards and I began to picture what happened. I just sort of walked in among the bushes to see where it had gone – the bird, if it was a bird. You could trace its path along the tops of the bushes. But there were no feathers, only ragged cuts. So . . . I looked about, and I found a stone.'

By now she was perplexed as well as anxious. She waited for a lull in traffic then pulled in to the side of the road and stopped. She turned to study him.

'What are you saying, Greg?'

'I think someone was waiting on the upward slope, among the foliage, and when Ruggiero came opposite I think he threw the stone.' He mimicked the gesture. 'It was one of those thin, flat stones that we all like to skim across a pond. And now we've thought it all through – about the insecticide and the poisonous berries, I've come to believe that Ernesto was the thrower. So that's item Number Four in our list of harmful things.'

'But throwing a stone . . . that seems so childish.'

'That was frustration. An angry attempt to do what had failed when Floria ate the first bunch of grapes – which I'm sure she did just so as to spite Ruggiero. She ruined Ernesto's plan.' He paused, then went off on a different tack. 'Ernesto's been working at the villa for about a year, I believe. He probably knows that Ruggiero's not a good horseman.'

'I would think so. Armeno probably chatted to him about things like that.'

'If Armeno had been riding with him, Ruggiero could have gone over the side. I had to grab his reins to control the mare.' He sighed to himself. 'If Armeno had been with him, Ruggiero could have broken his neck.'

Liz was listening to his account with growing alarm 'That all seems so . . . so *desperate*. Ernesto must absolutely *hate* Ruggiero.' She shuddered. 'And he's involved his wife in his hatred – she must be the one who slipped the privet berries among Flora's herbs.' She paused and thought. 'But then, your expert says privet berries wouldn't kill an adult.'

'No, only make him ill, cause him discomfort. That's a bit weird.'

'Perhaps we're wrong to think Cristina is responsible—'

'No, wait! If you think about it, if you were to kill a totally healthy person with poison, it would cause quite a lot of surprise, wouldn't it?'

'What?' She frowned, staring at him in a moment's perplexity. Then she said slowly, 'Oh, I see. If someone who suffered from gastric trouble were to succumb to an accidental dose of some garden spray, that would seem reasonable.' She put her hands up to her face and hunched in upon herself as if for protection. 'It's been *planned* – planned for a long, long time.'

He put an arm around her shoulders. 'Whatever the truth is, Ernesto got a terrible fright when Floria died. You said it yourself – he and Cristina were absolutely shattered. And the attempt to cause a riding accident didn't work. So I don't think he's going to be trying anything dangerous for the present. I think we should delay before we tell Ruggiero, and try to find out a motive.'

Liz said: 'We have to tell him about the privet berries. Rini knows we were going to consult an expert. She'll want us to report about that.'

'Oh, Lord! Yes, of course.' He kissed her on the top of her head, and said: 'Well, I apologize for dragging you into this. Next time my respected grandmother asks me to help one of her friends, I'm going to say no and run for the hills.'

That made her laugh. 'Me too. I'm scared.'

'But we're stuck with the situation now, Liz, so we have to do something. "*De l'audace, encore de l'audace, toujours de l'audace!*" as Danton once remarked.'

'Oh, did he? And wasn't he one of those revolution types that got murdered in his bath?'

'No, that was Marat. Danton got his head chopped off.'

'There you are then.'

He laughed and after a moment she produced a tremulous smile.

They drove on, still not sure how they were going to handle this tricky problem.

Ernesto came out of the lodge as they approached. He

opened the gates by using a gadget in his hand, and as they came through, actually spoke for once. 'The Signora is expecting you,' he said. He waited by the car, as if expecting a response.

'Thank you,' Greg replied. Then as they passed out of earshot, added to Liz: 'He almost never says a word. Why does he suddenly decide to speak to us today?'

'He did give us a bit of a stare, didn't he. I wonder why?'

'He's interested in us.' He was thinking it out. 'Perhaps . . . Cristina told him that we took away Floria's herbs yesterday. Remember, we asked her for a box.'

She made a muted sound of protest. 'It's such a tangle.' And then with an attempt at a laugh: 'I really am a bit scared.'

Ruggiero let them in when they came to the villa's door. He gave an angry glance at the box Greg was carrying. 'Don't know why you went along with that nonsense,' he growled, heading for the drawing-room.

They had clearly arrived in the middle of an ongoing storm. There were tears on Rini's cheeks. She was wearing one of her flamboyant silk dresses, mourning abandoned. Ruggiero's sallow features were flushed, perhaps with irritation, perhaps from a few too many drinks at lunch.

'Now you're a man of broad experience, Gregory,' he began, turning as they followed him into the room. 'You agree with me, I'm sure. That damned icon can't be kept in my house any more. It has to go to somewhere safe.'

'It was safe here,' protested his wife. 'Until that woman stole it!' She clasped her hands in appeal. 'You agree with me, don't you, Gregory? Saint Olga deserves to hang in a place where her devotee can offer prayers to her.'

'If you really can't pray without having her picture, for God's sake buy a modern one and pray to that—'

'No, no, dearest, she *lives* for me in that painting, she hears my prayers—'

'Oh, does she! And what good did it do, may I ask? Things have never been in a worse mess for me – if your saint can't do any better than that, I think you should try another one!'

'How can you be so cruel? You know it was for your sake that I adopted her as my intercessor—'

'Did I ask you to do that? Have you ever asked me if I want your prayers and pleadings? No, of course not – and you go blindly on your way, sure you know what's best, and the whole household is thrown into uproar because—'

'Because Floria hated me! Because she wanted me to suffer! If you must blame someone, blame that awful woman! She—'

'She had a bit of a crisis – a brainstorm – she didn't mean—'

'She scratched out my eyes in that portrait! You think that's nothing? She meant to harm me, and she did. She pierced me to the heart when she took away my saint, and she meant to harm you too!'

'That's just your crazy imagination.'

'No, you're wrong, she was secretly causing your ailments, and I'll prove it!' She swept round, her silk gown gleaming in the thin rays of sunshine coming through the shutters. 'I know you have something to tell us, my dear Gregory. Your botanist friend found poison among her herbs, did he not?'

'I don't want to hear another word about it!' shouted Ruggiero. 'Floria would never have harmed me! Floria—'

'Yes, say it, say it! Floria loved you! She couldn't bear it when you married me, and she has took her revenge!'

Her husband threw out a hand in a gesture that mimicked a blow. Greg thought the time had come to put an end to this furore. He set down the cardboard carton with a decided thump on a side table. Man and wife started in alarm, then stepped farther apart from each other, breathing in deeply, like opponents in a boxing ring when the bell rings.

'Let's all sit down and try to behave like civilized people, shall we?' Greg suggested. 'And when we do discuss what Liz and I have found out, can we do it without raising our voices?'

'Huh! I think I'm justified in saying what I think—'

'Ruggiero, you were shouting loud enough to be heard by Cristina in the kitchen,' Liz said, but with a soothing note in her voice. 'It's better to keep things a bit more gentle, don't you think?'

'Well, I suppose I . . .' Ruggiero was comforted a little by her manner. 'I've had a bad couple of days,' he groaned. 'Yesterday was bad enough with my party bosses, but when I came home . . .'

'When you came home Rini told you about finding the icon. Yes, I imagine it was a big shock to you,' Greg said.

'My God! I just couldn't believe it at first! Of all the things that could have happened to that confounded thing! Floria took it. I can't seem to come to terms with that.'

'Dearest,' murmured Rini, regret in the word, 'I should have been more considerate in my reaction. But I was in great, great distress.'

'There now,' said Liz with a smile, 'everybody forgives everybody else and we're all friends again, aren't we. And if it's no trouble, I'd be very glad of a cold drink.'

'Oh, good heavens, what a terrible hostess I am! Of course, dearest Liz, come, look at the drinks table, tell me what you would like and if you see nothing there, we'll ring for Cristina.'

Liz chose mineral water from the drinks. Everyone had something with which to ease their throats and give their hands something to do. They all sat down. Then Rini said, in very measured tones: 'You brought back the box of herbs that were stored in Floria's office, Gregory.'

'Yes.'

'And the expert? What did he find?'

'All the ingredients were harmless except for one.'

Ruggiero gasped. Rini smiled triumphantly.

'And what was the one exception, Gregory? She was trying to kill my Ruggiero, was she not? By little and little, like someone from the Borgia family!'

Greg sighed. 'The one harmful item is the berry from the privet bush.'

Since they were speaking English, he used the English word. Neither of the Ardiccis recognized it. '*Ligustro*,' he translated.

'The hedging plant?'

'Yes.'

'But that never has berries.'

'It never reaches that stage in most gardens because hedging is kept well clipped. But if you let it grow on, it flowers.'

'No it doesn't—'

'Yes it does,' Liz intervened. 'It has little bunches of cream flowerlets and to my mind they smell horrible, though some people don't mind it. But some people like mock orange, and I can't stand that either.'

She was chatting to take the gravity out of the situation.

Since neither of her listeners had the least idea what mock orange was, they listened in troubled silence, without passion.

'The berries of the privet bush,' Greg went on, 'are poisonous—'

'I knew it!' Rini cried.

'But not poisonous enough to kill an adult, Rini.'

'What?'

'That's what my botanist says. And he showed me a text book that supports it. Privet berries could kill a child if eaten in enough quantities, but an adult would survive.' He got up, went to the box, and picked out the jar labelled 'Vaccinium'. 'The quota of privet berries in this jar isn't large enough to do much harm.'

'But – but – they can have an effect?' She was insistent.

'I imagine so. They would cause digestive upsets.'

Ruggiero put his head in his hands. 'Dear God,' he whispered. 'Why?'

In a moment Rini was up and by his side. 'My darling,' she said, kneeling beside him, 'that's in the past. Everything will be fine now.' She put a protective arm around his bowed shoulder. Looking up, she said in a low voice, 'My treasured friends, forgive me if I ask you to go now. My poor love has had too much to bear for the moment.'

Anything else that might have been said was rather gladly forgone. As they gently closed the big front door behind them, Liz looked at Greg in relief.

'What d'you think will happen next?' she asked as they got in the car.

'I think they'll cry in each other's arms and then go to bed and make love.'

She smiled and sighed. 'There's a good idea in there somewhere,' she murmured.

She circled the parterre and made a slow turn into the drive. Greg said, 'Look!'

'At what?'

'The hedges! It never occurred to me before, but these are privet hedges.'

The bushes had been allowed to grow tall and thick over the years, but now she came to examine them, Liz could see that these were indeed ordinary, run-of-the-mill privet, as grown in gardens all over Europe.

'And once when I arrived here, there was a ladder and shears, and Ernesto had just been clipping them,' Greg went on.

'So he could leave a twig or two so that it put out flowers and then berries . . .'

'Yes, and collect them and . . . and give them to Cristina to put in one of Floria's little jars, because Floria's office is right next door to her kitchen.'

The car was creeping along as they spoke. She said, 'I hate this place,' and changed gear so that they went off with a tremendous jerk.

At the gates, Ernesto glanced out of his lodge window but didn't emerge. The gates opened. They drove out.

'Can it really be that the pair of them have been – scheming – plotting – to kill Ruggiero?' Liz asked in a wondering tone.

'It seems possible.'

'But he gave them this great job – posh little house next to the villa, decent salary, all sorts of perks like kitchen left-overs and stuff.'

'Didn't somebody once say that if you do somebody a good turn, they'll never forgive you?'

'Hmm.' She was silent while she negotiated the passage down the narrow track to the main road. Then she said: 'The trouble with that clever remark about doing good turns is . . . I can't imagine Ruggiero ever doing one. Not unless he was going to get something in return. Something important. So it makes you wonder why he gave the gate-keeping job to Ernesto, doesn't it?'

'It does, now you mention it.'

'So now the big question is: Why did Ruggiero give the jobs to the Stresos?'

'I wish I knew.'

'Should we stop off again in the village? Try to collect a bit of gossip?'

He shook his head. 'They're all still getting themselves together after their afternoon break. We could hang about for an hour or more before we actually got into conversation with anybody useful. No, let's call it a day.'

'That gets my vote.'

That evening there was a little report among the television news about the forthcoming funeral of Floria Massigna, rela-tive of former Senator Ruggiero Ardicci. Liz raised her eyebrows when she heard it. 'I wonder if Rini will attend now she knows what Floria did?'

'And if she does, will she wear your clever black dress or one of her multicoloured outfits, just to show how she really feels?'

'Oh, don't!'

'Are we going to go?'

'No, we are not!'

The phone rang on the bedside table. Greg picked up. It was Yuri Tamaldov. 'Gregory, I just wanted to explain. I have not yet had opportunity to explain myself to Rini, as you wished me to. You forgive me?'

'Why the delay?'

'Well, it seems there is trouble at Villa Stefani. I ring them, Rini's voice is thick with tears, she says no I mustn't come to see her, she doesn't wish to speak to me on telephone, and so I have put off that important interview. You understand it is not my fault.'

'Very well.'

'Do you know why there is this emotional disturbance?'

'You'd better wait until Rini wants to tell you herself.'

'Is something bad?' The deep voice was full of what seemed genuine concern and he was sounding more Russian than usual in his use of English.

'It's not very good – but it's not my place to say.'

'Atmosphere at villa seems very bad. I really should be there, to help make things more calm.'

'You must do as you think fit,' Greg said.

'But you don't advise me to go?'

'I'm not offering any advice.'

'Very discreet.' A hesitation. 'I think something serious is wrong in that house. Tell me if you agree.'

'Dr Tamaldov, I'm just going to go out to have dinner. If you don't mind, I'll say goodbye now.'

'Then goodbye, *bon appétit*, and now I am very worried.'

'What was that about?' Liz inquired, turning from the consideration of what to wear for the evening.

'Tamaldov doing a bit of fishing. Rini's told him not to go visiting at the villa and he claims he's very anxious.'

'Oh, you always seem to think the worst of him. He's not a bad person, Greg.'

'So you say. But the last thing Ruggiero needs at the moment is some handsome Russian interfering in his marriage.'

She gave a shrug that acknowledged the truth in that.

While she changed, the prince rang his grandmother to keep her au fait with what was going on. '*Du lieber Himmel!*' she exclaimed on hearing his brief summary. 'You're going to put all this before the police, of course?'

'Well, I'm not eager to do that because I've got no actual proof of the Stresos being the culprits. The poison spray has been accepted as an accident, and if anyone appears guilty about the privet berries, it's Floria.'

'Mmm . . . What does your little lady friend think?'

'She agrees that we need to find a reason for all this. Otherwise Inspector Novelli is going to tell me to get lost.' He smiled to himself. It seemed that his haughty grandmother was beginning to accept his attachment to a commoner. Not so long ago, if she referred to Liz at all, she called her 'that peasant' or 'that dress-shop girl'.

They went out to see an American film dubbed into Italian, had a late dinner, and fell into bed soon after midnight.

Their plan for Thursday was to get to the village of Tabardi while it was still engaged in its morning activities. They were foiled by a telephone call from Rini Ardicci.

'Darling Liz,' she carolled. 'Ruggiero and I are coming to Rome on business, and we would very much like to take you and Gregory out to lunch, as a thank you for all you've been doing for us. We have booked a table at *Il Libeccio*, where you know, they're famous for dishes from the south of Italy. Would that suit you?'

Liz consulted Greg, who thought about it and suggested they should accept. 'We need to know the score with those two,' he remarked. 'What do you think?'

'I think we should go. We can do our visit to Tabardi in the evening.'

Liz wanted to use the intervening hour or two before lunch to look at the department stores. Greg went with her to the city centre but spent the time in shops selling musical scores. A choir for whom he arranged recitals needed copies of an early work by Monteverdi. They met to take a taxi to *Il Libeccio*, which was in a street not far from the Pantheon. It proved to have a large courtyard covered by an awning, so that it was possible to have lunch in the open without being scorched by the afternoon sun.

Rini was back to wearing black, since she was out before the public and wicked gossip might start if she wore bright colours. Ruggiero was in a well-tailored suit of black wild silk. He took charge of ordering the meal with gusto.

The first course was linguini with lobster, then ravioli with mushrooms and lamb – at which Liz shuddered but made no remark, simply easing the meat away to the edge of her plate. With these came first a sharp white wine and then a rich red. Lastly there was a dessert consisting of layers of pastry laden with cream and chocolate.

Rini, thinking of her husband's health, attempted once or twice to influence the ordering but failed. He was in a strange mood – aggressively good-humoured, very managerial. His handsome pale features took on an unhealthy flush by the time they finished eating. Rini watched him with anxiety.

As their coffee was brought, he made the announcement that was clearly the main reason for having them to lunch.

'The . . . er . . . the icon . . . Rini and I went to the bank this morning and put it in our strongbox. I don't want any more anxiety over that relic. Rini agrees with me – don't you, darling?'

'Of course.' She said it with determination, but her expression was downcast. Liz felt a certain sympathy. To have found this missing treasure, only to have it locked away – that seemed hard. Yet it was good sense on Ruggiero's part.

'I want to ask you not to speak of the icon to anyone,' Ruggiero went on, with an earnest glance from Liz to Greg and back again. 'Rini and I have discussed the matter, and she agrees that it probably belongs . . . well . . . we can't tell where it belongs, I suppose, but surely it ought not to be in a private house.' He turned to his wife for assent, and she nodded.

'So it's to stay in a strongbox in your bank,' murmured Greg.

'It's safe there.'

'Yes.'

'You sound unconvinced.'

'I'm convinced it's safe, but I'm not sure that's where it belongs.'

'It belongs with someone who treasures it,' Rini burst out in protest.

'My love, we talked about this,' said Ruggiero sternly. 'Of course you love and revere Saint Olga, but the painting is clearly very old and may be very, very valuable. We cannot have it hanging on a wall in your boudoir.' He nodded towards his guests. 'Liz and Greg would not speak of it to anyone, I'm sure, yet good sense tells us it might be in danger if it were hanging there.'

Greg took a moment then said: 'Liz and I aren't the only people who know about it.'

'Oh, you mean Yuri?' Rini smiled in agreement. 'Of course, he was there when it first went missing and I admit, I wasn't discreet at that time. But Yuri is a good friend and a Russian. He understands the depth of my feeling for the painting.'

'That may be true. But he probably has a good idea of its value to the previous owners.' Rini frowned, but couldn't meet his eye. 'Where did it really come from, Rini?'

'I don't know,' she cried, 'I honestly don't know!'

Heads turned at her voice. 'Ssh,' warned her husband.

Liz felt that Greg had been left to handle this difficult matter on his own long enough. 'Rini dear,' she said, 'I think we all know that the icon must have come from a church or somewhere like that. Come on now, admit it. You must always have had the feeling that it might be stolen.'

'No!'

'Could you put your hand on the painting and swear by your saint that it was come by honestly?'

Rini's eyes filled with tears. She said nothing.

There was a little pause while they all gave her the chance to recover her composure. Then Greg said: 'Yuri is an exile from his homeland who might feel some responsibility for the icon.'

'Responsibility? What do you mean?' Rini demanded uncertainly.

'I think you should talk to him about it. He might not share your idea of keeping it, even safe in a bank vault.'

'But I know Yuri so well! I know his heart! He wouldn't want to deprive me of the comfort . . .' Her words trailed off. She stifled a sob, then stumbled to her feet. 'Excuse me – I don't feel very well.'

She hurried towards the archway that led to the restaurant interior. Liz glanced at Greg then went after her. She found her in the ornate ladies' cloakroom, sitting on a brocaded chair and crying her eyes out. Luckily there were no others present.

There was nothing to do except lean over her and wait for the tears to subside. Tissues in plenty were available from an enamelled box. Once the mopping process had been completed, Rini studied herself in the mirror.

'I look a wreck,' she groaned. 'Liz dear, would you go and fetch my handbag from the table? I need my make-up.'

'In a moment.' She stood behind her so as to meet her gaze in the mirror. 'Rini, there's something I must say to you. Greg wouldn't want to, because he feels he'd be . . . well . . . a tell-tale. But the fact is that Yuri is in touch with the Russian authorities.'

'Oh, of course, he has friends trying to arrange his return to—'

'That may be so, but he may also have suggested to them that he can find and return a missing relic.'

'No!' Rini threw up her hands and clutched at her dark hair.

'I don't want to go into all the details, but Greg and I know that Yuri might not have been absolutely straight with you on more than one matter.'

'What do you mean?'

'I think you should ask him yourself.'

'You are saying that I should accuse him? Of what? He has been so good to us, you cannot ask me to turn against him.'

Liz shook her head and looked away. 'I'll get your make-up. Then Greg and I are going to leave, and what you do about Yuri is up to you.'

Rini sat staring at her reflection. Liz hurried back to the patio where she found the two men engaged in a discussion about cars, just to bring life back to normal.

'She's better?' Ruggiero inquired, sympathetic yet impatient. 'My poor sweetheart, she lets her emotions run away with her rather too often.'

'She's just going to freshen up and then she'll be back.' As she leaned over to pick up Rini's handbag Liz said softly to Greg, 'I think we should make ourselves scarce. I've been telling Rini she ought to talk to Yuri.'

He was surprised but hid it well. Guessing that they were

about to escape from this debacle, Ruggiero said with some envy, 'Ah, you have such an easy, close relationship, you two. But then, you're young. You don't have troubles like us old *bavosi*.'

His guests could have told him they had had their troubles even though they weren't old and doddery. Instead Liz took out the make-up bag and hurried off. Ruggiero said to Greg: 'So can I rely on you not to speak of the painting? I'd like to have some time to think what to do about it.'

'It's possible Dr Tamaldov might be able to help you there.'

'You think so? You mean he's interested in religious things? I never got that impression.'

'But he might have connections in Russia who could help in getting the icon back to its proper place.'

'That would have to be handled with discretion,' Ruggiero said in alarm. 'I don't want the Vatican taking an interest! If it were known that I . . . that Rini . . .' He groaned. 'Well, I'd first have to persuade her that she must give it up.'

Liz returned. Greg rose. 'Thank you for a lovely lunch,' Liz said. 'This is a beautiful restaurant.'

'Oh, yes, and all the rage at the moment – although of course in August . . .' He rose, they shook hands in farewell, then he hesitated. 'I know I can rely on you not to breathe a word about the supposed theft, and the identity of the thief? Poor Floria – we wouldn't want her good name to suffer.'

'Certainly not,' Greg agreed. They asked to have their good wishes passed on to Rini, still in the cloakroom fixing her make-up. With some relief, they took their leave.

Outside in the street, it was hot and airless. 'Let's go back to the Pastorella and relax,' Liz sighed. 'I need to let that extraordinary lunch settle down a bit.'

'The next item on the agenda is our visit to Tabardi.'

'Where we may find a reason to believe Ernesto is a murderer.' She took his arm and leaned against him. 'I don't really want to go, Greg.'

He said nothing to that. Instead he hailed a passing taxi. Luckily it was an ultra-modern vehicle with perfect air-conditioning. They settled down in relief.

'I'll go,' he said. 'There's really no need to drag you there.'

'I wouldn't be any use anyway. I don't even speak the language.'

'Right.'

'But of course you feel you have to follow this up, because if you don't, Ernesto might actually succeed in killing Ruggiero.'

'Well . . . Only if our theories are correct.'

'But you think they are.'

He nodded.

'I knew you'd say that.' She patted his knee. 'Would it help if I came along and smiled at the locals?'

'My angel,' he said, 'your smile is always a boon and a blessing.'

# SIXTEEN

The evening air was cool and fresh. The village square was gleaming in the light of its elderly street lamps. A young trio of musicians was playing near the tourist information bureau, and a few couples were dancing.

Liz and Greg had agreed to have their evening meal in Tabardi. It seemed a good way to account for their presence, and in any case, as Liz remarked, they had to eat but it should be sparingly after that enormous lunch.

At first it seemed that the *albergo* could offer nothing but pizza. 'No, no,' groaned Liz. But after some discussion the proprietor agreed that he could provide a chilled soup, followed by an omelette and salad.

'And to drink?' he inquired.

'Not wine,' murmured Liz. 'I've had enough wine for one day.'

Greg entered into a discussion on the topic. The innkeeper grinned and said: 'Don't worry! I won't offer you anything made from the Stefani grapes!'

'What's happening about them?'

'The *signore* called in a contractor, who came this morning and carted them all away to be disposed of as hazardous waste.' He produced a rather worn wine list. 'All of these are quite healthy, I assure you, *signore*.'

To please him, Greg ordered a dry white wine and a large

bottle of mineral water with which to dilute it. They sat back to wait for their meal, studying their surroundings.

The inn had folding front doors, now open to the evening air. Outside there were half a dozen tables illuminated by a string of hanging lanterns. Three were occupied by visitors, some of them from abroad judging by the wisps of conversation they could hear. Within the restaurant there were a few tables for four and one long table where the locals were lounging. A television in one corner had a group of young men close by, watching football.

Their soup was brought by none other than Signora Federa, Armeno's mother. 'Good evening, *signorina*, *signore*,' she said, with a smile. 'It's nice to see you again.'

'You work long hours,' said Greg.

'Ah well, such is life.'

'How is Armeno?'

She clasped her hands and shook them before her in a token of thanksgiving. 'Improving. He begins to understand that the horses are gone and that he'll never see them again.' She stood a little closer to the table and added quietly, 'I found a little gift under a vase in my parlour. Thank you, *signore*.'

He nodded it away. 'Give my kind regards to Armeno.'

She bustled away. Liz asked, 'Is he OK?'

'She says he's getting there.'

They tried the soup, which proved to be a delicious thick mixture of green vegetables and herbs. When the omelette arrived, it was brought by the innkeeper himself. He laid everything before them then said, 'Pia tells me you're the foreigner who's been kind to Armeno.'

Greg gave an embarrassed shrug.

'We all appreciate that, you know, *signore*. There's not much kindness up at the villa as a rule.'

'They've had their troubles there.'

The innkeeper grunted and moved off.

'What was that about?'

'General grousing about the Ardiccis.'

'Never mind the Ardiccis. We want to get them talking about the Stresos.'

'Patience. Eat some omelette.'

She obeyed. 'This is jolly good!' To her surprise, she was quite hungry. And the salad was absolutely what she needed to satisfy her nagging conscience about the non-vegetarian lunch.

Pia Federa reappeared with a basket of fresh rolls and some butter. 'There's *torta di fragole* if you'd like it afterwards.'

'Thank you.' He asked Liz what she thought.

'Could we have yoghurt?' she wondered.

The word was recognizable. Signora Federa said eagerly, 'I'll ask Dino,' and hurried off.

'We've got to eat everything,' Greg suggested. 'It's their way of saying thank you for trying to help Armeno.'

Liz went on with her omelette, then said: 'We'd better drink some wine, then, and sit back and relax. Perhaps she'll come and chat if we do.'

The innkeeper arrived as they were finishing the main course. 'As to yoghurt,' he began, 'we don't offer it fresh, but would you like frozen? It's home-made. Strawberry, peach, melon, chocolate . . .'

'Everything's home-made, is it?' Greg inquired.

'Oh, yes, my wife's the cook except for the pizza, and that's made next door. That's what's ordered mostly. But Gabi – my wife – she's quite talented. She made the soup and your omelette.'

'My compliments to the chef,' Greg said, laughing.

'Thank you, sir, she'll be delighted. So what about this yoghurt, then?'

Greg reported the list of flavours. Liz chose melon. 'Tell him I've never had a melon yoghurt before.'

Dino was delighted to have her remark passed on to him. 'Ver' good,' he said. He smiled at her and she smiled back. He collected up their plates and went off to the kitchen, beaming with pleasure.

The yoghurt was delicious. Dino stood by while she sampled it, and laughed out loud when she said in her English-Italian, '*Benissimo!*'

They ordered coffee. It was brought by a plump, energetic woman in a blue dress and snowy-white apron. It was easy to guess that this was Gabriella, otherwise Gabi, the cook and wife to Dino.

She poured the coffee for them from an earthenware pot. 'You visiting the villa, no?' she said in English.

'Yes, my friend Liz here, she has been helping the *signora* with her mourning dresses.'

'*Cosa?*'

'Dresses for the funeral,' he translated.

'Ah.' She turned her attention to Liz. 'You are a . . .' she made stitching motions with her hands.

'Dressmaker. Yes. And I work for fashion shops.'

'Signora Ardicci, she wears the fine clothes.'

'Yes indeed. But of course, nothing suitable for a funeral.'

Gabi made a little grimace. 'Next week, the funeral. Some must go, of course, to show our respect. And a little, we approved Signorina Floria – buys not much from the village but some things. Signora Ardicci, she knows nothing of keeping the house. And when Cristina and Ernesto leave, perhaps nothing at all will be taken from the village shops, I think.'

'Ernesto and Cristina are leaving soon.'

'Yes, Armeno says one month.'

Her husband sauntered up to join the chat, bringing as his excuse a little bowl of mints. 'Ernesto . . .' he said, and added in English much poorer than his wife's, 'he not lasted long with the gates-keep.'

'When did he start at the job?' Greg asked. Dino looked puzzled. Greg put it into Italian. He said in apology to Liz, 'This will go better if they can speak easily.'

She nodded agreement.

Dino was eager to take over the conversation. 'The *signore* hired him just over a year ago. To drive the cars, look after them, and see to the gates. He was also to do a bit of gardening, and this tale that Ernesto somehow harmed Signorina Floria with the spray for the grapevine, that's nonsense.'

'What makes you say so?'

'Ernesto – he knows about things like that, so I say although he had to take the blame, I'd make a bet that it was that Russian wife.'

'Signora Ardicci?'

'Of course. You know the Russians, very tempestuous!'

'But how could Signora Ardicci be spraying the vine?'

'Oh, she doesn't need to spray the vine. Just paint the poison on the grapes Signorina Floria would eat.'

'But nobody knew the *signorina* would eat the grapes—'

'Oh, that's the story that we have to believe, and of course Ernesto has to take the blame but if you want my opinion it was the Russian woman. Either that, or Ardicci himself.'

Greg kept his expression very grave. 'You support Ernesto. He's a good friend of yours, I suppose – born here, you went to school together . . .'

'Ah . . .'

'Dino knows him a little,' said Gabi. 'But no one can say he's a good friend to Ernesto. Ernesto keeps himself to himself.'

'More since Chiara,' said her husband, nodding.

'Who's Chiara?'

There was a slight pause. Then Gabi said, 'We stand here gossiping and look, there's a customer waving at you from outside, Dino.'

'Where – Oh yes, of course. Excuse me, *signore*, duty calls.' He hurried out to the other diners.

'I'll fetch fresh coffee for you,' said Gabi, and went quickly towards the kitchen.

'Gee!' murmured Liz in surprise. 'What brought that on?'

'No idea. Dino mentioned somebody called Chiara, and his wife shut him up at once.'

'Who's Chiara?'

'No idea.' He gave her a summary of the conversation but it seemed uninformative.

'I tell you what, she's "the other woman",' Liz suggested with a faint hint of enjoyment. 'We stirred up a memory of a domestic drama.'

'Ha!' he rejoined. 'I don't think Ernesto ever had "another woman" – just remember how he and Cristina were absolutely wrapped up in each other when he'd been in trouble.'

'We–ell . . . That's true.'

They sipped what was left of the coffee in their cups. It was cold by now. When the fresh pot came, it was brought by Pia Federa.

By now it was nearing ten o'clock. 'Still here?' Greg remarked as she poured for them. 'When does your day finish?'

'When the last customer leaves, *signore*,' she said, without the least hint of complaint.

'You've always worked for the *albergo*?'

'Since my husband died, yes. Of course, in winter, I'm only needed part-time.'

'That must have made it hard for you when Armeno was little.'

'Well, then, of course, he was at school.' She sighed and smiled, pleased to have someone take an interest in her son. 'He never made much of his schooling, but the other children understood and played with him. And when I had to work at weekends, neighbours kept an eye on him.'

'Is that when Ernesto took an interest in him? He was a neighbour?'

'Nearby, yes. Cristina used to bake little cakes for my poor Armeno, and then he and his friends would play "picnic" in her garden.'

'Cristina is a very good cook.'

'Oh yes, a wonderful cake every Easter, and she used to make little sweets with sugar and almonds – the children loved those, so of course Chiara was very popular.'

Greg was about to ask: 'Who's Chiara?' but before he could utter a word Pia drew in a sharp breath and spoke first. 'Excuse me, I'm needed in the kitchen.' Within seconds she was gone.

Greg looked at Liz. 'I heard,' she said. 'The name seems to be an absolute show-stopper. You were talking about Armeno and then what happened?'

He explained.

'So Chiara's not "the other woman", she's a child.'

'*Was* a child. Played with Armeno. Armeno's what? Sixteen? So Chiara must be about the same age.'

'If she was still around, would Ernesto and Cristina have her with them at the gate-lodge?'

He thought about it. 'If you picture the house, there isn't enough room for a family, is there? I imagine it's always a couple that get the job.'

'I bet she packed up and left when they moved to the gate-house,' Liz suggested. 'Career prospects hereabouts seem rather limited.'

'Could be. Perhaps that's why they don't like to talk about her – perhaps she had a row with her parents about going away.'

They sipped their coffee. Greg poured wine and added mineral water. 'We've got to keep on drinking and ordering things or we'll have to leave,' he said.

The audience for the football match had grown. An old man with a head of thick grey hair had been left alone at the long table. There was a roar from the TV set, the watchers cheered. The old man struggled to his feet and with a glance of contempt limped across to their table.

'Absolute nonsense!' he said in Italian. 'Twenty-two strong young men paid huge sums of money to kick a ball about! What's the world coming to?'

Greg laughed. 'My grandmother says things like that.'

'Ah. She's the grand lady who was doing the decorations at the villa. Drove past quite often but she never stopped in the village.' He gave a wink. 'She was lucky! Managed to leave before the cops and all that.' He studied Greg for a moment. 'You're the foreigner I was talking to when this beautiful young lady drove up and took you away.'

'Quite right. I'm Greg, this is Liz.'

'*Leez* – now that's French for lily.' He gave her a gallant bow. '*Bienvenue à mon village, mademoiselle! Je m'appelle Filippo.*'

Liz understood that perfectly. '*Merci, monsieur, mais je ne suis pas Française, je suis Anglaise.*'

'Liz is short for Elizabeth,' Greg explained.

'Ah, difficult English name,' said the old man in English, not the least put out. 'I speak much languages, I chat to travellers, if they like history I tell about the village.'

'Sit down, have a drink,' Greg invited. He twitched a clean glass from an empty table to pour for him. The old man eased himself gingerly to a chair and accepted the glass of wine.

'So you're the local historian,' Greg prompted.

'If someone asks. Romans, the Pope, all that. But to tell truth, nothing much happen around here any more.'

'The death of Signorina Massigna doesn't count for much?'

'Oh, her. Housekeeper – she was OK but to us, no big deal. She is not missed.'

'But it had a big effect on Ernesto and Cristina. They lost their jobs.'

'Ah. But you see, nobody ever stay long at the villa. Rafaele and Alizia, they are fired to give the place to Ernesto and Cristina. That's the way it is.'

'I suppose Ernesto was chosen because he's good with cars. Or was it Cristina's cooking?'

Filippo's face cracked in a grin. 'You think Don Ruggiero knew anything about Cristina's cooking? *Macché!* Of course he had reasons but nothing to do with how good Cristina cook or how Ernesto drive cars.'

'Well, whatever the reason, he's sent them packing,' Liz pointed out.

'Packing?'

'He's sent them away with nothing.'

'Oh, he did that just while he was angry,' said Filippo. 'And of course they must go. But they'll get good *ricompensa*, I would take the bet.'

'I don't think so,' said Greg. 'Even if they were to take him to court—'

The old man was scornful. 'They don' need to go to court! They *get* the job, they *lose* the job, but they still have the string to pull.'

'You mean they got the job in the first place by pulling strings? What influence could they use?'

'You don' understand. Don Ruggiero must be good with his *rinomanza* – what is it, reputation? – for the politics. Bad enough he has a Russian wife, but also—' He broke off, as if he'd thought better of it.

'What?' urged Liz. 'He's done something his party wouldn't like? Bribed someone – something to do with money?'

'What does he care about money? Plenty in foreign places, those markets that do well all the time – no, it is a matter of family.'

'His family? Bringing disgrace on his family name?'

'Not *his* family,' growled Filippo.

For a moment no one spoke. Then Liz said, 'This is to do with Ernesto's daughter, isn't it?'

The old man looked down at the table. His shoulders sagged. After a long moment he said, 'I talk too much. And of course, it's all *fasullo*. A few glasses and all you hear is nonsense.'

He dragged himself to his feet. He looked at the crowd of men watching the television and sighed. He tossed off the remains of the wine in his glass. 'I should take up football,' he muttered and shaking his head, he made his way out to the street.

When he had disappeared from view Liz said, 'So now we know who Chiara is.'

'But we don't know what happened.'

'Whatever it was, it's why Ernesto and Cristina hate Ruggiero.'

'And to keep them quiet, he gave them the job at the gate-house.'

'And . . .' Greg fell silent then went on: 'They took the job so as to be there on the spot, and kill him off without being accused of murder.'

This thought kept them silent for some time. A group of new customers came in and settled at a table. Dino appeared to take their order. Though he had to pass Greg and Liz, he kept his head averted.

'We're not in favour any more,' Liz observed.

'So it seems. We might as well give up, Liz – let's go.'

He left an ample supply of money to pay the bill. They went out into the dining area lit by the hanging lanterns and there was Pia Federa clearing the crockery from the vacated tables.

'Speak to her again, Greg,' Liz urged. 'She's got a soft spot for you.'

He felt unwilling. It seemed like taking an unfair advantage. But after all, they were trying to prevent a killing. With an inward sigh, he stopped alongside the table where Pia was working.

Liz stood aside. If Pia could be persuaded to talk, it was likely she'd do it if there wasn't a witness.

She watched the exchange between the two, which was brief. At first reluctant, Pia seemed to change her mind and spoke rapidly to him. He listened, nodding or shaking his head as seemed appropriate to what he was told. Then Pia picked up her tray with determination and hurried away.

Liz took Greg's arm as he rejoined her. 'Well?'

'It's what you might expect, in some aspects.' He led her out of the café's dining area and into the street. They made their way towards the car park.

'Chiara Streso was a couple of years ahead of Armeno in school. A very pretty girl but headstrong. She got a job as chambermaid at the villa – I suppose she was the predecessor to Sara, that little shy woman. After a couple of months, she was seen to be wearing a pretty little pair of earrings – a present from the boss, no doubt. And her father gave her a lecture and made her give up the job.'

'That sounds good sense.'

'Next thing, Chiara runs away from home. The rumour is that she was seen in Rome wearing expensive clothes. The locals deduce that Ruggiero was keeping her. Ernesto went after her but she never came home. Nobody knows where she is now.'

'When did all this happen?'

'Early last year. Then just before Christmas it seems Ernesto went up to the villa and had an interview with Don Ruggiero, and then he and Cristina got the job at the lodge.'

They reached the car park and paused beside the Toyota. 'What do you think – blackmail?'

'It seems likely.'

'Oh Lord.'

Greg leaned against the car. 'The problem is, can we take this to the police? It's just village gossip, and you know the local cops don't seem keen to help Ruggiero.'

'Couldn't you go to someone higher up?'

'I don't know anybody higher up.'

'What about your musical friends? Don't they have any friends or relations in the police force?'

'I doubt it. Besides, *Liebchen*, most of them are away on holiday with their kids.'

She made a face. 'They've never let you down before.'

'Well, we've never been in Rome in August before.'

'Couldn't you go to your embassy and ask someone there to do something?'

'Oh, good heavens, that's the last thing I'd want to do! My family doesn't want to get involved with diplomats because we like to keep a low profile.'

Liz unlocked the car. As it chirped, Greg drew back. 'Although . . .' he murmured.

'Although what?'

'My grandmother might know somebody in Rome who could speak to someone a bit higher up in the police force . . .'

Liz gave him a glance of amazement. 'You want to ask dear old Grossmutti for some help?'

'It's not that I want to,' he protested. 'It's just that . . . I can't think of anything else.'

# SEVENTEEN

His grandmother's reply was simple. 'No.'

'You mean you really don't know anyone in Rome that could help us?'

'I'm not going to ask him. Last time I saw him was at a soirée here in Geneva – one of those United Nations things – and he practically ignored me.'

'But this is important!'

'Only to you!'

'It's quite important to Ruggiero, don't you think? He might end up dead if we don't do something.'

'I'm not sure I care what happens to Ruggiero.' It was clear that Nicoletta von Hirtenstein was in a bad mood.

'Grossmutti, talk sense! You've still got his ballroom to decorate. You're not likely to do that if he's dead.'

'Oh.'

'Please tell me someone I can approach.'

In the end she told him that she herself would telephone the Honourable Patrizio Rinaldi-Giuletto, deputed to parliament on behalf of the Centre for the Study of Juvenile Criminality.

'What am I to say to him?' she asked.

'Say that Ernesto Streso, at the gate-lodge of the Villa Stefani, should be retained for questioning about the use of a poisonous substance.'

'I thought you were telling me he was plotting to murder Ruggiero?'

'I think he is. But if we can scare him off by having him questioned, that's enough, perhaps.'

'But all that was already written off as an accident.'

'So it was, but the poison was meant for Ruggiero, not Floria, so he's killed one person already – and although it was an accident, it was intended to be a murder.'

'You're not asking me to say all that to Patri?'

'Say whatever will convince him to get in touch with the local force.'

'Well, it's rather late to be bothering an old man, but I'll see to it.'

'Ring me back and let me know what's happening.'

'Huh!' she said, and rang off.

Something more than an hour later, when they were back at the Pastorella, she got in touch on his mobile to say that Don Patrizio was already aware of some kind of trouble at the Villa Stefani. He was willing to speak to the commandante on behalf of Signor von Hirtenstein, of whom he had heard. He would do so in the morning.

'Thank you, Grossmutti.'

'You had better let Ruggiero know what's happening.'

'It's late. Tomorrow's the funeral – I'll leave it till that's all over.'

'Are you going?'

'No, you know I only met Floria a couple of times.'

'So when the police want you, they can reach you at . . . what's your girlfriend's hotel?'

'The Pastorella. And don't forget I'm known here as Signor Corona.' It was the family custom not to use any titles when abroad, but instead to use the local form of the word 'crown'.

'Very well. Goodnight.'

When he reported all this to Liz, she said with some hesitation: 'It's a good sign that she asked for the "girlfriend's hotel"?'

He grinned. 'Is that what you pick out as important?'

'Well, it's important to us, isn't it?'

That was true. They hugged and went to bed, very late. So in the morning they were slow to get going and only managed to scrape into the breakfast room before it closed. They were drinking their second cup of coffee when Greg was approached by their receptionist.

'*Signore*. Inspector Novelli just rang to ask if you were in the hotel, and he instructed me to ask you to remain until he can get here.'

'Tell him I'll be here.'

'Oh, excuse me, *signore*, he disconnected.'

So it was an instruction, not a request. Sighing inwardly, he resigned himself to another tetchy session with the inspector.

They waited for him in the hotel's little bar, still in the process of being cleaned. Novelli came stamping in about half an hour later.

'Signor Corona or Hirtenstein or whoever you are, you'll be pleased to hear that according to instructions handed down from the highest echelons, I interviewed Ernesto Streso first thing this morning and found nothing to add to the report already submitted.'

'What?' cried Greg, appalled. 'You went there without contacting me first?'

Novelli glared. 'Believe it or not, I'm quite capable of conducting a police inquiry without help from you! Haven't you done enough damage to that poor numbskull already? He had a busy day ahead of him what with the funeral and all that, and you make me go and stir up all his guilt-feelings about Signorina Massigna—'

'Be quiet!'

The inspector stopped in mid-tirade.

'If you'd just stop disliking everybody who doesn't share your view on society, you might learn something.'

'Not from you!'

'I've got something to tell you, and if you'll shut up and listen for five minutes, you might realize that Ruggiero Ardicci is in real danger.'

'Of what? Of having a bad attack of indigestion because he eats too much? Let me tell you—'

'Oh, for goodness sake,' exclaimed Liz in English, having listened to this Italian battle of words in growing impatience, 'will you sit down, Inspector, and have a civilized conversation?'

He checked himself, and his upbringing told him that he ought to be polite to a woman – especially a pretty woman. He subsided into a chair, sighing heavily, and glanced about for the barman so as to order a drink. Seeing no one, he banged on the table yelling '*Servizio*!' A startled man in an apron appeared, took Novelli's order, and hurried behind the bar.

Liz said: 'You and I have been extremely worried over things we've found out. Will he listen while we tell him about it? Ask him, Greg.'

Warily, Greg gave him a summary of their activities of the last couple of days. Novelli listened in silence, seizing the wine from the barman when it came and gulping down half the contents. Liz could see he was unimpressed, unconvinced, determined not to be forced to act.

'So you found a few poisonous berries in a set of little jars. Have you any proof that Cristina Streso put them there or even knew of their existence?'

'No, but—'

'And the grapes – if Signorina Massigna decided to eat them to spite Signor Ardicci, does that make Streso a murderer?'

'No, but—'

'And as for this fairytale about a bird flying by—'

'It was a stone.'

'Well, a stone. Can you prove Ernesto Streso threw it?'

'No. No, but that's three times Ruggiero's been in danger. He's been made ill for months by the tisanes his housekeeper was making.'

'And perhaps it was his housekeeper who put the poison berries in the brew.'

'No, Floria loved him. She might have done something foolish in a moment of irritation – like eating his precious grapes – but she would never have intentionally harmed him.'

'In your opinion.'

'In my opinion the intentional building-up of an appearance of ill health was a way of preparing Ruggiero for the final stroke – the parathion. And when that failed, the stone that startled his horse was intended to send him tumbling down a steep hillside where he could have broken his neck.'

Novelli drank the last of his wine. 'And you wanted me to hear all this and then confront Streso with it?'

'Yes.'

'And what – get my superiors to charge him? Any good lawyer would pull that case to pieces.'

'What will you say to your superiors when Streso finally pulls it off and Ruggiero Ardicci dies?'

Novelli made a face. It seemed to say, 'No great loss.'

'You *have* at least informed Ardicci that you're looking at Streso again?'

'What, while the caterers were carrying in all the food and drink for the funeral? Don't be silly, you don't bother a man at a time like that.'

'Inspector,' said Liz, 'please don't shrug this off. Signora Ardicci lives for her husband. Do you want to make her a widow?' She looked at Greg to translate for her.

He grinned. 'Oh, very melodramatic. Tell the *signorina*. I have a career in the police force. I don't want to look a fool and set myself back ten years by taking this tale to the boss.' He got to his feet. 'My advice to you, *Signor Principe Passato*, is to take up polo or stamp collecting.' With an ironic bow, he swept out.

Greg sat watching him go, thinking that the man had a turn for words. The ironic title he'd used meant not only 'former prince' but 'prince who's a bit overcooked'.

'He's an idiot,' cried Liz.

'No, he's got brains but he's biased because of party politics. Ruggiero was in the Senate for a party that Novelli despises, and things being as they are in Italy, that matters a lot.'

'Can you approach the man your grandmother mentioned?'

'I don't think he'd be keen to get involved any further.'

'What are we going to do?'

'I don't know.'

'We ought to tell Ruggiero what we think.'

'*Mon ange*, he'd summon Ernesto to his house and beat him up.'

'Oh, come on – Ruggiero's a bit thick but surely he wouldn't try to hit Ernesto! Ruggiero's a pudgy lazybones and Ernesto's a big, hardy-looking man.'

'All the same—'

'Greg, Ruggiero has to know some time, doesn't he?'

'I suppose so.'

'Ring him and tell him we've got something to say to him.'

'No, he'll have a house full of people now, after the funeral.'

'What does that matter?'

'It's not something you can explain in the middle of a crowd of mourners.'

'Well, we'll go, and hang around until they've left.'

He knew she was right – Ruggiero had to be warned that one of his servants seemed to be planning to kill him. But he also knew that there would be a violent scene when he was told. He didn't want Liz to be there.

'I'll tell you what,' he said. 'I'll go – I'll be offering condolences like everybody else, and then afterwards I'll give him the information.'

'I'm coming too.'

'No, why should you? You scarcely knew Floria, after all. And by the way, shouldn't you be having a run or something? It's days since you went jogging.'

'Oh, it's much too hot now.'

'Well, why don't you go for a swim? If I remember rightly, the hotel folder says a gym called the Marmoreo offers day membership for visitors.'

'We–ell . . .' It was true that she'd taken no exercise for a long time. And to be well-regarded in the fashion trade, you had to stay in trim. The idea of a swim and perhaps a massage in a hotel spa was a lot more appealing than a wake in the house of an Italian politician. 'But I didn't bring a swim-suit . . .'

'Do my ears deceive me? Is this the woman who in the past few days has been through every shopping centre in Rome?'

'Ah . . . You've got a point.'

He was to have the use of the car. He put her in a taxi then retrieved the Toyota from the hotel car park.

As he got on the side road leading to the Villa Stefani, he met several rather good-looking cars going the other way. He deduced that the wake for Floria Massigna was coming to an end. The gates stood wide open to allow the easy passage of visitors.

Cars were parked along the drive. He saw Tamaldov's worn little Fiat, one or two smart vehicles that might belong to the Ardicci circle of friends, some elderly cars and a pickup from some local farm.

In the little circular turn-around in front of the villa's entrance a very glossy limousine had its engine running. Ruggiero was engaged in saying goodbye to a trio of very well-dressed middle-aged men. Something seigneurial about them, and the way Ruggiero was treating them, made him think they were party bosses.

He parked some yards off, among the other cars. By the time he reached the front steps, Ruggiero had spotted him and was waiting to shake hands.

'Good of you to come,' he said. But there was a growl in his voice. He was clearly bored by the whole thing. He waved his guest on towards the dining-room, where canapés and drinks were still available. A cluster of village worthies were

still there, enjoying the largesse and growing somewhat merry
from the effects of too much wine. The catering staff were
beginning to collect up empty serving dishes and load them
on to trolleys to take away.

Ruggiero was summoned to say farewell to another guest.
At the serving table, Ruggiero's lawyer, Don Perriero, was
setting down an empty glass. He saw Greg and came at once
to join him.

'Good morning, *signore*. You didn't come to the church?'

'No, I knew Signora Massigna only briefly.'

'A sad business. However, we had a little conversation, his
colleagues and I, and it seems that the media have lost
interest in the accident with the garden spray. His chances of
standing in the next election have not been greatly harmed,
I'm glad to say.'

Greg listened and nodded. He wasn't the least interested in
Ruggiero's political career. What did attract his attention was
a little scene out on the shady terrace.

Rini Ardicci was deep in conversation with Yuri Tamaldov.
She was listening with both hands up to her cheeks, perhaps
to stem her tears. Tamaldov looked anything but happy.

So it seemed that today he'd decided to tell her the truth
about himself. Perhaps it was a good choice, thought Greg –
a miserable day from the outset that could hardly be made
worse by his confession.

The lawyer finished his little talk about safeguarding
Ruggiero's prospects, glanced at his watch, and took his leave.
Greg picked up a glass of wine and a concoction of seafood
on a sliver of toast. He had just taken a bite when Rini hurried
past him heading for the hall. After her, very slowly, came
Tamaldov. Sombre in a black tunic, grey trousers, and city
shoes, he looked the picture of remorse.

'She took it badly,' he said to Greg.

'I suppose you were expecting that.'

'She is right to despise me. I allowed myself to become
friends with her, instead of treating her as a client. She suffers
now because I was thoughtless.'

Greg wanted to say, 'Stop carrying on like Russian opera,'
but refrained.

Ruggiero was rather curtly getting rid of the mourners from
the village. They had reached the stage where one or two of

them were bursting into song. They were harmonizing the last verse of 'Santa Lucia' as their host urged them towards the door. Out they trooped, their voices rising in song and, from some, in argument. There were only a couple of women among the group, trying to shepherd them away. The men were so drunk that Greg wondered if they were fit to drive home.

Cristina was bustling about gathering up the villa's glasses and silverware to ensure it didn't get loaded with the caterer's supplies. Greg supposed her husband was at the gate-lodge, preparing to close up after the last car left. Ruggiero, after a quick survey of the room, went out to the loggia to make sure there was no guest there who ought to be encouraged to say goodbye.

Tamaldov was viewing the scene with gloom. 'I too shall go,' he announced. 'When Rini comes down again, tell her I leave my soul here, waiting for her forgiveness.'

'I will,' said Greg, doubting he could ever pass on the message in those actual words.

A few moments later the house had that feel of being suddenly deprived of animation. Ruggiero came marching into the drawing-room to pick up one of the remaining glasses of wine.

'Thank heaven that's all over,' he groaned.

'Could we have a word or two?' Greg asked. 'I've something quite important to tell you.'

'What? About the icon? Tamaldov said he had something he wanted to tell Rini on that score.'

'No, this is about Ernesto.'

Ruggiero frowned in perplexity. 'What now? The police were at the lodge early this morning but it seemed they were just checking for their final report.'

'I had a conversation with Inspector Novelli this morning. It seems he didn't speak to you at all?'

'No, why should he – that's all over.'

'No, it isn't, Ruggiero. Remember the privet berries in Floria's herb collection?'

Ruggiero took a big mouthful of his wine. 'Oh, I've decided that was just a mistake.'

'No it wasn't.'

'Look, I've moved on. Floria's in her grave, her stupid theft of the icon is all forgotten—'

There was a slight clash of crockery as one of the little catering trolleys was wheeling away. Cristina was on her hands and knees brushing dropped food into a dustpan. Better to say all this in a less busy place, he thought.

'Could we go to your study?' he suggested.

Ruggiero shrugged. He led the way. They crossed the hall and entered the gloomy room. He threw himself into the swivel chair behind his desk, waved Greg to another, then said: 'Well, what?'

'I believe you employed the daughter of Ernesto and Cristina last year?' Greg began.

Ruggiero sat up erect in his chair. 'What?'

'You've had a series of accidents over the past months. Your health has deteriorated, your housekeeper died from eating poisoned grapes, and you nearly came to grief when your horse shied on the mountain path.'

'What are you saying?'

'I think Cristina put the poison berries in Floria's ingredients so as to make you ill. The poisoned grapes were meant for *you* to eat. Your horse was frightened not by a bird, but by a stone thrown in front of her nose.' He put his hand in his pocket and produced the sliver of black basalt. 'This stone. And Ernesto threw it, I think.'

'But that's – they wouldn't *dare*!'

'Yes they would. In revenge for what happened to Chiara.' Greg leaned forwards so as to look into his face across the desk. 'Don't you see? They took the job you offered as reparation just so as to be near you, to find an opportunity to kill you.'

'No!' It was a cry of angry disbelief.

Greg waited a moment then went on: 'Of course you can disregard what I say. But I think you're in real danger. Ernesto and Cristina have less than a month now to finish the job they started when they came to work here.'

Ruggiero shook his head, but his sallow complexion had gone wax-white. Against the black of his suit, his pallor was startling. 'No,' he groaned. 'No!'

'Floria died, Ruggiero. But she died in your place. You would have sat down and eaten those grapes if they'd still been there, wouldn't you?'

'Oh God! Oh, don't say it! The first grapes from my vine . . . But it was an accident!'

'In one way, yes. Floria was never meant to die. But I think Ernesto knew what was in that old bottle. In fact he may have brought it with him when he moved into the lodge, because from what I hear in the village, he's quite an experienced gardener.'

'What?'

'He had a vine at the house where he used to live. And I'm told he grew very good vegetables. It's not likely he'd make a mistake.'

'But we made an agreement – he was to get a lot more as wages than I ever paid a gate-keeper before. He was doing very well out of it.'

'Out of the loss of his daughter?'

Ruggiero groaned.

'That *stupid* girl! She couldn't really imagine I was going to pay for that flat forever? And the bills she ran up – clothes and shoes and hairdressing and then she wanted jewellery – you know, real sapphires! The whole thing was getting out of hand.'

'So what did you do? You paid her off?'

'You needn't take that tone about it!' he replied with indignation. 'She did well out of it – she kept all her stuff and I gave her a very decent golden handshake.'

'And where did she go?'

'How should *I* know?'

'I was told that Ernesto looked for her. He must have asked you what happened?'

'He – well, he – you know, she'd left home of her own accord in the first place and he was angry with her and disowned her. But then after a while he – he got a letter from her—'

'What did it say?'

Ruggiero shook his head from side to side. 'I told you, she was a stupid girl! Why couldn't she come to terms with what happened? I mean, she could have sold her wardrobe of clothes, used the money I gave her, set herself up in business . . .'

Greg didn't ask, 'What kind of business?' He let a moment go by then asked: 'What was in the letter Ernesto got?'

'It was . . . it was a suicide note.' Ruggiero shuddered. 'But it wasn't my fault! She should have had more sense!'

Greg got up. 'Ruggiero,' he said, 'Novelli told me very

forcibly that he thought the police couldn't make a case in court against Ernesto. But if I were you, I'd pay him off *now* and get him to leave as soon as possible. And I think you should hire some personal security – because even after they've gone I don't think the Stresos will give up their plan very easily.'

# EIGHTEEN

F rom outside came a great hubbub – the grating of metal, angry voices, the shrieking of car alarms. Ruggiero leapt up to dash out to the hall. 'Good God, what now!' he roared.

Greg went after him. Rini came running downstairs. They followed her husband out to the drive, where three vehicles had been in collision – the catering van, the pickup, and the Toyota.

The Toyota had been stationary. It seemed that the old pick-up had been coming out recklessly from its parking spot and hit the van as it made its way towards the main drive. It careered on and barged into the Toyota. The Toyota's bonnet had sprung open, there was a great gash along its side.

Rini exclaimed in distressed Russian. The driver of the pickup was on his feet trying to drag the van driver out of his seat. He was accusing him in furious Italian.

'Stop that!' yelled Ruggiero. 'You! Nicolo Scriveni! Get back in that truck and clear the way!'

The pickup driver, starting back in alarm at the bellow of rage, let go of the van driver. He scrambled back into his vehicle and began to edge out of the path of the van.

'You in the van! Stay where you are until I tell you!'

The van driver locked his door and, much relieved, sat waiting. Ruggiero marched into the path of the van, faced it, and began to beckon it forward. All seemed well with the vehicle. Ruggiero stepped out of the way and with angry arm gestures signalled him to leave. He drove on gingerly. A friend from another car was directing the pickup to move forward and into the correct position to travel.

'Right!' shouted Ruggiero. 'On your way, Scriveni! I'll expect you here tomorrow, when you're sober. A full apology and payment for the damage you've caused. Now, out. The lot of you!'

Rini, now clutching Greg's arm, murmured in admiration, 'He's so *masterful*.'

With surprising quickness the drive was cleared, leaving only Greg's car looking like an invalid. The master of the domain, his wife and his guest looked at it ruefully. Ruggiero gave a gusty sigh.

'Come on in and have a drink,' he said.

'No, nothing to drink, thanks, I've got to go back to Rome.' Greg got out his mobile to call for a taxi.

'Oh, at least let me lend you a car,' cried Ruggiero, understanding his move and catching his arm. 'Come and pick what you'd like from the garage.'

'Now that's a wonderful idea, darling!' cooed Rini.

All three walked round the side of the villa to the garage. There were four cars there: the big limousine in which Greg had first been brought to Villa Stefani, an avant-garde Mercedes, a new silver Honda, and a Suzuki jeep-like vehicle in light blue.

It seemed to Greg that the jeep would be the car least in use. Moreover, it would fit more easily into the small car park at the Pastorella. He chose that. Ruggiero hooked the keys from the array on the wall. 'See how you like it,' he said, and pushed the garage door wide.

It was a sweet little vehicle, starting to life at a touch. Greg edged his way out.

'I wish you'd stay a little,' sighed Rini, leaning into the open driver window. 'I have so much to tell you.'

'About Yuri?'

She nodded, at once dejected.

'Another time, Rini.' He was longing to get away, back to normality.

Ruggiero went before him to ensure there was no unexpected loiterer hanging about in the semicircular drive by the house. Greg drove sedately out. They stood back, Rini holding out both hands in a theatrical gesture of farewell, Ruggiero looking very flushed and still very vexed.

Greg left the turn-around and steered rather cautiously on

to the drive, for the vehicle was new to him. It was now about four o'clock. Warm air flowed past his window but the big privet hedge cast a welcome shade.

As he came round the last bend he saw that the drive gates were still wide open. Presumably Ernesto was waiting to be told by telephone whether the last guest had left. He went ahead, out on to the minor road, turning carefully to his right.

From the undergrowth down the slope, a figure suddenly leapt. Greg stamped on the brakes.

Ernesto – wielding a sledgehammer.

'Argh!' It was a cry of raging frustration. 'I thought it would be His Lordliness himself – but you'll do!'

The sledgehammer rose above his head and came crashing down on the windscreen.

Greg threw up his arms to protect himself. The glass held although he felt a few tiny splinters stab into his forearms. His foot slipped off the brake. The jeep lurched ahead. He looked up, seeing almost nothing through the wrecked wind-screen, and grabbed the wheel.

There was a stamping and shuffling. Ernesto was on his left, his free hand reaching in the side window to grab him. Greg steered away from him in a tight curve. Ernesto came with him, carried by the impetus of the vehicle. He staggered, almost fell, crashing along the side of the vehicle. The sledge-hammer slipped out of his grasp. He lost his footing and was on the ground, almost in front of the jeep.

Greg reversed in a rush.

Ernesto was scrambling to his feet, reaching for the fallen sledgehammer.

*Which way to go?* As Greg hesitated, a figure suddenly came running out of the gateway.

Cristina. And carrying a shotgun.

He saw it aimed squarely at him. The driver's window was still open. Where was the button to raise it? His fingers couldn't find it. He went into fast reverse.

Ernesto was running, the sledgehammer between two hands, trying to heave it up for a throw. He didn't know which of them to look at. Which was the greater menace?

Then all at once Ernesto was yelling. He couldn't make out the words. Cristina was running to come abreast and aim directly into his side window.

Ernesto had dropped the hammer, throwing out his hands in horror. And now Greg could make out the words.

'No, Cristina, no! Don't!'

She had got the shotgun steady just a few feet away. He saw her pull the trigger.

The gun exploded.

The barrel disintegrated, the wooden stock splintered, there was a mess of blood and bone, of metal and wood, like a little dark cloud in the air.

'*No!*' shrieked Ernesto. 'No, my angel, my life! Oh, God, no!'

He ran. He threw himself on the body lying on the dusty roadway.

Greg had stalled the jeep. He sat stock-still, staring out at the scene. It was like a painting by Goya – death, blood, dust and despair.

Ernesto was kneeling now, his wife gathered close against him. His face was hidden against her bloodstained breast, his shoulders heaving.

No one could have sustained those injuries and lived. Greg felt the truth of it filter through his mind. Cristina was dead.

Ernesto was rocking her to and fro, speaking to her, begging her to answer. His voice was broken, raw and desperate.

It seemed to Greg that he had to wake from this dream. He forced himself to move again. What should he do?

Call an ambulance. Useless, of course, but he must do that. He felt for his mobile, got it out, and for a hopeless moment couldn't even remember which buttons to press.

But he was beginning to function better. He asked for both ambulance and police. Then he rang the number of the villa.

It was Rini who answered. 'Oh, I'm sorry, Gregory,' she said in a rueful tone, 'but Ruggiero has had such a bad day, I don't want him bothered any more.'

'Rini,' he said, 'get him to the phone.'

He heard her surprised gasp at his tone. 'Oh,' she said, hurt, 'please don't be annoyed with me!'

'I'm not annoyed, Rini. But I *must* speak to Ruggiero at once. Please get him.'

He sat in the jeep, waiting for Ruggiero. It took some minutes.

'*Now* what?' demanded the master of the Villa Stefani.

'I'm just outside the gates. Cristina is dead.'

'What?'

'Cristina is dead. Come down and see.'

'How can she—'

'I've called the police and ambulance. You ought to be here when they arrive.'

'Are you out of your mind?'

'Oh, for God's sake!' He disconnected.

After a minute or two he opened the car door and got out. He found it strange that he could stand up straight, breathe in and feel the coming freshness of the early evening.

Slowly, he moved towards the two figures huddled together in the dust. Ernesto was weeping now, wordlessly, a wail of grief and loss.

Greg stood by. He felt he ought to show respect in some way, but there was nothing he could do.

There was the sound of a powerful car, then the limousine jarred to a halt between the gateposts. Ruggiero got out, stamping in irritation. He walked a few paces then stopped short.

His hands flew up to his mouth to stop the cry of horror. It took him a moment to recover enough to cross himself.

And then, after a long moment, Ruggiero said with muted satisfaction, 'I think this probably ends any anxiety about the Stresos' vendetta.'

# NINETEEN

L iz Blair arrived at the villa about mid-evening. A near hysterical call from Rini – a jumble of Russian, Italian and English – had given her a terrible scare. It seemed Greg had been hurt and the police were at the villa.

She had no car, but the reception desk found a taxi for her. When it arrived at the gates of Villa Stefani, the driver drew up cautiously before a barrier of warning tape. Liz began to get out, offering a handful of Euro notes. '*Aspetta*!' she commanded.

The driver said something in Italian that could be translated easily even to a poor linguist as 'No fear!'

'*Pagaro doppio*,' she said, wondering if it really meant 'I'll pay double.'

The driver seemed pleased with the offer. He put on the brake and increased the volume on his music system. He was listening to a pop music station.

The next problem was the policeman on guard. He held up a hand and spoke with authority. It was an easy guess that he was saying she couldn't go any further.

'I'm a friend of Signora Ardicci,' she said. 'She telephoned me.' She mimed the telephoning.

She wasn't sure whether he understood. But he put his walkie-talkie to his ear and spoke into it. After a moment he was nodding in acceptance. He raised the police tape so that Liz could duck under it. She began to walk quickly up the drive. But that wasn't fast enough and in a minute she was running, saying a thank you to all those mornings she'd spent pounding the pavements of big cities.

It was growing dark. Light was shining from several of the villa's windows. A handsome BMW and a couple of police cars were drawn up close to the entrance. The man on duty let her pass at once. She hurried across the marble hall and dashed into the drawing-room from which she could hear voices.

Greg was sitting in the corner of the sofa. Cushions had been heaped around and behind him. Rini Ardicci was standing at the back of the sofa with one hand protectively on his shoulder. His forearms were resting on yet more cushions. They were bandaged. His shirt sleeves had been cut off.

Liz stopped short. Words rushed to her lips but she didn't say them. Not in front of Rini. After a moment she said: 'Well, get *you*!'

'Oh, Liz darling, don't be alarmed! The paramedics have taken good care of him. Haven't they, my dear?' cried Rini.

Greg smiled. 'Picked out a lot of little tiny bits of glass, and ruined a good shirt.'

She sat down beside him, but carefully, so as not to jog the protecting cushions. After drawing a deep and calming breath she inquired: 'What's been going on?'

Rini gave up her post of ministering angel to come and sit opposite on a small tapestry settle. 'It's really dreadful!' she burst out. 'Ruggiero is so distressed! How could they, after he's been so good to them!'

'How could they what?' Liz asked.

'Plot and scheme! And mean to *kill* him! But you see, Saint Olga was watching over him because she foiled their plan and now it's Cristina who's dead!'

'*Cristina?*'

Rini was about to rant onwards, but Greg spoke first. 'It was an accident, Liz.'

She touched one bandaged arm with a finger. 'This accident?'

'In a way. It all began when the Toyota got damaged.'

'The Toyota's damaged?'

'Yes, but Ruggiero saw to all that, Liz my dear, and the company is coming to tow it away tomorrow.'

'So you had an accident with the car—'

'No, it was one of the funeral guests,' Rini corrected.

Greg began again, speaking a little more firmly than last time. 'I was telling Ruggiero what we'd discovered and suggesting that he should send the Stresos away for his own safety. We were in his study, and the funeral guests were leaving. Then suddenly there was this great row outside and we both dashed out to find that somebody in a pickup truck had side-swiped the Toyota and then collided with the caterers' van.'

'So of course Ruggiero got them cleared away,' Rini took it up, 'but then we found out that the Toyota was so badly damaged that it couldn't be driven. So Ruggiero suggested that Greg should take one of our cars to drive back to Rome.'

Liz looked from one to the other. 'So you weren't hurt in the accident with our car?'

'No, and it wasn't an accident with the Suzuki, either.'

'Rini, let me tell it,' Greg said. 'Otherwise it's going to take all night to explain it.'

She was immediately subdued. 'Of course. I talk too much, Ruggiero always says so.'

Liz gave her a sympathetic smile, but turned to Greg for the rest.

'When I started to speak to Ruggiero, Cristina was around, clearing up the after-effects of the party, I realize now that she was watching us, but I didn't think anything about it at the time.'

'It's so awful,' cried Rini, unable to keep quiet. 'We trusted them!'

'Go on,' Liz urged.

'Well, I think she followed us to Ruggiero's office and eavesdropped on what I was saying. We didn't close the door completely so she could have heard. Ruggiero agreed that he would have to send the Stresos away, and I imagine Cristina went straight to the telephone in the kitchen to ring Ernesto and let him know. Then when I drove down to the gatehouse in the little blue jeep—'

'It looked as if it was Ruggiero driving,' Rini declared triumphantly, 'because it was one of the villa's cars!'

'And so?'

'So Ernesto jumped out of the roadside undergrowth wielding a great big hammer in front of the car,' said Greg.

'Oh!'

'The man just proved it there and then,' cried Rini. 'He's a murderer!'

'He . . . he hit you with the hammer?' Liz faltered.

'No, the windscreen.' Greg made a little movement of his bandaged arms. 'Hence the glass in my forearms – I put them up to protect my face. Unluckily I wasn't wearing my jacket because it was still very warm when I set off.'

'My God,' breathed Liz.

'It's too terrifying, isn't it, my dear? To think we had a man like that moving among us, for months and months, and never suspected—'

'And what was the thing about Cristina?' Liz asked, over-riding Rini's lament.

'Well, Ernesto was trying to land a blow at me through the open side window, and I was turning the jeep away from him as fast as I could . . .' He broke off, sighing. 'And then out ran Cristina with an ancient rifle—'

'Yes,' Rini put in, knowing she had information of import-ance. 'Ruggiero says it was practically a family heirloom, belonged to the Streso family since World War II. He says they brought it with them to the gatehouse and it was hanging on the wall in their living-room.'

'As Rini says, a very old piece,' Greg agreed. 'Ernesto says now he used it during last autumn's hunting season and hung it again on the wall without bothering to clean it or empty the breech. So when Cristina aimed it at me—' He broke off.

There was a sudden silence. Even Rini seemed unable to utter the words.

'W–what?' faltered Liz.

'Ernesto was yelling at her not to fire it, but she pulled the trigger and . . . and . . . it blew up in her face.'

'No.'

'It killed her outright. I expect the autopsy will show she got fragments of the barrel in her skull.'

'Oh, Greg . . .'

A long silence.

'Ruggiero's with his lawyer and the police, in his study, trying to give the background to the affair. Ernesto's been taken away. I gather they were going to put him in a safe ward in a hospital. He wasn't making much sense when they tried to question him.'

Liz nodded. She couldn't think of anything to say.

Rini looked from one to the other. 'My dears,' cried Rini, 'what a bad hostess I am! Let me offer refreshments – a drink? Something to eat?'

'No, nothing, thank you,' murmured Liz.

'We'll be going soon, I hope,' Greg said. 'We'll get something in Rome.'

'Really?' Rini brushed back her hair and sighed. 'Just as well, perhaps. I would have had to get it myself and I'm so unaccustomed to the kitchen . . .'

There were sounds of movement in the hall. Ruggiero came in, followed by his lawyer Perriero and a tall, solid man in a very good suit.

'This is Superintendent Di Grandi,' Ruggiero said, introducing Liz. 'Superintendent, this is the young lady I was telling you about.'

'Ah, yes, the friend of Signor von Hirtenstein.' The superintendent bowed slightly towards her. His English was very good. 'But I gather you had no part in today's events.'

'No, I stayed in Rome.' Swimming in a luxurious pool, being massaged by expert hands, having her nails done . . . Liz felt somehow guilty.

'Just as well,' said Di Grandi. 'A bad business.'

'Indeed, indeed,' murmured Perriero. 'But completely without the knowledge of Don Ruggiero, as we have agreed.'

'Quite so.'

'What will happen to Ernesto?' Liz asked, remembering how she had once saved the couple from being dismissed and wondering now why she cared.

Di Grandi gave her a solemn smile. 'Ah, the ladies. Always rather soft-hearted even towards a wrongdoer. I think he will be declared unfit to plead, *signorina*. He speaks only to lament the loss of his wife when we question him.'

No wonder, she thought. He's lost everything – his daughter, his wife, his home, his reason for living . . . But she put none of it into words.

'My dearest,' said Rini to her husband, 'what happens now?'

Ruggiero glanced at his man of law, inviting him to respond.

'Well, my dear Rini, I think it's agreed that the whole matter will be dealt with discreetly. There will have to be inquests, of course, but I think if you all give written depositions either tomorrow or the next day, that will be sufficient. You and Ruggiero should have a quiet evening and perhaps go away for a few days so as to avoid the press. It will all die down.' He sighed as he said it, and it occurred to Liz that he was thinking there would be bad repercussions for Ruggiero's career.

Greg got up from among his nest of cushions. 'We may go now?' he asked of the detective.

The superintendent returned to his native tongue, apparently feeling it would be more authoritative. 'Certainly, *signore*. I have the name of your hotel – perhaps tomorrow I may telephone and ask you to come to the Questura to sign the statement you have already made?'

Greg nodded agreement.

'Let me lend you one of my cars,' Ruggiero began.

'No, that's all right, I left a taxi waiting for us down by the gates,' Liz intervened. The last thing she wanted was to be indebted in any way to Ruggiero Ardicci.

The superintendent eyed Greg with a questioning gaze, clearly trying to assess whether he was to be considered walking wounded or whether, since he was a minor royalty, he should offer him and his lady transport to the gates. He decided in favour of the latter.

At the door he uttered a few rough commands. One of the uniformed men got into a police car and started the engine. Another opened the passenger door for them. Greg and Liz got in, she rather wondering whether they were about to be whisked off to jail.

But no, at the gates the car pulled up, the driver opened the passenger door and saluted as they got out. Liz's taxi driver emerged from his vehicle, looking very impressed, to open the passenger door for them. He muttered something to her as she got in, some sort of apology for not recognizing her importance earlier. At some other time it would have amused her. Now, she wanted only to be on their way out of the influence of the Villa Stefani.

She sat as close as she could to Greg. He put an arm around her. 'Oh, will that hurt?' she exclaimed.

'It's just scratches,' he said, and held her closer.

They sat in comforting silence until they were going through the village of Tabardi. The lights were on in the village square, the musicians were playing for a few dancers. A more peaceful scene could not have been imagined.

'I never want to see this place again,' Liz declared as they left the last house behind.

'*D'accord!*'

'I'm even going off Rini,' she went on, with a hint of regret. 'She just refuses to see anything wrong in him.'

'She doesn't know the whole story,' Greg suggested. 'About the affair with Chiara, for instance.'

'More likely, she doesn't want to know.'

'Perhaps.' He was thinking about the beginnings of his link with the Ardiccis. 'Grossmutti got me here on the proposition that someone had stolen a collection of diamonds. But you know, they never breathed a word about the icon until you worked it out and challenged them. She really seems to live to please him.'

'Sneaky pair.'

'Oh, don't forget Floria! She sat there while I tried to work out how the diamonds could have been stolen, and all the while they were in a suitcase in her room.'

'Oh, Floria . . .' She sighed. 'Poor soul. I didn't like her, but . . .'

'She didn't deserve to die.'

'No.'

'Ernesto Streso should have stopped then. He should have seen . . .'

'That what he was trying to do was terribly wrong?' She shook her head. 'What was that you said, about vengeance?'

'Hatred inspires vengeance.' He sighed. 'That was the problem; the Stresos just couldn't get over their hatred of Ruggiero for what he did to their daughter. And people died, but the wrong people – Floria, and Cristina too.'

'It's like something out of an opera,' she remarked, trying for a little lightness.

'*Rigoletto*. The Duke seduces Rigoletto's daughter, Rigoletto arranges for him to be murdered and instead he gets his daughter's body back in a sack.'

'Oh, *Greg!*'

He gave a little shake of the head. 'And you know, nobody is going to be punished. It's all going to be wished away.'

'Because of Ruggiero's political connections?'

'That's how it looks.'

'Greg, how can he be so important to his party? He's . . . he's not really much of an asset, surely – he's so self-engrossed, so . . . stupid!'

'He's got money. Winning elections takes money.'

'So you think they'll still send him to New York, after all the bad things that have been happening in his little kingdom?'

He could only shrug in response.

The taxi driver, having heard the word 'Rigoletto' among their English, had decided they didn't like the pop music his sound system was offering. He sought around until he found a broadcast of opera, and they swept along the *autostrada* to the strains of *Turandot*.

At the hotel, they had a drink at the little bar then went upstairs to freshen up. Their spirits should have been considerably lifted by the difficulty of getting Greg washed without wetting his bandages – he standing with arms outstretched while Liz wielded a sponge. Yet they hardly even laughed.

At about ten they were ready to go out for supper. But as Liz was heading for the door of their room, Greg called her back. 'I ought to ring my grandmother,' he said.

'Oh.'

'I really should, *Liebchen*. There might be something in

tomorrow's press about an accident and a death at the Ardicci home. I wouldn't want her to get a scare.'

'I suppose not,' she said, trying not to sound unwilling.

'I'd better do it now, on the landline. It's not the kind of thing you want to talk about on a mobile.'

'Right.' She dithered. She didn't want to sit here in the room while he made a long explanation to his fearsome grandmother. 'I'll go and get us a table at the restaurant. Where are we going?'

'We hadn't decided. Giotto's?'

'Sounds OK.' Giotto's had a reasonable menu of vegetarian dishes. 'So I'll see you there later, dove.'

'"Dove"?'

'It's a term of affection. Doves are famous for being faithful and patient. So I'll wait for you at Giotto's.'

He laughed, and she was pleased. It was another signal that he was more like himself. He'd been rather quiet since she came to fetch him from the villa.

They kissed and she went off to sit at the restaurant with a glass of wine and a borrowed copy of the evening paper. So far as she could tell, there was nothing in it about the happenings at the Villa Stefani.

When Greg appeared he looked troubled. He sat down beside her to give her a kiss on the cheek.

'How did it go?' she asked.

'Oh . . . Very perturbed. She was anxious that we – the Hirtensteins – shouldn't be involved.' He picked up the menu, sighing. 'Odd though it may seem, I'm hungry.'

'I should think so. It's hours since you had anything to eat unless you scoffed a lot of the finger food at the funeral.' She gave him a mock frown. 'Now it's time to have a proper meal, my lad, and you must eat it all up.'

He tried to smile but she knew it wasn't really very funny. She was in something of a quandary. He'd been through something she couldn't even imagine – the death of a woman by a very horrible accident – and she felt herself inadequate to deal with it.

He consulted the menu. The waiter who had been looking after Liz appeared at once, pencil and pad at the ready. They ordered food and wine, the waiter nodded approvingly and smiled at Liz. She rewarded him with a smile but wished him gone. She wanted to be alone with Greg, to find a way to ask him how he felt, without seeming insensitive.

'Now things at the villa seem to be cleared up, I mean about the supposed theft of the diamonds – is Grossmutti coming back to do the rest of the redecoration?'

'We didn't get that far. It was politics mainly. My grandmother . . . her main interest in life is that the Hirtensteins should keep the code, be upright and honourable, ready to return to rule in their homeland when the invitation comes.'

She didn't ask, 'And when's that likely to be?' She knew it was never going to happen, and so did Greg and so did the ex-queen mother, if she was honest with herself.

The wine came, a bottle of dry Orvieto. It seemed to help him relax, for he sat back in his chair and his attitude seemed easier.

'It's Saturday tomorrow,' he murmured. 'I've got a concert going on in Lisbon in the evening – I ought to ring and ask if everything's all right at the hall.'

'You can do that in the morning.'

'Yes, and I ought to look at my organizer to see if Amabelle is staying in Geneva over the weekend because she was talking about taking the children to some amusement park.'

'Too late to do that this evening – you can do that tomorrow too.'

'I've been too taken up with the Ardiccis,' he confessed. 'I haven't kept in touch with Amabelle.'

'Never mind. You'll catch up.'

'And what about you?' he went on. 'I dragged you into this horrible business . . .'

'I wasn't dragged. I wanted to come. Stop piling up a mass of things to blame yourself for.'

He shrugged and nodded. Then he said, rather awkwardly, 'I've got a message for you from Grossmutti.'

'What?' She was alarmed.

'She wants you to ring her.'

'Me?'

'Yes.'

'Why?'

Luckily he didn't have to answer the question because the waiter came with the antipasto. The truth was, he didn't know why.

# TWENTY

In the morning their telephone rang while they were still in the process of getting up and dressed. Greg had slept badly, they were late in waking up. The call was from Rini Ardicci, from the reception desk of the hotel.

'My dear,' she cried when Liz answered, 'we have to go to the Questura about the statements, so Ruggiero thought it would be a good idea to offer to take Gregory, since he must also sign his.'

She covered the receiver to relay this message to Greg, who groaned.

'I can say you're not ready,' she suggested.

He thought about it. 'Well, no . . . I have to go and I might as well get it over. What about you, cherie? Do you want to come?'

She at once looked so unwilling that he had to laugh. 'All right, tell her it's a single passenger.' She obeyed, and when she'd put down the phone he asked: 'What do you think you'll do?'

She hadn't thought about it until that moment but invented an immediate excuse. 'I thought I'd go and see Yuri.'

'Good heavens! What on earth for?'

'To ask if he's told his pals in Moscow about the icon. I mean to say, sweets, though I'm thoroughly disenchanted with the Ardiccis, I still wouldn't want Rini to have a visit from the Russian police force.'

'And if he's told them, what can you do about it?'

'Warn Rini.' She shrugged. 'Who, by the way, is waiting for you downstairs.'

She helped him put on his jacket. She collected her handbag and sunglasses. He stood hesitating. 'What?' she inquired.

He picked up his mobile from the nightstand. 'You still haven't telephoned Grossmutti.'

'Oh.'

'You don't have to, of course.'

'No.'

'But it's so strange that she should ask.'

'She only wants to read me a lecture.'

This was entirely possible. 'Well, I'll leave you my phone. She's on the speed dial list.'

She accepted it and put it in her handbag. She sat down on the bed. 'Where and when shall we meet?' she asked.

'Ah, well . . . officialdom doesn't work fast,' he replied. 'Let's say two o'clock, at the Bocca della Verita – you know it?'

'Oh, the place where you get your hand snapped off if you tell a lie? Sure. I'll be there.'

'Aren't you coming down to wave goodbye? I might be detained as a material witness,' he said, with a wry smile on his long face.

'I'm going to sit here until you and the Ardiccis have driven away. I never want to have to talk to Ruggiero again as long as I live.'

He put his arms around her, picked her up from the bed, and kissed her hard. 'What would I do without you?' he murmured as he let her go. Next moment he was gone, and she sat disconsolate for quite some time.

In the end she actually did ring Yuri Tamaldov to find out if he was available. He answered, surprised to hear from her. He agreed at once to meet, but said he had clients to see in their homes first. They arranged to meet at a café in the Piazza del Popolo.

'I like this place,' he said when she joined him there. 'They make tea in Russian manner but they use decaffeinated tea, which is better for health, of course.'

'How unusual,' she said, with no intention of trying it. Instead she had a long cold drink.

He was clad in a black shirt and trousers, above which his pale features and dark eyes were very striking. 'I'm so glad you should ring,' he began. 'Rini was in touch with me last night – what a truly dreadful thing to happen! And Ruggiero, of course, has stomach troubles because of stress, and is very worried. But yet she tells me I must not go to her, because his advisers say he must be very careful until trouble all settles down.'

She nodded acceptance of all this. It was just like Ruggiero to forbid his wife to see a friendly Russian while his party bosses were considering his future.

'So tell me all what happened,' he urged. 'From Rini I could only get some big events, which of course includes death of poor Cristina.'

She gave him an outline of the facts. He was shocked into a little outburst of Russian which she thought might actually be a prayer. She let a moment go by then asked: 'Have you done anything about the icon?'

'No–no . . . At the moment, I negotiate.'

'How does that go? You still getting official letters?'

'Ah, now they telephone me.' He looked pleased, although uncertain. 'I think it is good. They understand that Rini is wife of person of importance, nothing can be done by coercion, but I have explained I think I can persuade, so perhaps in time . . . a month . . . who knows?'

'We have a saying in English,' she remarked. 'Gently does it.'

He smiled. 'That is how I intend. And although of course I have great respect for Rini's devotion, yet I hope she will see that it is not good to keep such a treasure, so beloved by the faithful.'

'I think it might be a good idea to mention how dangerous it is to keep it.'

'Dangerous? To Rini?' His eyes flashed in defiance. 'I would not let anything bad happen to her!'

'To her husband's career.'

'Ah. But she has always known that.'

'It's a more significant danger now. I get the impression that Ruggiero is losing favour with his party bosses. They keep having to steer him out of one disaster after another. I think they may be losing patience with him.'

'And Rini would be so unhappy if she caused him harm.'

'Exactly.'

He sipped some tea and thought about it. 'I will try to counsel her,' he said. 'Perhaps I could say that to make this sacrifice is good. I mean, religiously good. Russian tradition esteems sacrifice.'

Whatever sails your boat, she said to herself, but merely nodded approval of his analysis.

She had something to say that she felt was more important. 'If you persuade her to return the icon,' she began, 'get her to return it to its original state before it goes.'

He frowned a little. 'She has altered it?'

'You've forgotten the diamond frame?'

'Oh . . . No, of course not.'

'That was why Greg was brought here in the first place. He was told Rini's diamonds had gone missing. And' – she waved an admonitory finger at him – 'he wasted a lot of time trying to find them until we worked out that Saint Olga hadn't been stolen for the gemstones but because it was a religious icon. Did you see it hanging in its sparkly frame?'

He looked affronted. 'It was hanging in her boudoir! Of course I never went there!'

'Oh, forgive me.' She hid a smile. 'Well, I don't know what they'd think of it if they saw it. You know Rini had her diamonds mounted as a frame. She wanted the diamonds to sparkle. So the frame-maker mounted the icon on a plate of glass and then glued on the diamonds.' She waited for his comment, but it seemed he was unable follow her trend of thought. 'It looks awful,' she said.

'Awful?'

'Theatrical. Do you know the English slang word "bling"?' He shook his head. 'Well, it means . . . fake, showy.'

'That is unkind.'

'It's *true*. It's not at all the kind of thing that would look right in a museum or a church. And the point I want to make is this: the frame-maker used some special adhesive of his own. The custodians in Moscow might not know how to detach the picture from the mount—'

She broke off. Tamaldov's grasp of English was failing him. 'Mount? Is this horse?'

'No, no. I'm talking about the glass that the icon's stuck on. The frame-maker has a special glue that he invented. *Invented*, you understand?'

'Oh yes, yes, now I understand.'

'I think only the frame-maker would know how to get the painting off. So tell Rini she's got to take it to him – otherwise in trying to detach it, they might damage it. It's painted on a very old piece of wood.'

'God forbid it.'

'I couldn't agree more.' She might only be a fashion designer for high street customers, but she still loved great art.

In this amicable frame of mind they parted.

It was still too early to meet Greg so she went window-shopping. She always wanted to take note of good window displays, for it was part of her business to help show fashion to passing shoppers. But the windows were uninspiring, many of the shops being closed until August was over. She found a very expensive hairdresser that was not only open but busy, so went in to have a luxurious shampoo.

From this she emerged feeling energized although Rome was still in the grip of August heat. She took a taxi to the car hire firm, expecting all kinds of trouble over the damage to the Toyota.

But no. 'Everything has been taken care of, *signorina*,' the manager cooed. 'Don Ruggiero Ardicci telephoned us and we accept that you were in no way responsible for the collision. Our insurance covers everything. If you would just sign here . . .?'

She took the Metro to the Circo Massimo and found a seat in the shade to wait for Greg. When her watch showed a few minutes before two, she made her way to the portico of the church, and there he was, considerably less formal than when he had left the hotel earlier. He'd taken off his jacket, removed his tie, and rolled up his shirt sleeves. The bandages had been replaced by strips of sticking plaster.

'I didn't put my hand in the *bocca*,' he said, grinning. 'I'm in a bad enough state already.'

'What? The cops rough you up?'

'Well, they weren't friendly. The superintendent dealt with Ruggiero's statement. I was left with the underlings, who were frigidly polite but wanted everything explained ten times over. But in the end they had to agree that I hadn't done anything wrong, so I was dismissed and went to a clinic to get the bandages replaced. And here I am.'

'Poor sweetheart.' She linked her arm in his and urged him out into the piazza. 'What you need now is a reviving drink and some lunch. Let's find a restaurant with good air-conditioning.'

They settled on a Thai restaurant with its tables set out around an indoor fish pool. The air was fresh with the scent of green leaves and blossoms. The place was still busy but the head waiter welcomed them cheerfully; before long they were drinking ice-cold Tiger beer and starting on a mango salad.

'Let's stay here forever,' Liz suggested, sighing with pleasure.

'So long as the Ardiccis never find us,' he agreed. Then, studying her, 'You look different.'

'So I ought to! This is the handiwork of one of Rome's best hairdressers.'

'Ha! So while I'm being roasted by the police, you are off enjoying yourself.'

'You always get that wrong,' she scolded. 'It's not "roasted", it's "grilled". And besides, I sorted out the car damage, so I wasn't just pampering myself. Anyhow, do you think I look good?'

'You always look good.'

'That was the right answer.' They smiled at each other. 'And of course besides the pampering, I had a long talk with Yuri.'

'Oh.' He never liked any talk about Yuri.

'He's going to persuade Rini to return the icon to the Russians.'

'That I rather doubt.'

'I think he will. He's going to use some argument about sacrifice being good for the soul.'

He accepted that with a shrug and gave his attention to the remains of his salad. He was about to ask her if she had telephoned ex-Queen Nicolette but at that moment the waiter brought their satay and he thought better of it. If she'd done so, she would have told him without prompting.

Her thoughts still being with Rini, Liz inquired, 'Did she have to give a statement to the police?'

'No, they aren't interested in her and I think Ruggiero told her to make herself scarce.'

'So it's all done and dusted?'

He laughed at the phrase. 'What a language! Yes, dusted and put away in a cupboard. Nobody wants any more trouble with the happenings at the Villa Stefani.'

'Ah well . . . That leaves us free to do whatever we like, doesn't it?'

'I ought to make that call to Amabelle. Have you still got my mobile?'

Some of the enjoyment went out of her expression at the mention of it. She knew he was wondering if she had made the call. But she found the phone in her handbag and handed it over without comment.

Later they were going into the little foyer of the Pastorella thinking that they would have a relaxing hour or two before going out for the evening. And there, to their dismay, was Rini Ardicci, sitting on a faux-Louis Fourteenth chair and sipping a Martini.

'Ah, my dear ones!' She sprang up, arms outstretched, eager to embrace them. 'It seems our sea of troubles is calmed at last! And Ruggiero asks me to say he will settle any money matters if you will send him your account, Gregory. He himself has been spirited away to report to his advisers – they were anxious to hear how things went with the police but all is well, I gather – yes?'

There were so many points in her greeting that all they could do was make sounds of assent. It was clear she wanted to talk, so Greg gathered the only other chairs in the foyer and they sat down with her.

She was glowing with enthusiasm. 'I wanted to tell you how much you have helped me in this bad time!' She indicated the black suit she was wearing. 'You recognize this, don't you? You bought it for me. And I have been to see your little dressmaker today and she will make me two more outfits which should see me through the period of mourning, I believe. So to thank you, Liz dearest, I have bought you a little present.' She snatched up a carrier bag by her feet and produced a gift-wrapped parcel.

'Oh, Rini, you shouldn't—'

'Yes, yes, I should! Because I know in my heart you will be leaving soon, and I wanted to give you something that will remind you of me, for whom you will always be an example of true kindness and friendship. Open it, open it. If you don't like it I can exchange it.'

The contents proved to be a narrow case with an elegant wristwatch inside. 'Oh, that's beautiful, Rini!'

'You like it? Oh, I'm so glad. And for you, Gregory—' She held out another package.

He took it, knowing it would be a waste of time to protest. He found her gift was a wallet of fine maroon leather by a famous maker. 'Thank you,' he said.

'It is too little. You have been our saviour! I wanted to celebrate the conclusion of this time of trial and . . . and . . . to tell you that I have made a decision about the icon.'

'You have?'

'Yes, Liz my darling. Yuri called me while I was shopping for these little presents and suggested that we meet. So I went to his clinic and we talked. He is so *good*! He told me he had been thinking about my icon and he felt that for my peace of mind I should return Saint Olga to her homeland.'

Liz hid a smile. 'That's a very big decision,' she said.

'Of course it is, and such a sacrifice – you can't imagine how much I shall miss her! And yet, you know, I should show my gratitude to her by sending her home. She protected my Ruggiero when everything seemed harsh and dangerous. She helped you to shed light on the Stresos and their schemes – oh, she has been so good to me, and although it makes me sad to give her up, I know it's the right thing to do.'

'Well, I think it's very brave of you.'

'Brave? Liz, my dear friend, I have been in anxiety all these past days and now – because Yuri explained it to me – I understand I must rid myself of the burden by giving Saint Olga back to her people.'

She was smiling, although there were tears glistening in the dark eyes. Liz thought that having such tempestuous emotions must indeed be a burden, but gave her a hug and kiss to comfort her for losing her saint.

She left at last, summoning her car by mobile from some car park. They waved her farewell as she was driven away.

Greg said rather drily: 'That was of course very loving and grateful, but I have a feeling it was a way of saying it's time for us to go.'

'Suits me,' she agreed. She held out her wrist for admiration of the new watch. 'This is the second goodie I've collected in Rome.'

'The second?'

'Yes, the other one's the little hair tag you gave me.'

'Oh, that? That cost a fraction of what the watch is worth.'

She put an arm around him as they made their way to the lift. 'I don't need to tell you which of them I value most, do I?'

They felt the need of a drink after the encounter with Rini, and found the ingredients in the mini-fridge in their room. Liz said: 'I wonder if Rini understands that Yuri will be going back to Russia too?'

He shrugged.

'She'll miss him. He's really the only friend she's got here.
And perhaps he's been more than just a friend.'

'No, no.'

'Oh, come on. He's a nice-looking bloke and she must often
feel the need for loving arms around her.'

'No, really. I think their relationship has been on a different
level. He's been her "*cicisbeo*".'

'Her what?'

'It's something that used to be quite common among the
upper classes in Italy. Your poet Byron was "*cicisbeo*" to an
Italian *contessa* during his stay here. It used to mean something like "attendant" or "devotee".'

'Get along with you! Byron? He got in bed with every
woman he met, by all accounts.'

'She was the exception. He wrote poems about her but he
admitted he never "conquered" her.'

'The things you know,' she marvelled. 'So you think Rini
and Yuri are really "just friends"? When I come to think about
it . . . Yuri got quite offended when I suggested he'd been in
her boudoir.'

'Well, now he's persuaded her to part with Saint Olga, he'll
get permission to go home to St Petersburg. But perhaps it
won't be so bad for Rini. Ruggiero might get the job at the
United Nations and she'll have all the thrill of furnishing a
new home in New York. She might even be offered operatic
roles – she's sung in New York in the past.'

'Poor Rini,' sighed Liz. 'She's just so . . . so bound up in
Ruggiero. And there are a lot of marvellously attractive women
in New York . . .'

By and by they began to think how they should spend the
evening. Today had been very stressful. They decided to go
to a café that advertised an entertainment of Italian folk songs.

Liz had showered and was putting on her make-up. Greg
was in the shower. Her eye alighted on his mobile, sitting on
the bedside table.

Should she ring Queen Nicoletta?

No. Why should she kow-tow to the wishes of this domin-
eering old woman?

But then . . . it was so strange that she'd asked. Liz had
shrugged it off: 'She only wants to give me a lecture.'

Had that been the right thing to do? After all, this old lady had been a surrogate mother to Greg. Whatever her faults, she had helped to make Greg what he was – the man who seemed to Liz her ideal partner: clever, kind-hearted, good-looking in his subdued fashion.

Perhaps she ought to ring Nicoletta.

She picked up the mobile and pressed the button that would connect her.

There was a slight pause, and then an elderly but crisp voice said: '*Allo*?'

She almost put the phone down. Instead she quavered: 'Madame von Hirtenstein? This is Liz Blair.'

There was a weighted silence. Then Nicoletta said: 'Good evening, Ms Blair.'

'Good evening. Greg said that you wanted to speak to me.'

'Yes.' Quite a distinct pause. 'Ms Blair, we have in the past been unfriendly.'

'Yes.' *You can say that again*, she remarked inwardly.

'I apologize for my manners. I've come to understand that I . . . er . . . I was under a misapprehension.'

*You can say that again too*, she thought. Aloud she said, 'Let's put that aside. Did you have some particular reason for wanting to speak to me?'

'Well, you see . . . you are there with him, and I am not. I mean, some strange things have happened. When he spoke to me recently he didn't seem himself.'

Liz nodded though no one could see her. 'He'd just seen a woman die rather horribly in front of his eyes. He took it quite hard, madame.'

'Of course. Yes, I understand that. But some time has passed and Gregory is resilient. How is he now?'

'Ah, well, he spent two or three hours with officialdom today and I think it brought out his fighting spirit. He's more himself this evening.'

'He was with the police? About the death of Cristina?'

'Yes, and Ruggiero was there too, and as far as I can learn everything is being smoothed over because Ruggiero hands out pots of money to his political pals.'

'So I gather.'

'So he's going to come out of it covered in roses and then he'll go flying off to New York to be an ambassador.'

'Oh, that's not going to happen,' said Nicoletta with complete conviction.

'No? Why not?'

'Because he's a fool. Because he married for love – if that's what it was – and his wife is a handicap. Because too many unfortunate things happen around his family – his housekeeper dies because his gardener is careless, and then the gardener turns out to be trying to kill him and the gardener's *wife* dies in a gun accident. Does this sound to you like the background for a diplomat at the United Nations?'

'But the political bosses keep clearing up after him,' she protested.

'They're growing tired of that.'

'How can you be sure?'

'Ah, my dear . . . I wasn't always a bad-tempered old woman. I used to be able to make hearts beat fast, and some of those hearts are still beating in very influential places.' There was pride and some amusement in her voice. 'I asked among my acquaintances in the diplomatic world, and the opinion is that Ruggiero Ardicci will not be going to New York.'

'Oh . . .' said Liz. 'That's rather a shame for Rini. Greg was saying that if they went there, she might be asked to sing opera again.'

A snort of disbelief. 'Dear Gregory, he often thinks the best of people who really don't deserve it. While I was staying at the villa she murmured that she didn't like New York – the artistic directors were unkind to her there.'

'Artistic director. That means the guy who's in charge of rehearsals and stuff, doesn't it? Ye–es, I seem to remember that Greg said she often disappeared to go to church.'

'That kind of behaviour brings out impatience in those trying to manage an orchestra and cast, I imagine. *Hélas*, fond though I am of Rini, I have to admit she can be irritating.'

Liz made a little sound of agreement. 'You have to come back and put up with her again though, don't you? You still have some work to do at the villa.'

'Ah no, my dear. I am going to write a polite little letter to Ruggiero saying the delay would cause me problems with other clients, and enclose my bill. I do not plan to return to the Villa Stefani. Life's too short to waste it on people like Ruggiero.'

'I couldn't agree more.'

There was a little pause, then Nicoletta remarked, 'It seems you and I have more in common than I had understood.'

'Well, we both want things to go well for Greg.'

'Indeed.' Liz could hear that Nicoletta was now trying to put some words together for a special reason. *Here it comes,* she thought. She's going to ask me to stop seeing him.

But what Nicoletta said in the end was: 'You know, Ms Blair, if you are ever in Geneva, it might be quite pleasant to meet for a drink.'

Liz stifled a gasp. 'Oh . . . Thank you,' she said.

An embarrassed pause.

After some hesitation, Liz plucked up courage to say: 'You know, madame, Greg will want to know why you asked to speak to me. Er . . . what shall I tell him?'

Nicoletta laughed. 'Tell him I've decided to use you as a way of checking up on him!'

'That should work,' said Liz. With an unexpected feeling of agreement, they said goodbye.

Her hair still needed some attention to return it to the neatness achieved by the new style. She was trying the hair tag that Greg had bought when, clad in bathrobe, he appeared behind her in the mirror. He dropped a kiss on the top of her head. 'Don't do any more,' he ordered. 'It's perfect already.'

She turned to face him, smiling. 'You have the knack of always saying the right thing.'

'It's my diplomatic training. Grossmutti had this wild idea that I might one day have to deal with world events.'

She pulled herself to her feet by holding on to his bathrobe. Close against him, she said softly, 'I've just been speaking to her.'

'Who?'

'Her. Your grandma. You asked me to ring her.'

'Good heavens!'

'Yes, wonderful, isn't it. Here I am, post-conversation, and still in one piece.'

He lowered them both on to the bed with one arm around her. 'Tell me the worst,' he said in a rather doleful tone.

'The worst? Well, that seemed to be that she won't be coming back to finish decorating Ruggiero's house.'

'What?'

'She doesn't like Ruggiero. She doesn't have much patience

with Rini. To tell the truth, she more or less shares our view of that pair.'

'You were talking about the Ardiccis?'

'Part of the time.'

He drew in a slow breath. Then he said: 'I cannot believe that my grandmother wanted to talk to you about the Ardiccis.'

'No, of course not. She wanted to talk about you. She was worried about you.'

'Well, that's normal. She's always worried I'm going to do something to blight the family name.'

'No, she was worried about . . . well, just how you are and so forth. So I told her you were more or less normal and she was pleased.'

'*Pleased?*'

'Definitely.'

He put a hand to her face and turned it so that they were staring at each other. 'You're glossing over what she really said.'

'No. No, honestly, love, she was . . . er . . . she was quite nice to me.' He frowned a little but said nothing so she went on: 'I think she's beginning to like me a little bit.'

'You really think so?'

She got up. 'Come on, let's get dressed and go out. Let's go somewhere where we can celebrate with some champagne.'

A little later they were walking along the Via Veneto. The atmosphere was oppressive with the aftermath of the day's heat and the fumes from the traffic.

'You know,' he said, 'I've had enough of Rome for the moment, and we've done all we were asked to do for the Ardiccis – we found their precious diamonds, after all. So what do you say – let's pack up and go somewhere cooler and less demanding.'

She smiled to herself. 'What about Geneva?'

'*Geneva?*'

'Yes, should be cooler up in the mountains, shouldn't it?'

'But we might bump into . . . well . . . you know . . .'

'Might be fun,' she said. 'Why don't we go there and see?'